TRAITOR'S BLOOD

REGINALD HILL

TRAITOR'S BLOOD

WARNER BOOKS

A Warner Communications Company

WARNER BOOKS EDITION

Copyright © 1983 by Reginald Hill
All rights reserved.

This Warner Books Edition is published by arrangement with
The Countryman Press, Woodstock, Vermont

Cover illustration by Ben Perini
Cover design by Don Puckey

Warner Books, Inc.
666 Fifth Avenue
New York, N.Y. 10103

A Warner Communications Company

Printed in the United States of America

First Warner Books Printing: December, 1987

10 9 8 7 6 5 4 3 2 1

for
DAVID and HELEN
Trail-blazers
after Rome, Africa!

Thou old unhappy traitor,
Briefly thyself remember: the sword is out
That must destroy thee.

KING LEAR, Act IV, Scene 6

I

. . . over by Christmas . . .

Dr Quintero was drunk when he diagnosed my stomach cancer but that was no reason for disbelieving him.

He'd been drunk when he arrived on Isla da Margarita eight years before, shortly after the folding of his fashionable Caracas practice. Once I'd established that the scandal had been moral rather than medical, I hired him. He'd been drunk when he diagnosed my prickly heat, my hepatitis, my tape-worm and my psycho-neurosis, and it hadn't stopped him from being right yet.

He seemed genuinely upset when he gave me the results of my tests. I asked him, how long? and there were tears in his eyes as he told me it could all be over by Christmas. Six months. It wasn't long to make up for a wasted forty years. I doubted I could do it. Quintero told me to take it easy, but I decided to follow his example rather than his advice.

Luis drove me back up to the *hacienda* where I picked up a bottle of Rémy Martin and a jug of ice and lay back in the *chinchorro* slung between two pillars of the verandah. A flight of scarlet ibis sailed past to roost on the lagoon. I paid them little heed, but drank steadily till the sun sank with scarcely a hiss into the twenty-mile strait that separated the island from mainland Venezuela. Numero Siete came and sat beside me for a while but went away when I ignored her. It occurred to me that there would be no Numero Ocho. Only Numero Uno had had a name. She'd lasted two years, long enough to give her delusions of permanency. I gave commands and thereafter avoided the same mistake by frequent changes. Somewhere deep inside I knew that I was disabled from deep relationships, perhaps forever.

The light faded fast. Luis appeared at the foot of the verandah and regarded me uneasily. He wanted me to go inside so he could switch on the floodlights and let the dogs loose. Security hardly seemed a priority at that moment but it was a still, clammy evening and the mosquitoes would soon be out. I rolled out of the hammock and bore my half-empty bottle inside. Towards midnight I rang Kate. The drink had confused me and I was working on the principle that Venezuela was about four hours ahead of London time. It wasn't.

I doubt if she'd have been polite to me, sober, in the middle of the day. Drunk, at four a.m., I was allowed only the speaking space permitted by her incredulity.

'It's Lem,' I said.

'Who?'

'Lem. Your ex-husband. Listen, Kate, I've got to see Angelica . . .'

'What do you mean, "got to see"? Do you know what time it is?'

'For Christ's sake,' I shouted. 'Who's worried about the sodding time? I've got to see Angelica. I've a right to see her! She's my daughter.'

'Right? You gave up all your rights ten years ago, or have you forgotten? You disgusting bastard, if you want to see her, you get on a plane and come back here and she can look at you behind bars where you belong.'

'I might just do that, you cow,' I yelled. 'And if I did, you'd be sorry, you'd all be sorry, the bloody lot of you!'

The phone went dead. I went back to my bottle. An hour later I fell across my bed. Behind me the door opened. Numero Siete stood there, slim, brown, naked. Our eyes met. She turned and went, quietly closing the door behind her.

I fell asleep and almost immediately my dream came. Pa was drowning in a raging sea. He stretched out his hands to me and cried. 'Help me, Lem! Please help me!' I swam towards him with a powerful, easy stroke, reached my hands tantilizingly close, laughing at his efforts to catch them. Then with a last despairing lunge he seized my wrists just as he sank and drew me down after him beneath the stifling waves.

I woke suddenly. There was half an ounce left at the

bottom of the cognac bottle. I tossed it down and returned to a black uncharted sleep.

Next morning I was still drunk. I breakfasted on black coffee, worked out the time difference correctly, and rang Uncle Percy at his Gloucester Place flat.

Uncle Percy, more properly Sir Percy Nostrand, my godfather, was the only person in England I could call a friend and the only visitor I'd ever received on Margarita, apart from a few journalists that Luis set the dogs on. And even his visit had had to wait until just a couple of months earlier when his retirement from a fairly muted career in Whitehall had, as he put it, 'released him from the constraints of public duty'. Well, perhaps it was an old-fashioned notion of duty which prohibited an unimportant Civil Servant from accepting the hospitality of an escaped criminal, but it was an equally old-fashioned notion of loyalty which had made him my only defender and kept him my only friend when the balloon went up, and for that I was eternally grateful.

The line was bad, but he wasn't unprepared to hear from.

'Kate was on to me first thing this morning,' he shouted. 'Lem, you really shouldn't have contacted her like that. She was most distressed.'

'No. I'm sorry,' I yelled. 'Tell her I'm sorry. Uncle Percy, I have to see Angelica. Soon. Please, can you get her to fly out here as soon as possible? Perhaps you could bring her yourself.'

'Lem, we've been through this before. Kate still feels bitter and threatening phone calls in the middle of the night haven't altered the situation for the better. In two years, when Angie's eighteen, she can make up her own mind. But sixteen's a sensitive age. I can't help seeing Kate's point of view. Lem, why the sudden urgency? It's only a few weeks since I saw you and you seemed content enough to be patient then.'

I thought of telling him. But what good would it do unless he then told Kate and that smacked of begging. I didn't want to see my daughter under such conditions.

I said, 'Oh, put it down to a bad bout of depression, Uncle Percy. Thanks for trying.'

I returned to the bottle and made it my constant companion for the next few days. That wasn't unusual. But I started to do my drinking very noisily in the Bella Vista or the Concorde in Porlamar, and that was. I'd lived a very quiet life, partly for security reasons but mainly because my situation in Venezuela had been very ambivalent ever since I arrived in Caracas ten years before, not quietly as planned, but with Chief Superintendent Hunnicut of Scotland Yard hot on my trail.

I'd done the groundwork, knew a lot of the right people and was able to make out some kind of case for citizenship on the grounds of Mama's nationality. But it was Hunnicut himself who tipped the balance. His shout-loudly-at-the-thick-Dagoes attitude got right up the thick Dagoes' noses. I was allowed to stay. But I didn't get a passport, and the unwritten condition was that I lived quietly on Mama's old estate on Margarita Island and gave plenty of warning if I visited the mainland.

For ten years this had suited me very well. For ten years I'd been so self-effacing that there'd probably been complaints in Caracas that I wasn't even a tourist attraction.

Well, all that had changed now. You don't get too many British visitors on Margarita Isalnd but those who did come were soon quickly aware of the identity of the noisy drunk with the generous disposition. Antonio Lemuel Ernest Sebastian Stanhope-Swift, 6th Viscount Bessacarr, the well-known charity embezzler, illegal arms dealer and fugitive from justice. Not that that bothered them. Most were only too keen to rub shoulders with a headline-maker. Only on that last night in the Bella Vista's patio restaurant looking out across the wide sweep of the bay did I run into any active opposition.

I had taken Numero Siete with me and I was in fine and noisy form. Hearing the bray of Home Counties English across the room, I despatched Eduardo, the head waiter, with a jeroboam of champagne for the party.

Five minutes later he was back, small worry lines crinkling his sallow skin around the eyes, followed by an acolyte pushing the ice-tub trolley.

'*Que passa, Eduardo?*' I demanded.

He ironed out the worry lines with one of his most golden smiles and said, 'Your friends are desolated, Señor Swift. They have drunk so much already that they cannot do justice to your gift. They thank you and beg that they may be allowed to postpone their enjoyment to another evening.'

I smiled back as I draped my napkin across my lobster thermidor and stood up. Numero Siete watched me with indifference, Eduardo with alarm, while at the bar Luis instinctively slid his hand down to the waist-belt where he liked to tuck his .38 Special.

'*Por favor*,' I said to the acolyte, relieving him of the champagne trolley. Pushing it before me, I threaded my way across the room to the party of English diners. The source of the trouble was evident at a glance, a slim grey-haired man with that look of calm certainty which sits equally well on the faces of elder statesmen and the backside of elder baboons.

'*Mira, chico*,' I said to him. 'I hear you don't like my drink.'

Some of the others looked a little embarrassed at my approach. He didn't even twitch a muscle.

'Thank you, no,' he said as if refusing to let a waiter top up his glass.

'What's wrong with it?' I demanded.

Now he looked me full in the face.

'With the drink, nothing. It's an excellent wine,' he said.

'OK. So drink,' I said.

'But we do not care to share the profits of crime,' he continued. 'So you must excuse us on this occasion, Señor Swift. Good evening.'

It was the veneer of politeness that got to me. It reduced the incident to a good story for a St James's club, a piece of propaganda for true breeding.

'Have it your own way, *chico*,' I said, seizing the jeroboam and untwisting the wire round the cork. 'If you won't drink, you can drown!'

The cork popped. I put my thumbs over the neck of the bottle and shook it violently like a racing driver celebrating a Grand Prix victory. The champagne fizzed and fountained out, spraying everyone at the Englishman's table and also at most of the neighbouring tables. There was a babble of protest, a scraping of chairs. I roared with triumphant laughter, not at the consternation I was causing but at the look of sheer animal fury I had provoked on those well-bred, controlled features.

Somewhere at the edge of the room there was another pop, as if some other reveller had decided to join in the fun. Then more screams of outrage. But somehow these had a different note, the pitch of real terror. I saw the look of fury on the white-headed Englishman's face fade as he looked beyond me.

Slowly I turned.

At the seaward entrance to the patio stood four men. Over their heads they wore nylon stocking masks. In their hands they carried machine-pistols. Immediately before them, arms raised, were three men I recognized as hotel security officers, probably attracted, and distracted, by the scene I had caused with the champagne. While at the bar, more alert than they but still not alert enough, Luis was sliding off his stool with his right hand dangling at his waist-belt and his left exploring a rapidly spreading patch of red at his right shoulder.

That was the pop I had heard. I took my thumbs off the neck of the bottle and the jet of champagne immediately detumesced to a gurgling overflow and then fell silent altogether.

'Mr Swift, over here,' commanded one of the intruders.

I didn't move.

'Quickly, or we start firing.'

The gun barrels jerked menacingly, not in my direction but towards the terrified diners.

Carefully I set the jeroboam down in front of the Englishman. The fellow was really cool, I had to give him that.

'Perhaps I will have a glass after all,' he said.

'Move it!' screamed the gunman.

I went towards him.

'Listen, you bastard,' I said. 'What the hell . . .'

The pistol barrel came round and crashed against my jaw. I almost went down but one of the others caught me under the arm and I was dragged half-conscious from the room.

Behind me I could hear the gang-leader screaming, 'Tell

them this is the work of the Bravo Commando of FALN. Tell them that we intend to scour this foreign scum from our land and put their criminal wealth in the people's pockets. Tell them . . .'

What else *they* were to be told I didn't hear. I was half dragged, half carried a short distance on to the beach, then I was flung face down into the back of a sand-buggy and as it raced along the beach my arms were pinioned and broad bands of surgical tape slapped across my eyes and mouth. A couple of minutes later I was dragged out of the buggy and tossed into some kind of motorboat. I lost interest in externals after that, concentrating all my efforts on not choking on my own spittle and vomit. I was aware of being transferred to another land vehicle whose movement was marginally less distressing than the boat's. That too finally halted. I was dragged out, frog-marched into a building (I heard a door slam behind me), bumped down a flight of stairs and deposited with a stunning crash on to a concrete floor. There was a babble of voices, relieved, self-congratulatory. Then one commanding voice spoke, footsteps retreated, a door closed.

Next minute the surgical tape was ripped from my face taking chunks of my beard and moustache with it.

Standing over me removing the nylon mask from his face, was the FALN guerrilla leader.

I looked up at him in loathing.

'You fucking idiot, Dario,' I said. 'You nearly killed me!'

He grinned unconcernedly and stooped to untie my bonds.

'Shut up, Señor Swift,' he said. 'We've got a lot to do.'

2

. . . welcome home! . . .

We spent the next hour making tapes and taking photos.

The tapes were easy. I just let my voice sound progressively weaker and more stumbling as I read the prepared script. The photos we did in reverse order, that is, the worst first. We started with one of me looking half conscious, cheeks sucked in, hair and beard unkempt and combed out to look as long as possible, a grimy blood-stained bandage wrapped around my right hand.

'Better give me the ring now,' he said.

I handed it over.

'Where will you get the finger?' I asked.

'No shortage of fingers in the *ranchitos!*' He laughed.

We then worked backwards, taking half a dozen of me looking progressively better, the last one being done after I'd given my hair and beard an initial trim. No one was likely to remember the state of my coiffure immediately before my sudden departure from the Bella Vista.

Finally I opened the US passport Dario produced. It was in the name of William Banks. There was an entry stamp showing that Mr. Banks had landed at Simon Bolivar airport at Maiquetia two days earlier. The photograph of me was eight years old. I'd given out word that I was suffering from ring-worm and not moved from the *hacienda* for two months till the hair grew again. Now I set it alongside the shaving mirror and consulted it from time to time as I worked on my face.

Dario sat and watched, a foul-smelling cigarillo dangling like a fuse from his lips.

'Still working at the university, are you?' I asked. Despite myself, I was nervous and needed conversation to steady the hand wielding the cut-throat razor.

'In line for senior lecturer,' he said proudly.

'In moral philosophy?' I laughed. He looked offended, but I wasn't impressed. He'd looked offended eight years ago when I'd offered him his first bribe. He and a couple of FALN militants (the guerrilla wing of FLN, the National Liberation Front) had broken into my ranch-house to assassinate me. Dario, a first-year university student, had come along out of bravado and had saved himself by collapsing in a dead faint when Luis had cut his two companions in half with a machine-pistol. He'd wanted to effect the same division on Dario, only more slowly, but I'd taken pity on the boy's youth and also his good sense as he spilled everything he knew about FALN into my tape-recorder. After he'd finished, I pointed out to him how distressed his friends would be to hear that tape and then offered him a very large retainer if he'd care to work for me. I'd read the man right. The combination of bribery and blackmail was irresistible and he returned to his FALN cell as the heroic survivor of a desperate assault on the vastly superior might of the English criminal fascist. My idea at first was merely to use him as a listening-post in the midst of my enemies. But then it had occurred to me that if ever I should need to get out of Venezuela without anyone knowing I'd gone, someone like Dario could be very useful. Just to disappear would have been easy enough, but what I really wanted was to be able to convince the powers that be, on both sides of the Atlantic, that I was safely taken care of.

So was born the plan. I'd never really thought I'd have to use it.

I winced now as I drew the razor down my left jawbone. There was a large bruise where the pistol had hit me.

'Look what that lunatic's done!' I said angrily.

Dario shrugged.

'You're lucky it's not worse. He thought it was for real. They all did.'

'Who are *they*?'

'Some of my students. Enthusiasts for the cause. Don't worry about the bruise. I brought some make-up to cover the white skin where the sun hasn't burnt you. It should do the trick.'

It wasn't perfect but it helped. I rubbed it along my jaw and into my scalp where I'd thinned twin tracks into my hair to give a widow's peak. A pair of spectacles finished the job. William Banks stared back at me out of the mirror, bespectacled, balding, with a neatly clipped blonde moustache. I didn't look exactly like the passport photograph, but who the hell does?

Dario looked at me critically, nodded his approval and said, 'You'll pass. Señor, about my money . . .'

'It'll be in your account tomorrow.' I glanced at William Banks's Omega digital. 'Three hours, is that right? You'll have things to do. Do them quietly, OK? I'll catch some sleep.'

He looked at me in disbelief for a moment. How he looked after a moment I don't know.

Seated on the hard chair in front of the rough table which held the shaving mirror, I sank rapidly into a deep and precisely measured sleep.

As I waited for my flight to be called at Simon Bolivar the following morning, I bought a copy of *El Universal*. My kidnapping got a big splash. The text of a FALN message was printed with only minor omissions, notably the obscene adjectives which always introduced the President and his government. There was some nice rhetoric.

The world vomits to see how our beloved country harbours the criminal detritus of other nations. Only a government of criminals would extend the hand of friendship to other criminals. How much of Swift's stolen millions has gone into the pockets of our corrupt officials? The FLN does not attack the people nor does it want money belonging to the people. All it wants for the safe release of this evil man is the chance to use his ill-gotten wealth for the true benefit of the people. Plus the following legitimate demands.

The list of 'legitimate demands' was long and comprehensive. The editor of *El Universal* suggested wryly that it wasn't very skilful bargaining to stress so emphatically the worthlessness of what you were selling. I smiled. It was going to give the British press a problem too. I mean, they couldn't really express their customary jingoistic indignation when they didn't give a damn, could they?

Personally I didn't mind what they said as long as it kept all interested parties happy that I wasn't on the Isla da Margarita only because I was tied up in some stinking cellar in Caracas.

My flight to New York was called. I boarded the plane without incident and it took off dead on time. I settled down to read the American newspapers provided with the in-flight literature. Below me Venezuela faded away. I'd spent the last ten years, a quarter of my life there, besides many happy weeks on vacation with Mama when I was a child. I didn't reckon I'd see it again. I really meant to take one last nostalgic backward look.

But somehow I forgot.

New York took me unawares. Last time I'd been here, I was one step ahead of Hunnicut and not in a very impressionistic mood. Since then I'd spent most of my life seeing more trees than people. Now these buildings, these crowds, suddenly sensitized an area of my mind I'd forgotten existed, an area even Quintero and his stumbling introduction of the word 'cancer' hadn't really reached – panic.

It passed quickly. I paid off my cab on Fifth Avenue and walked across to Madison, an intuitive rather than a necessary precaution. I'd booked a room at the Biltmore from the airport. The lobby was packed with a party of Japs fighting for their room keys. I pushed through them with no more concern than if they'd been pampas grass, and when I had my meal alone in my room later, it wasn't because I was frightened of being among people, but simply because I was exhausted.

The next day I felt much better, indeed the best I'd felt in weeks. Quintero had told me that initially deterioration would be slow and there might even be times when the discomfort which had taken me to him in the first place might temporarily disappear. As I washed his tablets down with a cup of that bitter black goo the American like to claim is the best coffee in the world, I wondered about getting a second opinion. On Margarita it would have been impossible without inviting everyone to know my business and that was the last thing I'd wanted. Suddenly it struck me that in one respect a second opinion was pointless. Healthy or dying, I was committed now. I was on my way home.

Yes, I'd get a second opinion all right. I'd be a fool not to. But in the only place an educated, well-heeled English gentleman would dream of looking for a second opinion: Harley Street.

There was one more change of identity.

My Viscount Bessacarr passport was locked away somewhere in the Venezuelan Ministry of Justice, but I hadn't let them lay hands on that of my *alterapersona*, Alexander Evans. I'd had to update it a little, but there'd been plenty of time on Margarita to do a good job.

I crossed the border into Canada as William Banks, shaved my moustache off in a motel room that same night, and arrived in Montreal as Alexander Evans.

There I spent three days allegedly letting the dust settle and making sure that no one was taking any undue interest in me. I say 'allegedly' for on the third day I woke up knowing that I'd been merely procrastinating.

Once out of Venezuela, I was as unsafe in one place as in any other, and in a Commonwealth country I might just as well have been in England.

I bought my ticket to London.

I travelled tourist on a cut-price night flight. There was no point in being ostentatious. We arrived at Heathrow at five-thirty in the morning. Unchallenged, I walked through the green-light channel. Then and only then as I emerged into the outer reception area of Heathrow did it really strike me that I was back.

I stood still and took it all in. There were signs directing me towards an Underground link with central London. That was new since last time I was here, I thought.

Outside through the plate glass I could see that the skies were heavy and grey. Or perhaps it was just morning mist, I thought generously. I wanted it to feel good to be back.

Someone bumped into the back of me and I realized I was blocking the way. I began to move forward again and the person behind moved with me.

18

But now there was a hand on my arm gripping it firmly but not yet painfully above the elbow. Jesus reckoned he knew when someone was touching him with intent and purpose. Me too. And I knew who it was even before he spoke.

'Mr Evans? Or is it Señor Swift?' said Hunnicut's familiar voice. 'No, let's be properly formal now you're back on English soil. Welcome home, my lord!'

3

. . . just the job . . .

I hadn't seen Hunnicut since we sweated out the Venezuelan government's decision on extradition ten years before. They kept me under a sort of house-restraint in one of Caracas's best hotels. Hunnicut was six floors below me and on the noisy front, while my suite overlooked the garden. They kept a much closer eye on him than they did on me. After all, I was a paying customer, while the chauvinist Hunnicut was a very undesirable alien.

'Hello, Honey,' I said, 'Still Chief Superintendent, is it?'

'Commander now,' he said. 'I could have retired last year, but I always had this feeling, if I waited long enough I'd see you again, Swifty.'

'Well, congratulations,' I said. 'On your promotion and your premonition.'

I stopped now and turned to face him. He released my arm but kept close. The years had been good to him. Or rather they'd stamped forty on his face at birth and now at fifty he was at last in credit. He was stuffed full of the prejudices and the conventional wisdom of the British working man. But he was dogged in pursuit and incorruptible in negotiation. He'd never even let me buy him a drink, and I mean in private as well as in public. I liked him for that.

Now I looked at him standing warily before me, deep-set grey eyes watchful, heavy shoulders hunched, Gibraltarian jaw thrust invitingly forward. But anyone who took a swing at that would be a fool.

I smiled, put down my suitcase and held out my right hand.

'I was just thinking,' I said. 'It's not right coming home with no one to meet you. It's nice to see you, Honey.'

Instinctively he took my hand. I pulled him towards me

and swung the attaché case in my left hand hard between his legs. His eyes came further out of their deep caves then they'd been in half a century and his mouth rounded in a rather feminine pout. Pride, or shock, didn't let any sound come out, but his leathery cheeks switched quickly from dark to light tan. He still tried to hold on to me, but I pulled free and then I was off; where, I didn't know, but why, I knew full well. I wanted to see my daughter before I died and I didn't want it to be across a prison table with a gaggle of screws looking on.

I should have known better. Hunnicut had slipped up by letting me get close enough to groin him, but there'd been no looseness about the rest of his reception plans. There were men on every exit. I met the first at the bottom of the stairway. More by luck than judgment my flailing hand took him across the nose and temporarily fended him off. The next stood innocently by till I was almost past him then he tripped me and jumped with both knees into my kidneys. A third 'accidentally' trod on my left hand and I let go of the attaché case. By this time the first had joined the party, signalling his arrival by burying his size eleven in my ribs and showering my lightweight mohair with blood from his nose.

Once there'd have been a fascinated crowd around such a scene in ten seconds flat, but now disturbances at international airports so often mean bombs and bullets that the initial instinct is to flee, or at least fall flat, rather than gather. So my captors managed to get in several more telling blows before deciding that they were running the risk of offending the delicate public.

I was dragged to a waiting car. Hunnicut climbed painfully into the front passenger seat.

'Want a free swing, guv?' offered one of the men sandwiching me in to the rear.

Hunnicut looked sorely tempted but to his credit shook his head. Not that it did me much good. As the car drew away, the sycophant in the back gave me two pile drivers in the belly. At least I think it was two. I really only felt the first before sliding to the floor in a darkness as sudden and complete as nightfall in the Caribbean.

At what stage it was decided that I'd be better off in a

hospital ward than in a cell at West End Central, I don't know. The thumps I got must have been par for the course in most resisted arrests, but I'd banged my head on the floor when I went down and I guess I was a bit concussed. Anyhow, I vaguely remember getting the full medical bit and I spent most of my first day back in Blighty asleep in a bright white hospital room. Of course my sleep was medicated and intermittent. I was brought out of it from time to time to be examined every which way and I had enough clarity of thought and vision to spot the bars on the window and the muscle on the door.

Finally about six in the evening I woke up feeling if not like a new man at least reconizably like the old one and also very hungry.

I shouted to the Herculean cop and demanded food. He didn't look as if he understood me and when he came back with Hunnicut, I said, 'How come someone as xenophobic as you has started hiring non-English-speaking cops?'

He smiled wanly. He looked very down, I thought. It was not the way a man should look who had finally removed the one obstacle to his happy and honoured retirement.

I said, 'What's the food like here, Honey? I'd appreciate a decent last meal before you take me to the dungeons.'

He offered me a Woodbine. I shook my head and watched as he lit one himself. He used to rather fancy himself with smoke-rings, but it just came out in a steady jet today.

'I'll see you get something just now,' he said.

'Just for the book, Honey,' I said, 'how'd you know I was coming?'

'Simple,' he said. 'It's all computers now, Swifty. Soon as I heard you'd gone missing, I put out a scan for an Alexander Evans on all incoming transatlantic flights, just in case.'

Simple indeed. I should have stuck with William Banks.

'Cheer up, Honey,' I said. 'They'll make you commissioner for this.'

He tossed his half-smoked cigarette into the washbasin and turned the tap on it, his back towards me.

'Swifty,' he said over the gush of water, 'I've been talking to the doctor.'

Then I had it. I realized I'd saved myself a Harley Street

fee. I'd got my second opinion on the National Health.

He turned and looked at me so unhappily that I found myself putting on a comforting tone. *Me* comforting *him* already!

'It's OK, Honey,' I said. 'I know. That's why I came.'

He started to answer but the door opened at the same time as his mouth and what entered was far more distracting than what could possibly have emerged.

The man was unremarkable though not undistinguished. About fifty, small but very erect, finely chiselled features, neat, greying military moustache and dressed in a traditionally cut charcoal grey suit which he wore like a uniform. Brigadier in mufti, I categorized.

But the woman defied categorizing. She was younger, perhaps in her early thirties, but heavy, almost theatrical make-up made it difficult to be sure. Her not unattractively squashed-up features were topped with a spiky haircut far too red to be natural. And she was wearing two hundred pounds' worth of indigo velvet jacket over a grubby yellow T-shirt and patched jeans. I'd missed out on punk but this had to be it.

'Thank you, Commander,' said the Brigadier dismissively.

Hunnicut looked at him angrily.

'I don't like this,' he began.

I didn't care to hear that. If Honey didn't like it, I guessed I wasn't going to be ecstatic either. But his protest was cut short by the punk woman, who thrust back the door till it crashed against the wall and jerked her incredible head at the opening.

Hunnicut's shoulders hunched, not in aggression but defeat, and he left without looking at me.

The punk slammed the door behind him and leaned against it, eyeing me dispassionately. The Brigadier drew up a chair to the bedside.

'Hello,' I said. 'You're not meals-on-wheels, I suppose?'

'Lord Bessacarr. Or, if you prefer it, Mr Swift,' he began in a cold, clear, court-martial-verdict kind of voice. 'You are suffering from a cancerous condition which is almost certainly terminal. You have come back to England presumably to see your daughter for the last time and no doubt to put your affairs in order. I am here to tell you that you have no hope of carrying out this plan.'

'Hold on,' I said. 'You mean if I just lie here and slowly die over the next few months, no one will let my lawyer in? Or any other legitimate visitors? You're talking nonsense! You couldn't do that, not even to a recaptured escapee and I'm not that, remember? There's been no trial, no verdict. Hell, I haven't even been formally arrested yet.'

I pushed back the sheets and swung my legs out of bed. I felt a bit woozy but nothing that a bit of gentle exercise and a few deep breaths of fresh air wouldn't throw off. Not that I expected to get beyond the door, but it would be interesting to see how the brigadier would react. He didn't, but then he didn't need to, not with me in a hospital nightgown like a parachute and no clothes anywhere in sight.

So I washed my hands carefully instead and said, 'Look, couldn't we discuss this thing over a kilo of steak?'

'Let me make the position clear,' said the Brigadier. 'As far as we're concerned, you're Mr Alexander Evans. You are being held for breaking the currency regulations. You will be remanded in custody pending further investigation. If you attempt to tell the court that you are really Lemuel Swift (who, incidentally, you resemble not at all and who is currently well known to be in the hands of FALN terrorists somewhere in Venezuela) you will be remanded in custody for pyschiatric examination. These remands will continue till they are no longer necessary, which medical prognosis suggests will be not earlier than eight, not later than sixteen weeks. Once you are bedridden, of course, you cease to be of interest to anyone and can tell the world whatever you like.'

'One newspaper picture of me coming out of court after shouting to the press that I'm Lem Swift and I'll be of interest to a lot of people.'

'I doubt it. The chances of anyone taking such a picture are remote, and even if they did, I repeat, you don't look much like the hirsute exile whose picture appeared in all the papers last week.'

'My wife would recognize me,' I said.

'I dare say she would,' said the Brigadier. 'And if she did, this would merely confirm what has already been suggested to her; to wit, that your kidnapping was a cover to get you back to England undetected where you purpose considerable harm to your enemies, including your former wife and daughter.'

'You told her that?' I said aghast. 'She'd never believe that.'

'On the contrary, she found it quite easy to believe. Your recent phone call seemed to her an evident symptom of your paranoiac state, brought on, she has now been told, by long isolation and various tropical deseases.'

'And Angelica . . .?'

He nodded and said, 'I fear so. She had to be put fully in the picture so that she wouldn't inadvertently leave a trail a journalist, say, might follow.'

'A trail?'

'Oh yes. Didn't I say? They've left the country, ostensibly to avoid being pestered by the papers. But they believe you're the real threat, Mr Swift. You'll need my help both to find them and to persuade them otherwise.

I wanted to hit him. Instead I managed an unconcerned shrug and said, 'OK, doc. Here's the deal. You get me my clothes and buy me dinner, and we'll talk this thing through. I mean, it may be all you want is my signature on a blankets-for-Oxfam list, OK?'

'This creep's lower than dog-dirt,' said the woman, opening her orange-gash-vermilion mouth for the first time. Her voice was not unpleasant, husky and very Irish.

'Hey, doc,' I said. 'You did that without moving your lips.'

'Mr Swift,' said the Brigadier. 'You know I'm not a doctor just as I know that a man of your background does not speak naturally like a stray from some Yankee hard-nosed detective series. Can we remove at once both those sources of irritation?'

'Brigadier,' I said, 'for my clothes and a meal I'll be delighted to remove anything you care to suggest.'

He started slightly as though my change of title had struck home, then he said, 'Miss Reilly, would you mind?'

'*Miss?*' I chortled. 'You mean she's an unclaimed treasure?'

The woman shot me a glance full of hate and a promise I hoped she'd never get the chance to keep. Then she went out, returning a moment later with my clothes, cleaned and pressed.

I looked at Reilly for a minute. She showed no sign of leaving so I removed my nightgown and did a careful examination of my body, checking the bruised and anointed spots carefully.

'Is this really necessary?' said the Brigadier impatiently.

I pretended to think the protest was a moral one and replied, 'She can always look away.'

'From what?' said Reilly scornfully.

I got dressed.

The air outside was probably more contaminated than the air within, but I gulped at it like Bacardi on the rocks. The street in front of the hospital was narrow and relatively quiet, but it ran into a well-lit and busy highway. I watched the London traffic and people go pouring by in a never-ending stream. It seemed that I just had to plunge into that and I'd be swept away out of sight and out of reach in seconds. But there were things I needed to find out. And in any case, I guessed the apparent ease of exit was illusory.

We went to a small French restaurant a stone's throw from Fitzroy Square. Ten years ago it had been a pizzeria. I knew because *Vita 3's* offices had been just around the corner in the Square as I was sure the Brigadier and his aggressive companion were very aware. We were expected, and ushered to a reserved booth which offered some privacy but not as much as the general bustle and hubbub of the place, which was crowded.

'Are there any dietary restrictions?' enquired the Brigadier.

'What? Oh, I see. Well, I don't chew many raw chillies,' I said.

'The *rognons* are highly thought of. Or the veal.'

'Both,' I said. 'Preferably though not necessarily in that order.'

He ordered in good French. He had an omelette and Reilly stuck at Perrier water and stick biscuits.

'Have you two seen in their kitchens, or what?' I wondered. 'I'm the one with the busted gut, remember?'

'You're doing Sam Spade again,' said the Brigadier in a pained voice.

'Sorry. All right. I'll try to eat like a gentleman.'

The meal continued in silence. The food was excellent, though rather let down by the wine which affected to be a 1970 Médoc of the most impeccable provenance but which wasn't a patch on the Chilean red which I imported into Margarita by the barrelful.

I felt able to express this opinion to the Brigadier, whom I could not feel to be my host in the real, that is the financial sense. He seemed to be genuinely interested and made a note of my recommendation, saying that he had a certain advisory responsibility to his club cellar committee.

'You won't regret it,' I said. 'No, no pudding for me. A lot of black coffee, an ounce of armagnac and about six inches of Cuban tobacco will round things off nicely.' I got them except that the Cuban was Jamaican and the armagnac was cooking brandy. At least it all confirmed the restaurant was genuinely French. They cheat on everything but food.

'Ok,' I said, drawing luxuriously on my cigar. 'What's the pitch? Or, if you prefer, isn't it about time you put me in the picture, sir?'

The Brigadier shook his head slightly as though irritated by a fly and said, 'Mr Swift, please don't let this pleasant treatment you're receiving go to your head. We can afford to be gentlemanly with you because we simply don't need to be anything else. We hold all the cards, believe me. You hold nothing. You *are* nothing.'

'You think so?' I replied with an effort at jauntiness. 'Even criminals have rights in a free society, Brig. And I've still got a few influential friends.'

'I doubt it,' said the Brigadier. 'And even if you had, I do not think that they'd care to match their influence against mine.'

There it was, a gentle reminder of the official clout this cold-eyed ringmaster and his attendant clown must carry. I didn't really need reminding. I remembered how unhappy old Honey had looked in the hospital. But when the Brigadier had cracked the whip, Honey had gone trotting off as obedient as any high-stepping circus horse. Anybody who can make a Scotland Yard Commander jump has every reason to be confident he can make a cancerous criminal fugitive leap like a performing flea.

'OK,' I said. 'I've got no rights and I've got no friends. But I must have something, else why the big welcome?'

The Brigadier smiled and nodded.

'Indeed you have, Mr Swift,' he said. 'Though you weren't to know it, your move came at almost the perfect time for us.'

'Makes you believe in God, does it, Brig?' I asked.

'He is certainly providing us with the big guns,' he replied. 'You see, when we heard you'd been caught, our interest was aroused for reasons that will become apparent. But as your usefulness to us would involve giving you a certain amount of freedom, and as your lack of freedom looked to be our main bargaining counter, well, we could see that it was going to be difficult to hold you to your side of any deal.'

'You could have asked for my word,' I said.

'Once, perhaps. But I don't think you'd find a man in England willing to accept your word now,' he said. 'Nevertheless I sent Miss Reilly down here to keep an eye on the situation. And when she called in to tell me that the doctors had diagnosed a terminal cancer, that put a different complexion on things. Not only did it explain your sudden desire to come back to the UK, but it gave us a real lever.'

'That's what makes *me* believe in God,' said Reilly. 'Crap like you getting cancer at just the right moment.'

'You see, all you can do now is give us a straight *yes* or *no*,' said the Brigadier. 'If you say *no*, I've spelt out to you what the rest of your brief life will be like.'

'I heard you, and I remember things, sometimes for a couple of hours together,' I said impatiently. '*No* to what? *Yes* to what?'

The red-headed woman leaned forward, her face close to mine. The proximity made her features look even more squashed than they were but her breath was sweet.

She said, 'We want you to kill someone for us.'

I smiled incredulously. I'd been busy examining all my possible areas of expertise and had been hard put to come up with any single one which would make me a desirable property. But being a hit-man didn't even figure at the bottom end of the list.

'You've got the wrong Swift,' I assured her. 'Boy, have you got the wrong Swift!'

'They're the only two that we know of,' said the Brigadier. 'And we're pretty sure we've got the right one.'

'What the hell does that mean?' I said, suddenly alert. 'Who is it you want me to kill?'

'Who is it in the whole world you'd most like to see dead?' murmured the Brigadier. 'We wouldn't dream of asking you to do anything that would go against the grain.'

'No!' rasped Reilly in her bog-brogue. 'It's just the job for a creepy cockroach like yourself. We want you to kill your father!'

4

. . . Friday's footprint . . .

I sat very still for a while after that.

The Brigadier must have done another of his finger-waggles, for a waiter sloshed some more cooking brandy from his armagnac flask into my glass.

'Drink up,' advised the Brigadier. 'Get your breath back. I'm afraid we've taken you by surprise.'

'Don't waste your sympathy,' said Reilly. 'The bastard's just working out whether he should use a knife or a gun.'

'Brig,' I said. 'Just one thing – do we really need this- . . . this *amphibian?*'

'Miss Reilly is my right-hand – er person on this exercise,' said the Brigadier reprovingly. 'Where I go, she goes.'

'Even when you go for a leak?' I said, standing up. 'Well, not with me.'

I didn't want to be like a kid in class putting his hand up but it seemed wisest to get some kind of agreement. So I looked interrogatively at the Brigadier, who smiled slightly and nodded, before I set off down the open corridor at the back of the restaurant. To my right was the kitchen. Straight ahead was the rear entrance. It was tempting, but no doubt the Brigadier had stationed one of his yo-yos there among the dustbins. Added to which, I was in full view of the table still.

To the left were the loos. I opened the door and glanced back. The Brigadier was deep in reverie but red Reilly was watching me like a bug she was preparing to swat. I smiled invitingly at her and went through the door.

If she'd accepted my invitation she wouldn't have been out of place. I was in the Ladies. Fortunately it was unoccupied.

More years ago than I care to remember, I'd realized I was fully committed to the crooked path when I found myself always checking exits shortly after making entrances. When

I used to chew rubbery pizzas in this place after a late night at the office, there'd been two rear doors, the one in the corridor plus one in the kitchen, both easily covered by one man. The Gents didn't even have a window.

But the Ladies did.

It was high and it was narrow and it probably hadn't been open since the Frogs moved in. They don't like draughts. They spoil the soufflés.

Balancing on one foot on the handle of the lavatory door, I tried the window. It was firm as a rock. Fortunately there was a space of about three feet between the top of the door and the ceiling. I was able to swing myself astride and apply more direct pressure. It still didn't budge.

So I wriggled round on my back, not an easy trick on two inches of wood, and drove my right foot hard against it.

Now it budged. In the confined space of the loo it sounded like an explosion. But in the restaurant it had the din of the kitchen to contend with. Outside, at the end of the narrow service alley into which I now dropped, it had the riot of London's night traffic.

I dusted myself down and glanced up at the window, which looked so small I could hardly believe I'd got through it. The moral, I told myself as I strolled away, is – if you want to get slim, get cancer.

It didn't sound like one of my better jokes.

One of the gifts sparsely scattered into my infant cradle was an antibrood regulator. Or perhaps it was a legacy of Pa's self-sufficiency conditioning. Anyway, as my career to date has shown, I guess, I can be very single-minded. I rarely get hung up on irrelevancies, no matter how emotionally compelling. So now within a few paces I was able to put the Brigadier's crazy scheme right out of my mind and concentrate on the matter in hand. Which was to check the truth of what he'd said about Kate and Angelica.

Six or seven minutes not too conspicuously brisk walking brought me to the quiet Bloomsbury cul-de-sac where Kate and I had spent most of our uneasy marriage. The lease of the house had been in Kate's name from the start, a legal precaution rather than a token of love. But it had worked out well enough. There was no way they could suck the house in when the Charity Commissioners and the Law came vacuuming through the debris of *Vita 3*. There was also the steady income from the trust I'd established for Angelica's upbringing and education. The papers had it that the marriage cracked because of the scandal, but it was just the final blow, though Kate had reacted with surprising bitterness. There'd been one outraged letter, then I'd communicated with her via Uncle Percy. Not that there'd ever been any question of her rejecting my generous financial arrangements! I sometimes wondered what she would have done if I'd asked her to share a life of luxury in exile with me. But I'd never really seriously considered it. Margarita Island was no place for a girl to grow up. At least that was my bullshit reason. My asshole reason was that I didn't need the lumber, that I was better off travelling light.

All motivation claims are either asshole or bullshit; that revelation was another of the gifts that had hit me in the eye as I gurgled my first disbelieving disgust at the world. Bullshit reasons are those which are strongly laced with altruism; asshole reasons those shot through with selfishness. They are equally false. Our altruism rarely helps others. Our egotism rarely helps ourselves. There's something else, I don't know what, but when you wake up in the night racked by nameless terrors, then you must be getting close.

The house was dark. I took out my leather key-pouch. Probably Honey had taken impressions of the lot, but at least he'd put them back. Without looking, I selected a key by touch alone and slipped it into the lock. Another woman might have changed the locks in ten years, but not Kate. She was mean in every sense.

I examined the street carefully before closing the door. It looked empty enough, but I couldn't believe the Brigadier wouldn't send a yo-yo round here as soon as he discovered my flight. The house was empty too. I stood in the hallway and felt it. I'm rarely wrong. Even if there'd been the faintest stir of life in the most distant room, I'd have picked it up.

There was no time for a nostalgic tour. I went quickly up the stairs and checked the bedrooms. In the main one, the wardrobes though not empty were well depleted and on the dressing-table there was no sign of the apothecary's shop range of junk that Kate imagined she needed to magic her face back to life each day.

In the adjoining bathroom, the same evidence of departure was present. Pills, potions, shampoos, toothbrushes, all gone. But in the wall cabinet I found a man's razor and an empty tin of denture cleansing paste. I clicked my own almost unsullied teeth together with some satisfaction till it struck me I'd be willing to give up the lot for a healthy gut. I hoped the bastard shaving in my mirror got leprosy. Angelica's bedroom I'd expected to be a trial, but if anything it presented less problems than her mother's. Despite Uncle Percy's bulletins and the occasional snapshot, I guess I was still thinking in terms of hair-ribbons, teddy bears and the kind of elfin clothes a girl of six wears. Punk posters and an unhygienic knot of jeans in a corner of the wardrobe did nothing for me.

But one thing was clear. The Brigadier hadn't lied. They were gone, and on no short visit either.

I would have liked to have a good poke around, read a few letters, checked appointment books, to get some line on their destination. But I was short of time.

I went back to the big bedroom, clambered on the dressing table stool and removed the Picasso print from the wall. You'd have thought the cow would at least have chosen her own pictures. I bet myself she wouldn't even have gone to the expense of having the combination changed on the safe behind the picture.

I'd have won. It clicked open and the door swung back. It was empty. Well, that wasn't surprising. Kate had an old-sock-under-the-mattress mentality.

I took out my key pouch and selected a small latchkey. In the jamb of the safe just visible when the door was open as far as it would go, that is, barely more than ninety degrees from the wall, was a faint groove. In fact it consisted of three indentations joined by a narrow channel. I fitted the teeth of my key into them and pressed down, once, twice, three times.

There was a gentle click. I reached into the safe and with my fingertips slid the back panel to one side. It was still there, the small washleather bag. I thought of Kate; all those years of screwing with her toothless lover, and a quarter of a million in industrial diamonds a few feet over her head.

There was something else too. A gun. I didn't like guns. Only a fool makes plans that need guns. But even a wise man needs protection against the unforseeable. What's the point of fooling the world if some yo-yo after your wallet puts you in hospital at the crucial moment? So I got a gun. I had to leave it behind of course. Even ten years ago you didn't turn up at Heathrow with a gun in your suitcase. So I left it with my cache. Every where I go I leave caches, like a cat marking out its boundary trees. Come the thirtieth century and they'll probably be as eagerly sought after as hordes of Roman coins.

I pocketed the washleather bag. Then I reached for the gun too. I was deep into the world of the unforeseeable.

Just how deep I began to realize when I picked it up. There was a small envelope underneath it. That hadn't been left by me. That was as startling as Friday's footprint.

I picked it up. I had my name on it.

I put it in my pocket and carefully wiped my fingerprints off the surfaces of the safe before closing both the inner and outer doors.

That was my way of showing I was still in control.

I stepped down from the stool, replaced it before the dressing-table, and sat on it.

Only now did I open the envelope.

It contained a single sheet of paper with a single line of type.

Room 272 has been reserved for Mr Alexander Evans at the Abbotsford Hotel.

Shit, I thought. You clever little brigadier, you! He knew about the window in the ladies' loo. And guessed that I'd know too. He just wanted me to have a little run around in the fresh air, expend my excess energy, show I was independent, then come to heel.

I took the gun out and checked it carefully. Firing pin, action, ammunition, I went through the lot, then put it back together again.

At least at my next interview with the Brigadier if I didn't like what he was doing with his mouth, I could shoot it off.

34

Reilly's too. That thought cheered me up a lot.

Quietly I let myself out of the house. If they thought I was going to go quietly to the Abbotsford with my tail between my legs, they didn't know me yet.

I picked up a taxi in New Oxford Street and told him to take me to Gloucester Place. Here Uncle Percy had had his modest apartment for thirty odd years. If I had any slight hope of getting out of the Brigadier's stranglehold, I'd find it here. Not that Percy Nostrand was a man of very great influence. His Whitehall career hadn't carried him to the heights and he had spent the last twenty years of it in some quiet backwater of the Home Office. But I knew that there was much character behind that benevolent, almost simple exterior, especially when he felt that an injustice had been done. Indeed this had caused our only main point of disagreement for he steadfastly refused to acknowledge my father's guilt all those years ago. I suspect that this blind setting of friendship above all evidence had been partially responsible for his low-key career thereafter.

Later, I'd been only too pleased to benefit from the same flawed judgment. No one knew better than myself how guilty I was, but Uncle Percy had stuck by me and defended me when every other hand in the country was raised against me. I hadn't realized how much I'd need a friend. Without him, even the small contact I'd preserved with Angelica might have been denied by my ex-wife whose keenness to clear herself of the Bessacarr taint, while hanging on to the Bessacarr money, had been phenomenal.

Now I needed a friend again. At the very least he might have some idea where Kate and Angelica had gone.

I approached the apartment with caution but I needn't have bothered. One glance at Uncle Percy would have made me suspect the Brigadier had anticipated my visit here even if his greeting had not beem, 'Lem, they said you'd probably come. Step in, dear boy, step in.'

It was only a couple of months since I'd seen him but he seemed much older now. His face was as round and as ruddy as ever, but there was something hectic about his colouring. He led me into the book-lined living-room, musty with the smell of old paper and leather bindings and heated by an antique gas fire to an almost unbearable temperature despite the warmth of the summer night outside.

He said, 'Lem, it's good to see you, it really is. I was worried silly when I read about the kidnapping. I could hardly believe it when they told me you were back in England and might make contact.'

'*They?*' I said.

'They're very high up,' he said unhappily. 'People I respect. They have top-level authority.'

I nodded. He had been a Home Office civil servant all his life. *They* would know how to tighten the screws.

I said, 'Listen, Uncle Percy. Whatever they told you, forget it. Here's the truth. I'm dying of cancer. All I want to do is see Angelica before I die, but they won't let me. They want me to become involved in some lunatic scheme to assassinate Pa! You're the only person I can turn to for help.'

He shook his head disbelievingly. 'Oh Lem, Lem. Cancer, you say? I'm so sorry, so sorry. And killing Billy? It's a mad world. I never thought to live to hear such madness.'

His distress made me feel guilty for dumping this mess on his carpet, but I had to persist.

'Kate and Angelica have disappeared. Do you have any idea where?'

He shook his head.

'I'm sorry, Lem. I haven't spoken to Kate since she told me about your phone call. She was very angry, very upset. Why didn't you tell me about the cancer when you rang me the next day?'

'Would it have made any difference?' I said bitterly. 'Percy, can you try to find out for me? You must still have contacts. These people have got them stowed away somewhere safe. You could winkle it out, I'm sure.'

He shook his head. He looked at the same time obdurate, ashamed, and afraid.

'Percy,' I said, 'for God's sake, they can't have conned you into thinking it's your patriotic duty not to help me.'

He shook his head again and said, 'Please, believe me, Lem. There's nothing I can do. Please go now.'

I was completely taken aback and the shock of rejection stung me to nastiness.

I said, 'You're afraid, Percy. What of? You used to be frightened of nothing. What have they threatened you with? Cutting off your index-linked pension?'

He looked at me in angry reproach and I was immediately overcome with shame as I recalled my long debt of gratitude to this man.

'I apologize for that,' I said. 'I didn't meant it. I'm overwrought.'

'That's all right, Lem,' he said. 'No offence, no offence.'

He hesitated, then went on. 'A man came. He knew a vast deal about me. A vast deal. And about my friends. All my friends.'

I nodded, beginning to see the picture. Uncle Percy's fondness for handsome young men was a Whitehall commonplace, hardly worth remarking on, indeed almost normal in some corridors of power. I could not see Percy bowing before blackmail attempts aimed at him personally, but ...

I said gently, 'This man hinted at ... unpleasantness for your friends?'

He nodded, distressed and ashamed.

I said, 'It's OK. I understand. Really I do.'

'Believe me, Lem, if I knew anything that would help, I'd still tell you, no matter what,' he said, stuttering in his eagerness to convince me.

'I believe you,' I said. 'I believe you. Goodbye, Uncle Percy. I'll see myself out.'

I left him with tears in his eyes. Of all the nastinesses that were being perpetrated by the Brigadier and his chums, this was the worst yet.

Outside in the street, I stood uncertain for a moment or two. It was getting late and I was very tired. Finally I shrugged. The least these bastards owed me was bed and breakfast. I hailed a taxi and told him to take me to the Abbotsford.

It turned out to be one of those discreetly classy hotels tucked away in St James's. I was greeted with quiet enthusiasm and shown to my room where everything from toothbrush to bedroom slippers had been provided for me. There was even a bottle of Chivas Regal on the coffee table. I poured myself a nightcap and drank it in the shower. It was good and

37

I was about to treat myself to another when a sharp pain in my gut reminded me I had a house-guest to look after. Quintero's tablets were in my pocket. I took a couple, resisting the temptation to wash them down with more whisky.

Soon the pain subsided, but worry and fear kept me awake for some time before I finally swam into sleep and dreamt almost immediately I was being dragged under the dark waters by my drowning father.

5

. . . it'll stand hot water . . .

When I awoke it was eleven a.m. and there was a tapping at my door. I opened it and a waiter brought in a trayful of breakfast. Two pints of strong Colombian coffee, hot croissants, unsalted butter, Morello cherry conserve and half a pint of fresh orange juice. Someone knew my habits.

My stomach felt normal again and working on the principle that a man's only as sick as he feels, I set to with good appetite.

'Breakfast to your taste, Mr Swift?' said the Brigadier.

He was standing by the open door which I had locked behind the waiter. I said, 'They might try tossing a few cherries into their monosodium glutamate.'

He came in followed by red Reilly. She had changed the grubby T-shirt for a St Laurent blouse in fine silk, but as this was topped off with a creased and frayed bomber jacket, the overall impression was the same. The jeans too.

The Brigadier wore a dark jacket and pin-stripes. He looked like a traditional city gent till you got in the way of his eyes. He used his gaze like a dentist uses a high-speed drill.

'Have a seat,' I said. 'If we're going to be chums, I'd better have something to call you.'

'By chance you have hit upon the last military rank I happened to hold,' he said, sitting on the bed. 'Many people still use it, so I see no objection to your doing so. It was by chance, I take it?'

'Omniscience is commoner than you think,' I said. 'And there doesn't seem to be any bar to ubiquity these days either. Which brings me to the question; you're so bloody clever, why do you want me?'

He leaned forward and fixed me with his gaze.

'When did you last see your father?' he said.

'1963,' I said promptly. 'As I'm sure you know.'

'Yes,' he said. 'He would be – what? Fifty-one then?'

'Right,' I said. 'Now he's nearly seventy. Well past retirement age.'

'On the contrary,' said the Brigadier. 'He seems to be as active as ever. Yet we would very much like to see him retire.'

He let the words hang. I poured myself some more coffee.

'Listen,' I said. 'You've given me a pretty good imitation of a man who can fix anything. What's the problem in rubbing out a septuagenarian traitor slumming it in downtown Moscow?'

The Brigadier said, 'You have a distorted picture of your father's status. He has been treated well, indeed he is a Hero of the Soviet Union and his defection has never been declassed from Category A – that is, the category into which all top political, military and scientific defectors are put, though often for no more than a couple of years. You look surprised.'

'He's a wanted criminal, a murderer,' I said evenly.

'Must run in the family,' grated Reilly.

'Please,' said the Brigadier reproachfully. 'You must at least have read about him, Mr Swift?'

I shook my head. In England, my associates had rapidly become conditioned to never mentioning his name. If I came across a reference to him in a newspaper or magazine I read no further. Even journalists eventually gave up chucking their impudent, insensitive questions at me. And in Venezuela I had stopped reading the English newspapers from the day it was confirmed that I could stay. I didn't start again till Dr Quintero fed me his little dish of barium meal.

The Brigadier said, 'Time is of the essence. No, I'm not referring to your condition, Mr Swift. What we want you to do is subject to an even stricter temporal limitation. Succeed, and you'll be able to pursue your own concerns at your leisure.'

I said, 'If that's the case, you'd better start being precise, Brig. So far, I'm not even sure what time of day it is.'

Reilly said, 'This creep's no use to us. Lock him up somewhere till he starts shitting blood.'

I smiled at her.

'Listen, you Celtic hermaphrodite,' I said. 'I could easily forget the one per cent of you that's female and crack that prognathic skull wide open.'

We were like children squaring up to each other with a long mileage of sneers to cover before we reached blows. But looking into those contemptuously vivid blue eyes, I didn't feel it was an impossible destination.

'Please,' said the Brigadier again. 'Mr Swift, I cannot begin to give you details until I am sure of one thing. Could you do it?'

I didn't say, *what?* I knew what he meant. The time for evasions and delays was over.

Could I kill my father?

Twenty years ago the answer would have been easy. Now in the morning light, in this plush hotel bedroom, with a half-eaten croissant in my hand, the question seemed grotesque.

But it had to be answered.

The phone rang.

Reilly picked it up, listened, handed it to the Brigadier.

He listened, said, 'When?' looked at his watch, said, 'All right,' and dropped the receiver on to the rest.

He said, 'I have to go for a while. No more than half an hour.'

Reilly asked, 'Shall I come?'

He shook his head.

'No. You stay and keep Mr Swift company. I'll want his answer when I return.'

He left and I finished my croissant. The butter had congealed.

I said, 'You make a habit of catching me in my night clothes, Reilly.'

She shrugged and said, 'I wouldn't sell tickets.'

I drank the lukewarm remains of my coffee and said, 'Now I'm going to shower and get dressed. Why don't you step outside?'

'I don't mind. I've got a strong stomach,' she said.

I said, 'I meant, outside the window.'

She didn't smile. She didn't even look offended. I was beginning to be pretty pissed off with Red Reilly.

I said, 'OK. I'll settle for the door. Anywhere, so long as you're out of sight.'

I took her arm and tried to lead her gently – well, fairly gently – to the door.

She chopped the other edge of her other hand sharply against my wrist. It wasn't much of a blow but I thought she'd broken it.

'Jesus!' I said, letting go.

'Don't touch me again,' she warned, 'without you want to make it a full-scale fight.'

I said, 'Touch you if I could help it? You've spent so long in your Killarney bog that your brain's gone fibrous. Just go. Or at least get out of my way.'

She was standing between me and the bathroom door. I took a step towards her and she said in her low husky voice, 'I've warned you. Touch me and you'll pay for it. Not that you'll be able to recall the last time you touched a woman without paying for it.'

I swung the flat of my hand at her face. She ducked easily, seized my arm, and used my own momentum to fling me across the bed. I kept on rolling and came up on my feet on the other side.

'Reilly,' I said, 'forgetting you're a lady is easy. Much more of this and I could forget I'm a gentleman.'

She said, 'Crap, Swift. You've been a cockroach for twenty years, mebbe all your life. All this gentleman crap is because you're a scared cockroach.'

I did a standing jump on to the bed and used it as a springboard to get height for a side-kick at her neck. I was barefooted but it would have laid her out like a pole-axe.

She caught my foot and twisted. I went with the twist – the only alternative was to hear my ankle snap – and somersaulted on to my breakfast tray. Again I kept going and came up with the coffee-pot in my hand. She was coming after me in an expert-looking attack crouch so I threw the coffee-pot at her.

To my surprise she turned away in a very womanly fashion so that the pot hit her on the back and spilled grounds down her grubby bomber jacket.

'Hold it,' she said. 'If it's going to get rough, I don't want to risk any serious damage.'

For a second I wondered if this was some kind of surrender, but next moment she slipped her jacket off, very carefully removed the silk blouse, went to the wardrobe, put it on a hanger and closed the door.

'Right,' she said. 'Let's go.'

She wore a cutaway bra, more cutaway than bra. There was nothing ambiguous about her breasts. Suddenly she was wholly a woman to me, which was what made it so easy for her to crash the point of one of her stylish little court shoes under my knee-cap, and as I screamed, to stifle the sound in my throat with the angle of her elbow.

'What's up, creep?' she said. 'Like what you see, is that it? Mind on other things, all of a sudden? Tell you what. Anything you can take, you can have. No yells, no court case. Creep like you must have been an old-time rapist before you came into money. What do you say?'

'Reilly,' I gasped, 'the prize isn't worth spit.'

I turned my back on her, kept turning and came round to find that her guard had slipped sufficiently for me to get a left hook high to her temple. She staggered sideways and I drove my left again into her kidneys. After that it should just have been origami with me folding her as I pleased like a sheet of rice paper.

But she was a tough cookie. As she went down she drove her head at my crotch. Six inches lower and the damage might have been decisive. As it was, she caught me at the base of my solar plexus and it was my turn to fold.

I was still the first to recover, but only just. She went scrambling away from me over the bed, and inflicted some superficial damage with a couple of vicious back-heels. My uncharacteristic outburst of temper had already abated and I had no desire to hurt her any more. Even less did I have any desire to screw her, but it somehow seemed important to establish my victory, symbolically at least, and evading the kicking legs, I grabbed the waistband of her jeans and yanked back till the zip burst open and they began to slide over the swell of her buttocks. After a while she relaxed and suddenly rolled over on her back. Dishevelled and distressed, she looked younger, the lines of her face softer.

I looked down at her warily, suspecting a renewed assault.

'OK,' she said.

'OK?' I echoed.

'Yes. OK. You win. You're the champ.'

I was still doubtful, still suspicious.

She said, 'Jesus, what are you waiting for? The national anthem?'

This should have been the moment when I really finished her off by telling her *No, thanks, I'm a bit choosy*. But I found I couldn't. My bullshit reason was that I felt it would be unchivalrous. My asshole reason was that I'd earned it. What my real reason was I don't know, but I stood up, in every sense of the phrase, and peeled her faded jeans off her shapely well-fleshed legs.

Her bush was the same electric red as her hair.

'Is that *real?*' I said wonderingly.

'It'll stand hot water and anything *you* can give it, mister,' she said challengingly.

And it did.

6

. . . the hard . . .

Post coitum fessum est.

I'd kept myself pretty fit on Margarita, working out two or three times a week with one of Luis's boys. But I was nearly forty, and hadn't been in a real fight for years till first Hunnicut's lads and now this mad Mick had roughed me up.

It was all right as we lay locked together in that timeless post-eruptive trance which even volcanic lava banging at the door can't disturb. But when finally she sighed and gave a small wriggle and I, like a good little gent, rolled my weight off her, my back felt like it had been rearranged by a jackboot.

'Holy Mary, what a weak thing is an Englishman,' she said when I groaned. 'If you'd caught me at my peak, I'd have killed you for sure. Lie on your belly now.'

I obeyed. She rose up, straddled my buttocks and began to massage my back. Her fingers were strong and pliant and knew where to probe. I groaned again but this time in pleasure.

'Reilly,' I said, 'I take back five per cent of everything I've thought about you.'

'Don't get ideas,' she warned. 'You've got to beat me three times to get to keep me. And I don't think you're in shape.'

'That seems to be the popular medical opinion,' I said.

'The fingers paused for a moment.

'Not that it bothers me, Swift, but that wasn't my meaning. I just forgot for a sec.'

'Me too, Reilly,' I assured her. 'That's a great anti-mnemonic you've got there.'

'Is that what they call it?' she said, resuming the massage. 'Tell me something that puzzles me, Swift. For a man who's so fond of forgetting, why did you come back to England?'

'You know why,' I said.

'No,' she said. 'I know about the cancer and all that, but it still surprises me. You're a hard man, Swift, it's in your file. But here you are doing something which is a bit soft-centred, sentimental almost.'

'That's how you view patricide, is it?'

Again the fingers paused, but only for a second this time.

Then she said, 'You're not really going to kill your father, are you, Swift? This whole bloody thing's been a waste of time, I've thought so from the start. How can a man even contemplate such a thing?'

'You've read the files,' I said sleepily. 'You tell me.'

'No,' she said, increasing the length and the pressure of her stroke. 'You tell me. The files are paper and words, dry and dusty, dead. This is flesh and blood, muscle and tissue, I have beneath me here. I want to hear what it has to say. I like to draw my pictures from life.'

'Is that what you like?' I said, my face buried deep in the pillow which held the warmth of her head and the scent of her hair. As she slid her hands in their soothing rhythm up and down my spine, I was dimly aware of the movement of her thighs against my haunches. Eventually there would be a time to do something about it, but for the moment nothing seemed better than to lie here.

Dimly, distantly, almost to myself, I began to talk.

'When I was a boy, I used to think the sun shone out of Pa's arsehole. Certainly if anyone could have fixed it there, it would have been William, 5th Viscount Bessacarr, "the last of the Renaissance men", as the popular press liked to call him before they found other less flattering and more contemporary terms. You name it and Billy Bessacarr could do it well. People used to say he needed a dozen lives to achieve his full potential. The truth was, he got his dozen lives, and more. The trouble was, they belonged to other people.

'In the war, for instance, he soon grew tired of being a brilliant backroom boy while amiable nobodies like his old school fag, Percy Nostrand, were commissioned officers on active service. Learning that Percy was concerned with the setting up under the auspices of S.O.E. of an operation behind enemy lines in Jugoslavia, he did not rest till he got in on the act, supposedly as a 'scientific observer' – of what, God alone knew. The operation was a total balls-up, and Pa spent the next couple of years running around with the partisans. But if the British have one strength, it's being able to judge things in terms of individual behaviour rather than by strict tactical standards. Pa emerged from all this as a hero, was awarded a medal and was the universal acclaim of the Press. This huge fiasco became Billy Bessacarr's triumph instead of S.O.E.'s cock-up. Poor Press! They were never lucky in the long term with their Bessacarr heroes!

'While Pa was in Jugoslavia, I was emerging from my mother's womb. Mama was Angelica Mercedes Emilia da Madariaga, only child of a wealthy Venezuelan diplomat. It was Uncle Percy who introduced her to Pa and within a fortnight, fast work even for those hectic times, they were married. In those early years with Pa busy saving the world for democracy, Mama had to be the centre of my universe. And the centre of many other people's too. Everyone adored her. Young, beautiful, rich, she put her shoulder to the British war-wheel with all the energy of the proselyte, but never neglecting me. I don't suppose I can have many real memories of those years, but I seem to have and they're all good.

'I didn't really begin to know Pa till after the war. And even then I knew him not so much as a person as an elemental force, a power, whose absence meant peace and calm but whose presence brought a sometimes rather frightening excitement. We met in bursts. He would come down to Bessacarr House and pull the telephone out of the wall, announcing he wanted an uninterrupted fortnight. He took me camping in Snowdonia and sailing on the Solent and, once the post-war restrictions were lifted, we started spending several weeks each year abroad, particularly in Italy. The Bessacarr men always had a penchant for Latin women and my grandfather had married an Italian girl. They were both now dead, but my great-grandmama, the Contessa Dianti, was still living and spent the summer months at her Campanian villa near Amalfi to which we had an open invitation. She had another grandson besides my father, his cousin,

Giulio, but he showed no sign of producing children, so this blond-haired, olive-skinned Bessacarr boy was the last of her family *bambini* and she would have had me there all year if she could.

'Sometimes I felt as if I wouldn't have minded. It was there at the Villa Colonna that I was most under my father's spell. There was an old sailing dinghy moored in the rocky cove at the foot of the cliffs on which the villa was built. It was in essence I think a 15 ft 6 ins Snipe, though what it had been used for in the war years, God alone knows. Pa set about refurbishing it, and though I doubt if the result would have altogether satisfied the I.Y.R.U., it seemed like the most beautiful boat in the world to me. We named it *Ariel* and I was never so happy as when we were planing across the Bay of Salerno under full sail in a stiff wind.

'I learned my sailing the hard way. In fact with Pa you learned everything the hard way. His technique was to answer questions with questions, to force me to work things out for myself. I think he'd have stopped short of letting me kill myself, but, by Christ, he let me take many a hard knock in the interests of education!

'Back in England, for the most part Mama took over again. I was her boy. She was the one who visited me at school, she the one whom I loved to impress with my developing athletic prowess. Her delight when I won a race or scored a try was complete and undiluted. Pa's (on the rare occasions he was there) was always accompanied by some question about technique or tactics.

'Pa's scientific work began to run into trouble in the late 'forties and the 'fifties. Basically an ideas man rather than a hard-grafting researcher, his interests ranged wide across the whole physical-chemical gamut. But suddenly he started finding that the old easy access he had enjoyed to people and places in the world of science was being denied him. The trouble was not far to seek. Since the war, more particularly since his time in Jugoslavia and since Hiroshima, he had moved significantly to the left. Not in any specific party sense, not yet. Men like Pa don't easily belong to parties. Rather, they expect parties to belong to them.

'No, his frequently expressed creed was that shared

science benefited all mankind, secret science was merely alchemy and therefore diabolical. Naturally in those neurotic cold war years this meant he rapidly degenerated from being the government's golden boy to having the kind of security clearance they'd give to Krushchev's cousin.

'Not that this bothered him for the moment. In the mid-'fifties all his energies were directed into the foundation of the Bessacarr Trust, later to be called *Vita 3*, the Third World Self-Help Action Group. The aim of science should be to eradicate poverty and privation for the many, not to provide affluence for the few. *Vita 3* was registered as a charity, but its aims weren't charitable, he claimed. The Third World had to find out how to help itself. The Bessacarr Trust would merely provide the tools and the stimulus. It was Pa's old 'hard way' theory of education on a national scale.

'He threw himself into the Trust, heart and soul. This was to be his monument. The name Bessacarr would be a term of honour throughout the world for evermore. Mama and I saw less and less of him. Not that we were lonely. Mama, who grew more beautiful as the years passed, was at the centre of the European social scene. And in case the companionship of my friends at school was not enough, Pa kept on depositing a steady stream of orphaned children at Bessacarr House, picked up from anywhere in the world which happened to have a refugee problem. Two of them became permanent fixtures. One was a Korean girl of about my age whose name we anglicized to Kim; the other was Joe, a Kenyan boy a little younger who had been badly injured in the anti-Mau Mau fighting which killed his parents. Their status in the house was slightly ambiguous, but Kim, who picked up everything very quickly, became a kind of general secretary to my father, while Joe, who was not so sharp but was tremendously strong, helped out in the garden and became rural Hampshire's first black Teddy Boy.

'In 1960 I went to do my National Service, one of the last conscripts before the system was halted. I was commissioned in the Royal Marines and two years later I emerged a tougher, harder, and more lethal man, but not a very much wiser one.

'But I was wise enough to see that there was now a

49

disturbingly wide rift between my parents created mainly (so it seemed to me) by my father's obsession with *Vita 3*.

'Next step for me was three years at Cambridge. Well, that was the theory. I didn't spend much time working at my books. Sport was the only area in which I could come close to Pa and though that wasn't my only motivation, I suppose it helped. I got my rugger blue in my first term without difficulty. Fourteen stones of Marine commando was a useful adjunct to any pack. Rowing I couldn't be bothered with, I wanted my boats to have sails. But I was a pretty fair swimmer. Pa had seen to that after I'd gone overboard once in the Gulf of Salerno and nearly drowned. I was fast and I could keep going for a long time. But it's a sport you need to work at constantly at the highest competition levels and the training soon became a drag, especially when I realized that, though good, I was never going to be better than in the top ten at my distance. Still I was good enough to be called on at short notice, mainly because I was the only possibility handy, when the English first string went down with 'flu just before a student international in London. On recorded times, I was due to come in last by a long though not disgraceful distance. But as I was introduced to the crowd before the event, a localized burst of enthusiasm amid the polite but hopeful applause drew my attention.

'Mama was there. God knows how she'd found out and God knows what a hole she'd caved in her busy social life, but there she was, gorgeous as a film star, but with none of a film star's vanity to be worried about admitting that this hulking twenty-year-old was her son.

'Just what that did to me was hard to say. I'd been feeling pretty much down that summer for all kinds of reasons. I'd failed Part One of my Tripos and didn't know if I wanted to go back or not (Pa was typically unhelpful). I was planning to spend some time that vacation in the States but there was some hold-up on my visa. Pa's political profile had clearly been fed into some State Department computer and all his connections were being washed faintly pink. And it hadn't helped when some organ of the Yellow Press had started dropping hints that he was under investigation by Special Branch. And of course it was a pretty sour summer generally, with the Great British Public pruriently agog for every detail of the Profumo scandal and the whole nasty mess culminating in Stephen Ward's suicide at the end of July.

'But now Mama simply by her unexpected presence wiped all that away. I amazed myself, the opposition and the selectors by taking an early lead and knocking a vast chunk off my previous best time. When the others realized that I wasn't coming back to them as expected they came flailing after me, but I kept going, exhausted in everything but spirit, I kept going and won by a fingertip. I heard Mama's loving applause above all the rest and when I climbed out of the pool, she was there to embrace me, ignoring all official efforts to keep her in her seat. It was a perfect moment. Since then, when I've been curious to remember what happiness was, my mind takes me back to that moment. It was a moment of pure joy. And it was the last. But of course no one ever tells you that.

'I went back to Cambridge that autumn determined to give it another try, but I soon began to feel the uselessness of it all once again. I could make no decision, however, but in the end a decision was made for me. Or perhaps I forced it to be made.

'Playing rugger in South Wales one muddy November Saturday, I got tired of having my balls twisted in every scrum and tireder of the ref's indifference to my protests. Finally I thumped the twister and we left the field together, he broken-jawed, me dismissed for foul play. In Cambridge terms this was a considerable disgrace, but the Welsh bore no grudge, reckoning I'd only done what any one of them would have done but a lot earlier. The night went well. I won a bet that I couldn't run through the wall of the old wooden pavilion and the team coach left me full of splinters and ale to the Celtic ministrations of my hosts. At four o'clock in the morning we parted with much mutual expression of esteem and affection. Muddy, bloody, and still drunk, I re-entered my college at eleven o'clock on Sunday morning, and like a good lapsed Catholic I felt that my first task should be to offer thanksgiving, which I did, sorely testing the Christian charity of the congregation in the college chapel.

'They waited till I was sober before summoning me and

sending me down, so it was Monday evening that I climbed aboard the London train for what was probably the last time.

'I felt little regret. In fact, I felt rather pleased that the decision had been irrevocably made. Now I could look at the future squarely. The Army seemed a very real possibility. Alternatively, I knew it would please Pa if I offered to help with the administration of *Vita 3*. It occurred to me suddenly that what I was really considering as I sat on this train was a choice between going abroad to (probably) help the poor natives or going abroad to (possibly) shoot the buggers. When you're twenty-one such a choice can be at the same time real and amusing!

'From Liverpool Street I made my way by tube to Oxford Circus and then on foot to our London house in a quiet terrace off Wigmore Street. I had no idea who, if anyone, I would find there and indeed the place seemed deserted as I let myself in. There were signs of habitation downstairs however, and I thought I heard a noise from the next floor. I was about to shout to make my presence known but I didn't. It was only five o'clock in the afternoon, but at the back end of November already dark. A good time for an ingenious burglar, I thought. To catch such a one in the act would be a bit of a sweetener to the sour draught of my academic disgrace.

'I tiptoed up the stairs. The noise was coming from the master bedroom. The door was narrowly ajar letting out a thin line of dim light. I approached and peered through the crack.

'The noises had told me what to expect. A quick confirmatory glance was all I intended – no lingering voyeurism. I recognized my father's silvered patrician head at once and for a second expectation overcame actuality and I saw the limbs wrapped round as Mama's. But almost simultaneously I realized my mistake. Even in the muffled light of the single lamp which illuminated the room I could see the sallow yellowness of that skin, the bluey-blackness of that hair.

'It was Kim who grunted and groaned and rolled and wrestled about the bed with him.

'Another instant reaction, so fleeting I hardly registered it

– relief. Yes, for a thin sliver of time I was relieved not to be seeing Mama like this.

'Then the wave of horror and indignation came rolling over me. It carried me down stairs and out of the house. There was no way I could have interrupted them, made my presence known. I wanted to be away, to be out of their reach. I wanted to be with my mother, to offer her comfort for wrongs I prayed to God she did not know she had suffered.

'Christ, what a revolting thing it is to be young!

'I kept on running and did not slow down till I hit the slow-moving sludge of homeward-bound workers in Oxford Street. I drifted with them for a while, finally turning into a pub near the Tottenham Court Road. I don't know how long I stood at the crowded bar nor how much I drank, but finally the need to talk to Mama became irresistible and I pushed my way to the telephone in the entrance and rang Bessacarr House where I knew she'd had some friends staying for the weekend.

'The news I was given alarmed me. Mama was no longer there. The guests had departed during the course of the day and late that afternoon the last of them, my godfather, Percy Nostrand, had driven her up to town where she expected to be staying a few days.

'Immediately I rang Uncle Percy. He told me that he'd given Mama tea in his apartment but that she had left a little while ago with the intention, so he understood, of going straight to our town house. My agitated manner had alerted him to trouble and he started to ask me what was the matter, but I had no time to talk.

'The thought of Mama stumbling upon the sight that I had seen horrified me. Once more I set off at a run, but my limbs felt dull and lifeless as though weighed down with the certainty of impending disaster.

'I wasn't wrong.

'There were cars outside the house. And an ambulance. A policeman stood at the door but it would have taken more than him and a whole pack of Welshmen besides to bar my entrance.

'My mother lay in the hallway at the foot of the stairs.

There were men all around, with cameras, notebooks, finger-printing equipment. But all I could see was Mama. Her hand gripped the telephone which she had pulled to the ground as she fell. I could see her left profile. The eye stared, the lips were slightly parted, but her expression was her customary one of mild, unmalicious amusement. It did not go with the huge and bloody damage to the side of her skull where fragments of bone gleamed white through the clotted blood and matted tangles of her lustrous black hair.

'The rest is public history. Nothing emerged to contradict the police theory which the newspapers soon felt able to print as proven fact. My mother had caught my father in bed with Kim. Enraged, she had threatened to expose the full extent of his links with the Soviets to Special Branch or the Press, it doesn't matter. He had pursued her downstairs and in his fury struck her with an eighteenth-century brass crucifix which hung in the hallway. It was found by the body covered with her blood and his fingerprints. He may not have intended to kill her but so violent had been the one blow that it had easily sufficed. Then he and Kim had fled in panic. Ironically, said the papers, Mama's threat and its consequences had in fact saved my father. The yellow press had got it right. Special Branch officers who had been amassing a file on him for some time were on their way to interview him that very evening. They arrived an hour later armed with powers to enter and search which, when there was no reply, they used.

'My father, of course, denied everything. But as his denial took the form of a statement issued to a Moscow press conference, it cut little ice in the West. He refused to answer questions, talked stridently of Fascist persecution and accepted gratefully the Soviet offer of political asylum. There was a diplomatic furore, of course. There was, after all, a warrant out for his arrest on a charge of murder. But the Russians were intransigent, time passed, he sank out of sight, the world forgot.

'But I didn't forget. Pa was right, when you learned things the hard way, you didn't forget.

'I'd learned the truth about him the hardest way possible. And the world would end before I forgot.'

7

. . . home thoughts . . .

Reilly had stopped massaging me at some point in my story, I hadn't noticed when. Now she was sitting upright on my buttocks and I could feel the moist warmth of her crotch against my flesh, but it wasn't doing anything for me.

'Did you never hear from him?'

'Oh yes. He wrote me a letter. It had a French postmark. It was written in haste, so he said. But it didn't show any signs of haste other than being short, and he was never a man to waste words on the obvious. The obvious here was that what had happened was explicable in terms which would exonerate him of all blame. I could hear his voice as I read it. Confident. Assertive. *Reasonable!*'

'If he didn't write to explain, why *did* he write?' wondered Reilly.

I laughed gratingly. 'To comfort me,' I said. 'He knew how much I'd miss my mother. It was a sodding message of condolence!'

'And did you write to him?'

'Only once. After getting his letter. I wrote to him c/o The Kremlin. I said I hoped never to see him again in my life. But if I did, I would kill him.'

But of course the Brigadier and Reilly must know that. That's why I was here. She turned me over now and recommenced work on my shoulder and neck. I watched her through half-closed eyes. Beneath the make-up, I saw now, her face was puckishly young, thirty at the most.

'And since then, what? Tell me it all, my bucko.'

'Oh come on, Reilly!' I said. 'You must have every last dot and dash of me in your records!'

'Maybe we have,' she said. 'But this is the interesting part, isn't it? The part that records can never explain.'

I said, 'The Brigadier will be back soon,' and tried to push myself upright, but the sinewy fingers at my throat dissuaded me.

'He'll not be back,' she assured me. 'Not yet awhile, anyway. And what if he is? This'll not be the most shocking sight he's seen this side of Christmas. Now, what really interests me, Mr Lemuel Swift, is how soon did you decide to do what you did?'

How soon?

I thought about it.

How soon?

It was impossible to say. Lives aren't lived according to plans laid after carefully-thought-out decisions. They're shaped by the gradual interaction of personality and situation. For almost a year, I had been cold, emotionally frozen. The papers were full of Pa for a long time. The Vassall case, the Profumo scandal, Philby's defection, all made it a time of vast uncertainty, and when you finally lose a hero, you need to prove he wasn't such a hero after all. The press tried to prove that his scientific and philanthropic achievements had been grossly overestimated and that his war service had been pretty negligible. A few voices, Uncle Percy's loud among them, were raised in protest, but this was smothered by the news that Pa had married Kim and taken Soviet citizenship, formally renouncing all his UK titles and honours. An indignant Parliament saved him the bother by equally formally stripping them from him. By this time for some reason the papers had decided I was to be a sympathetic character, and it was almost as if I accepted the role for want of a better. There was a lot of crap written about not visiting the sins of the father, etc., and how they all applauded when I accepted the family title, saying it came from the Queen, but renounced all the Bessacarr monies and estates, saying they should belong to the people!

As usual, I had my twin reasons.

My bullshit reason was that I wanted to be my own man without any help from my paternal inheritance. My asshole reason was that the legal position as far as the property went was exceedingly complicated (the state can take a man's title but not his money, it seems) and I had inherited enough from Mama to keep me comfortable.

56

My real reason I didn't yet know, any more than I understood the real reason for my decision to take over the running of the Bessacarr Trust, though the Press praised my bullshit reasons to the heavens, particularly when I stripped it of all its suspect political tendencies, re-registered its name as *Vita 3* and relaunched it as a worldwide relief organization on the lines of Oxfam and the Red Cross. It was curious. There was the British Press holding me up as the perfect example of a brave young Englishman living down his wicked father's crimes, while over in Moscow I knew for certain Pa would be preening himself that he had forced me 'the hard way' to take stock of myself and do something useful with my life! Not only that, but in his egocentric universe, *Vita 3* would still be *his* idea, *his* creation, *his* monument. No matter what grandiloquent acts of renunciation I might make, I was still living on inherited capital.

Curiously, early in 1965 the incident which finally confirmed me as the *Boy's Own* hero also gave me my first clear view of what I was really doing and my first opportunity to begin doing it.

I was in the Ethiopian-Somali borderlands. To tell the truth, I'm not sure which country I was in. There was no overt political trouble in either at the time but there had been a long drought and *Vita 3* had offered to help. I was superintending the distribution of flour in a remote settlement. I had discovered in myself a considerable talent for administration but also discovered that such a talent, if overexposed, could keep you on your butt end in an office twenty hours a day. So as often as possible I accompanied *Vita 3* missions on the ground.

As we were humping the flour off our ten-tonner, a group of men came drifting in from the bush. Nothing unusual in that. Relief vehicles attract crowds the Third World over.

It wasn't until one of them approached me politely and stuck a dangerously antique Luger automatic into my ribs that I realized this was something different.

And so began my first experience of being kidnapped by guerrillas.

I lived with them rough for four months and I think I

learned more about the arts of surviving and killing during those four months than during the twenty-four I spent in the Royal Marines. They weren't quite sure what to do with me at first. They'd simply wanted the flour and had taken me along as some kind of protection against immediate pursuit. Only their leader, a sad-eyed, intelligent youth who invited me to call him Ras, spoke English, and he was much concerned to make a profit out of me. As we became cautious friends, we would sit together in the evenings and discuss what I might be worth by way of ransom. What he wanted was guns and it took all my powers of argument to persuade him that there was no way anyone was going to hand over arms for my release.

'Why not settle for money?' I urged. 'Then you can buy them.'

Ras shook his head.

'Money we have. More we can get. What use is it? Where can we buy what we need?'

'There must be plenty of arms dealers,' I said.

'Oh yes. For this kind of rubbish.' He held up his ancient pistol. 'We need new, modern weapons. Where shall we purchase these? It is a matter of trust as well as organization. We need a good friend in the West.'

His sad eyes looked at me questioningly. I wasn't yet ready to buy my freedom with promises I intended to break (the Bessacarr motto was *Trust Me*) but a few weeks later, half-starved and lousy, with a bullet graze across my skull to show me that government forces were incapable of making distinctions through rifle sights, I was ready to promise anything. I doubt if Ras was really convinced but we made our arrangements like a pair of honest dealers and shook hands on the deal.

The day after that, I 'escaped' from the guerrillas and made my way back to a hot bath, an iced lager and eventually, in London, a hero's reception.

Also waiting for me in London was Kate Hailey. Kate was a Whitehall career girl who at twenty-four was already discovering that the Civil Service was still a male club. The 'sixties were swinging, but the swinging stopped at Westminster and Whitehall, except for the indiscreet few like poor Profumo. Later I came to suspect Kate was ruthless enough to have slept her way to the top, but as she worked in Uncle Percy's department perhaps that particular avenue of advancement was a cul-de-sac. Percy at least did her the 'favour' of introducing her to me. It was semi-official to start with. Percy was a generous and energetic supporter of *Vita 3* and he 'loaned' me Kate to help sort out some legal difficulties at the UK end. We hit it off pretty well. Soon she'd moved in with me and shortly after she'd announced, not with any great enthusiasm, that she was pregnant, we got married.

Possibly that was her aim from the start. I can't complain. If she was using me, I was abusing her. There was something dead inside of me. I insisted that our daughter should be named after my mother, but even that was a symbolic rather than an emotional act. Perhaps I married Kate because I sensed that the relationship would make no real emotional demands on me. As for Angelica, I played the proud parent, indeed I felt real affection, but always there was a barrier. Unstinting love for my daughter would have set limits on unstinting hate for my father.

I shudder now to think how unbalanced I must have been. There was no plan. I even half persuaded myself that my first exercise in arms smuggling, which consisted of sticking a few automatic rifles at the bottom of a few relief crates and letting Ras know where he could hi-jack them, was merely the necessary act of an honest Englishman. News spreads fast in the subversive world. A short while later I was approached by another group of 'freedom fighters' at the other end of Africa. I tried to persuade myself that this time I was being blackmailed into it.

But even if there was still no plan, at least my motives were becoming clear.

I was out to destroy *Vita 3*, the Bessacarr Trust.

The Trust *was* my father. It symbolized his self-righteousness, his self-advertisement, his self-justification. I wanted it to become a model of that universal benevolence which ignores the pain and needs of those who should be nearest and dearest. I wanted my father to understand that his marvellous creation had been dealing out death in the guise of peace and love just as surely as he had dealt out death to Mama.

For my revenge to succeed, *Vita 3* had to succeed. I threw myself whole heartedly into turning it into one of the UK's primary relief organizations. And at the same time, I threw my alternative persona, christened Alexander Evans, into the illicit arms business.

Getting hold of weapons was the most difficult thing. I had to find out which corrupt officials of which indifferent governments were willing to sell the end-user certificates which are the official documents authorizing purchase of arms. I had to find whom to bribe, whom to trust, whom to threaten, whom to deceive. I soon realized that where there's a need for food, there's usually a need for bullets too.

I was for a while completely schizophrenic, I believe. Lem Swift and Alex Evans hadly knew each other, yet the latter desperately wanted to merge with the former once more. As Evans, I seemed to bear a charmed life. Difficulties smoothed themselves at my approach. I took larger and larger risks, made more and more outrageous deals, yet everything worked. The thing was, I wanted to be found out! I wanted this huge heap of agony to descend on to Pa. And at the same time I suppose I wanted to be whole again.

It finally occurred to me that I might have to precipitate discovery myself. And with that decision, some instinct of self-preservation returned to life in me. Before, I'd been content to die Samson-like in the wreck of Pa's dreams. Now it began to seem to me that Pa's pain would be exacerbated if I managed to escape scot-free! Survival is a great persuader!

It seemed an ironic bonus that Venezuela, Mama's birth-place, should be the obvious bolt-hole. I had inherited Mama's family estate on the Isla da Margarita, established there long before it became a tourist trap. I had influential friends in Caracas, some vague claim to citizenship, and I had never put through any deals with South American guerrilla groups.

So I set about triggering the blow-up.

Having decided on survival, I also decided it made sense to maximize my personal fortune. I could by now demand and get one hundred per cent advance payment from my customers and in the early months of 1971, I "sold" every subversive group I had contacts with precisely what they wanted. I was into Europe by this time and I even contracted to supply the Red Brigade with several thousand fragmentation grenades and fifty Sam 7 missiles. It caused me a certain perverse amusement to cheat these 'freedom fighters'. I'd long since been sickened by the left-wing self-righteousness of most of them. It reminded me of Pa. It was right they too should pay.

So everything was set. My last act was to make sure that in every *Vita 3* shipment scheduled to go out in the next month there was a crate of guns. No special markings. They would be opened with the other crates. And then the balloon would go up. And when they came looking for Antonio Lemuel Ernest Sebastian Stanhope-Swift, 6th Viscount Bessacarr, they would find nothing except a detailed account of Alexander Evans's activities over the last eight years.

So I was almost ready to depart. One thing remained to do and that was to say my goodbyes. I'd half persuaded myself that the more obviously ignorant Kate was when the scandal broke, the better it would be for her. But that was 'bullshit' reasoning. 'Asshole' reasoning urged me to silence also. But in the event I found I couldn't leave without seeing Angelica and without giving Kate some explanation and some warning against the press and police assault that was bound to come.

Kate and Angelica had been spending some time visiting Kate's family in Lancashire and were driving back that day. My plane ticket was booked for early the following morning. I was alone in the Bloomsbury house feeling the afternoon pile its minutes on me like stones and wondering if I could really go through with it. When the doorbell rang, I experienced a moment of sheer terror, thinking that Kate and Angelica had got back early.

But they wouldn't need to ring, of course. I was still mightily relieved when I opened the door and saw on the doorstep a man; middle-aged, solidly built, smiling lips, watchful eyes.

'Sorry to trouble you, my lord,' he said. 'But I wonder if I could have a word. Hunnicut's the name. Detective Chief Superintendent Hunnicut.'

I returned his smile and invited him in.

'What can I do for you, Chief Superintendent?' I asked with a puzzled air.

I was able to look genuinely puzzled as he began to explain he was in charge of a Special Fraud Squad section. Surely what I had been doing was unlikely to be investigated by the Fraud Squad? But gradually the truth emerged and I was hard put not to laugh out loud at the absurdity of it.

The thing was, *Vita 3*'s figures never lied. No one would ever believe that later, but it was true. If we said we'd received x thousand pounds and spent it on y tons of rice to be sent to Thailand, that's precisely what happened. The trouble was the arms shipments which went too. Some nosey bastard had worked out that to move a stated payload of relief supplies, we should have needed one transport less than we used. Or rather *claimed* to have used, for the accusation was that *Vita 3* was padding out its statement of expenses to make a few hundred quid on the side!

Hence the Fraud Squad. And because young Lord Bessacarr, whom everyone loved, was at the top of the pile, Detective Chief Superintendent Hunnicut had been told off to look into the matter.

I ceased to be amused when he mentioned that as a matter of routine, a *Vita 3* shipment currently awaiting dispatch from Gatwick was going to be carefully checked, and would I care to be present when this was done?

I regretted, but a meeting with the Minister for Overseas Development would prevent me from doing that, but if the Chief Superintendent would care to meet me at *Vita 3*'s offices at six p.m. when the staff had gone home, he could browse at his leisure through the records. He agreed and departed. I watched him drive away, then went into top gear myself. The case was altered. Or rather it would be as soon as those other cases at Gatwick were opened. I'd planned to be safely settled in Venezuela before the first discovery of illicit arms was made. Now I was going to be pushed to be out of the country. But I found myself surprisingly unworried as I grabbed my already packed case and headed for Heathrow. The reason was not far to seek. I was relieved at being given an excuse to avoid the confrontation with Kate, the farewell scene with Angelica.

At Heathrow the first available plane was going to Barcelona. I took it. From Barcelona to Rome. From Rome to New York. Once you've made up your mind to move, move fast and keep moving. That was Pa's advice. Good advice should never be ignored, whatever its source.

I was wise to take it. The hunt was up even more rapidly than I'd expected. Hunnicut was a wily old fox. Two minutes after they opened the crate with the guns in, he'd been on to the Ministry of Overseas Development to check if I had an appointment with the Minister. And when he learned I hadn't, he came after me personally. The guns meant that strictly speaking I was no longer his department's concern, but he didn't wait for the top brass to define parameters of responsibility. He'd got the first sniff and I was his prey.

We almost dead-heated in Caracas. It's curious. Nothing that I'd actually *done* had changed, but because the balloon had gone up rather earlier than planned, I was now regarded even by my influential acquaintances as a fugitive from justice rather than a rich and welcome incipient citizen. That was all Hunnicut's fault. But now I had occasion to bless the man. For, as I've said before, his attitude to the Venezuelan authorities rapidly undid all his own good work. By the time Scotland Yard got one of their international charm school graduates out there, it was too late, thank God!

Meanwhile *Vita 3* became the greatest scandal of the day. To most people its full extent was never known. Subversive groups weren't eager to advertise to their enemies what arms they'd got, still less to their friends how much money they'd been conned out of by my final coup! And all those politicians and officials the world over who'd been taking quieteners for years were now keeping quiet for free. So as far as the Great British Public was concerned, it was simply a huge and particularly unpleasant fraud. Everyone who'd ever listened to one of *Vita 3*'s broadcast appeals and pushed a fiver into an envelope was now convinced it had gone straight into my pocket.

I didn't mind. I sat back and waited for the feeling of triumph to well up inside me. It never did. I had done untold harm. I had abandoned my family and it gradually dawned on me that I had contrived to destroy whatever chance of meaning, fulfilment and happiness there might have been in my life.

And for what?

A triumph that never came. I tried to imagine my father's face as he heard the news about *Vita 3* and the final destruction of the Bessacarr name. I could never envisage the lineaments of pain and distress, only that characteristic expression of mingled pain and complacency as yet another disaster, uniquely forecast by himself, confirmed once more the wisdom of his ways.

So self-disgust warred in me with self-pity, and finally self-preservation won. I set up my security screen to protect my body. I set up barriers against involvement and friendship to protect my emotions, and I set up my arrangements with Dario to protect my future. It was always my plan to see England and Angelica again before I died. At least, so I assured myself at moments of maximum depression and fear – when I'd had the dream, for instance, or after sex. Home thoughts from a succession of broads!

All this, or most of it, I think I spilled out to Reilly. The first religion whose confessionals are conducted by a naked female priest straddling the repentant sinner's body is going to sweep the world.

But instead of going into penances all she said in a rather bored voice was, 'Lem Swift, you called yourself. Is that the family name?'

'Stanhope-Swift,' I said. 'I kept the title which pleased the traditionalists, but answered to plain Lem Swift which pleased the radicals. Lemuel, of course, was my father's idea of wit. My mother never liked it.'

I reached up and tried to pull her down towards me. If she wasn't going to be moved by my confession, at least she could offer some form of absolution.

'No, thanks,' she said. 'You'll need another fight for that.'

She swung easily off the bed and went through to the bathroom. I head the sound of the shower. After a while I followed her.

She was towelling herself.

'I've left it running,' she said. 'You'll need a shower. You're a sweaty fighter.'

There didn't seem to be anything to say so I stepped in.

By the time I'd finished, she'd left the bathroom. I dried myself for a moment, then returned to the bedroom with the towel round my waist.

Reilly was zipping herself into her jeans. The Brigadier was sitting in the armchair. I had a sudden daft feeling that he'd been sitting there all along and I just hadn't noticed him. I also had a not so daft feeling that he might as well have been. Suddenly Reilly's easy capitulation at the end of our struggle made sense.

'Decision time, Mr Swift,' said the Brigadier briskly.

'What's your trick cyclist say?' I asked, nodding at Reilly. 'Though I doubt the BMA would approve her bedside manner!'

'I said I thought you'd do it,' she replied unabashed, cradling her breasts into her inadequate bra and opening the wardrobe to retrieve her precious blouse.

'Go to Moscow and blow one of their favourite defectors away?' I said mockingly. 'You must be joking! With cancer I've got maybe three months. With the KGB I'd have maybe three minutes.'

'Less,' said Reilly. 'You're out of shape.'

She said it with a grin rather than a sneer and I didn't resent it. All right, she'd used me, but still there was between us the bond of our coupling. She might have faked the occasion, but she hadn't faked the fun, and that put us a bit above the mutual indifference of whore and client.

'You're probably right,' I said. 'So, even less reason for me to go to Moscow. Even if I was prepared to assassinate my father.'

'No need to go to Moscow, bucko,' said Reilly. 'If your da was staying in Moscow, there'd be no need to blow him away.'

'Not staying in Moscow?' I said in bewilderment. 'What do you mean?'

It was to the Brigadier that I addressed myself, but again Reilly replied.

'The Bessacarrs are on the move,' she said. 'It must be Bessacarr reunion time. Our information is that just like you, your old man, bless him, is heading back to the land of his fathers!'

'Back to England?' I said, astonished. 'But why, for God's sake? Why?'

'Why?' echoed Reilly. 'To surrender himself to the authorities and stand trial for the murder of your mother, of course. Why else, bucko? Why else?'

8

. . . good in the garden . . .

I got dressed.

My mind was a maelstrom of speculation but some atavistic sense of decorum insisted I should be properly clothed before hearing what was to come next. Also it gave me a few moments to get a grip of myself.

'OK,' I said, tying my final shoelace. 'Now tell me; why the hell should my father want to come back here and give himself up.'

'As to that, Mr Swift, you are probably in a better position than anyone else to understand his personal motives,' said the Brigadier. 'We can merely hope to interpret the motives of his political masters. Let me fill in the picture as best I can. Your father has now been in Russia for twenty years. He is almost seventy . . .'

'This month,' I said. 'He'll be seventy this month.'

'He is a widower. I mean for the second time,' continued the Brigadier. 'The woman, Kim, died earlier this year. Perhaps you knew that?'

I shook my head. So Kim was dead. It meant nothing. Once I had quite liked her as a person; once her oriental prettiness had played a large part in my teenage onanistic fantasies. But for many years she had just been a length of flesh thrashing around beneath my father's unfaithful body.

'It is many years since his hosts have felt it worthwhile to employ him as an active scientist,' said the Brigadier. 'He did some useful work for them on the biomass, I believe, but he seems to have alienated his fellow workers by his impatience and his irritability, which seemed to increase as he became aware of a decline in his own powers of creative scientific thought.'

That figured too. God spotting a grey hair.

'So he's coming back because he's a superannuated widower?' I said in half-feigned stupidity.

'Come on, bucko!' interjected Reilly, who could never be quiet for long. 'Think about it; the great Billy Bessacarr, last of the Renaissance men, how do you think he's always envisaged celebrating his seventieth birthday?'

I thought about it.

'Under a bright spotlight. Making a long speech. To a huge, appreciative, admiring audience,' I said.

'Right on! And his masters aren't about to lay on a fiesta in Red Square. But they have shown him how he can get close to it. And that's at the Old Bailey.'

I shook my head. 'But why? I can see that it might have some attractions for him, but what's in it for the Politburo? It'll be great for the media, of course, but at the end of the day what's the great message for the Western World? All they'll hear is a lot of old red propaganda crap which will be even less potent than usual, coming from an antique defector who also happens to be a condemned murderer!'

The Brigadier smiled and glanced at his watch.

'That's the nub of it,' he murmured. 'Suppose, just suppose, he were not to be condemned.'

'You mean *pardoned*?' I said stupidly.

'I mean, found *not guilty*,' he replied.

'Oh yes, it's a possibility we have to face,' he continued after he had let this sink in. 'His masters aren't letting him come back here to make a fool of himself and them, you can be sure of that. There's a long-term plan here, longer than even your father guesses, I suspect. It's our understanding that some of their best legal brains have been working on his defence for more than two years.'

'His defence? *What* defence?' I cried. 'I mean, look at the facts. Motive, opportunity, murder weapon covered with his prints, flight – Christ, how do you talk you way out of that lot? Surely no British lawyer would touch it?'

I don't know why I sounded so incredulous. The Brigadier and Reilly exchanged amused glances.

'Lawyers by their very nature work for a vast number of undesirable people, Mr Swift. Traitors are not excluded. And this promises to be a *cause célèbre* of the kind that most of them would give their partner's right hand to be involved with. It will have everything. *Everything*. It is our understanding that the defence will fall into two main areas. First, it will attack the assertion of motive.'

'What? I saw him! I told the police! I saw him at it on the bed with that ... with ... with Kim!'

'There's no proof your mother did,' said the Brigadier mildly. 'But the defence will, we understand, assert that even if she did, she was unlikely to have reacted as an outraged wife.'

'How then?' I asked in a low voice.

'As a woman of the world in the widest sense,' said the Brigadier. 'As a woman whose promiscuity was a byword in certain quarters. As a woman whose appetites were so voracious and so broad that they had driven your father into the chaste arms of his Korean secretary who later became and remained his faithful and loving wife for eighteen years.'

He paused. I opened my mouth to speak, couldn't, tried again.

'This is monstrous. No one would believe . . . monstrous . . . what evidence . . .'

'There will be photographs, letters,' he said. 'The KGB have technical skills of the highest order. You will recall that earlier in 1963 the year of your father's defection, there occurred the Profumo scandal, consequent to which Dr Stephen Ward was tried for living off the earnings of prostitution.'

'Yes, I remember. The poor bastard killed himself before the verdict came in,' I said.

'Yes. You may also remember that there were all kinds of wild stories circulating about the involvement in these, shall we say, sexually liberated circles of all kinds of eminent and respected figures?'

'Yes, but the speculation all died away, publicly at least, after Ward's suicide.'

'It died because it had no roots,' said the Brigadier. 'But there were those even then who suggested it died because Ward died and anyone who speculated too loud was likely to follow him. Absurd, of course, but this is the line your father's defence will follow. Mr Swift, in order to blacken your dead mother's name, a systematic attempt will be made to blacken the names of many of the living. You will recall the security implications of the Profumo affair? Among the admitted clientele of the chief lady in the affair was the Russian Naval Attaché, Captain Ivanov. The defence will claim to have been given access, (on humanitarian grounds!) to certain KGB classified material. Its alleged contents we can only guess at, but you can be certain it will be plausible and, as I've said, technically immaculate. The British public is always ready to believe the worst of the ruling classes. They will receive every encouragement. And even if the laws of libel and of contempt do not permit publication of all the so-called evidence, rumour has a wider circulation than even *The Sun* and I fear your mother's name at least could be tarnished beyond recovery.'

He spoke in a matter of fact rather than a sympathetic way and this made his monstrous scenario all the more realistic.

'But they'd need witnesses,' I insisted. 'Documents, photos even, wouldn't be enough, not at this remove. Who the hell can they put in the stand to support these allegations?'

'Grow up, Swifty!' interjected Reilly. 'Pimps and whores will sell anything for hard cash. And there's a couple of pretty respectable ladies and gents who're not above bending their memories for a fistful of the necessary. And what would you say to a KGB officer, now retired, who'd admit to being in charge of the political side of the whole nasty operation?'

'They'd never admit him,' I said.

'Want to bet?' she gibed.

'And then there's Joe,' said the Brigadier.

'Joe?'

'You remember Joe. The Kenyan boy. He wasn't too bright, but big and strong. Very good in the garden, I believe.'

'Yes, I remember Joe. What's he got to do with this?'

'It's our understanding,' said the Brigadier, 'that the defence will claim that your mother had a relationship with Joe when he was living at Bessacarr House in Hampshire.'

'*What?*'

'That she involved him in her circle and its . . . games.

70

That because of his youth, and his colour, and his . . . *size*, he was a special attraction. There will be photographs.'

'No!' I protested.

He went inexorably on.

'And what is more, Joe will be produced as a witness. Big, simple, transparently honest Joe.'

He glanced at his watch again and said to Reilly, 'I have to go. I'm sorry. Perhaps you will finish briefing Mr Swift. I feel sure he is with us in this matter. Mr Swift, we'll meet again later. I am sorry to have been the bearer of such distressing tidings. Good day.'

He left. I hardly noticed. I was feeling so sick that I went into the bathroom and after a while I flushed away the croissants, orange juice and morello cherry conserve. I filled the washbasin with cold water and plunged my face in, holding my breath till I was forced, gasping, back into the unchanged air.

I went back into the bedroom. Reilly had produced a bottle of vodka from somewhere and she slopped some of it into a glass which she handed to me.

'The rest isn't so painful,' she said. 'Not to you anyway. We said there were two main areas of defence. The first was to attack motive. Why should a lecherous slut like your ma get upset at the sight of your old man rogering the oriental help? OK, down, boy! It's not me speaking, it's the defence. That out of the way, they'll come on to the question, if your da didn't kill your ma, who did? And the answer they've come up with is, *us*. That is to say, British Intelligence. How do you like that? The same lot, they will suggest, as rubbed out Stephen Ward in case he got so uptight he spilled everything he knew about the Westminster-Mayfair connection. What do you say to that?'

She looked at me, eyes wide, inviting me to share her incredulity.

I said, 'OK, Reilly. So I've got the broad picture. My old man's planning to go out in a blaze of glory at No 1 Court, Old Bailey, throwing so much shit at the fan, everyone's bound to get a piece. And for why? For the greater glory of the Soviet Union? I don't buy that. Whatever else was phoney about him, his supra-nationalism wasn't.'

'Suppose I said, to justify himself to himself?' said Reilly. 'Would that make sense?'

'You don't justify murder by fixing the evidence,' I said.

'You don't imagine he ever thought of it as murder?' asked Reilly. 'That letter he wrote you, I bet what he said was that he was innocent *of murder*. And he'd believe it. Justifiable homicide, that's how he'd see it. But he's not going to be able to get a jury to bring in that verdict, is he? So he's going after the symbolic *not guilty*, and if the facts have to be altered a bit, it's only because an English jury isn't competent to deal with the truth.'

I thought about this. The letter I couldn't remember precisely, but it all rang true. I felt sick again, not physically this time, but in the very pores of my being.

'Reilly,' I said, 'he deserves to die. Once I'd have begged to be allowed to do it. If what you tell me is true, he deserves it even more. But I've changed too. I don't need persuading that he ought to be killed, but whether I . . .'

'Swift,' she interrupted, unsmiling now. 'I hope you haven't mistaken any of this for *persuasion*. The Brigadier spelt out the deal. Believe me, he means it, every last threat of it.'

'I believe you,' I said. 'But if my father's coming back here, surely you've got experts who can blow him away without any difficulty. Why do you want me?'

'Listen,' she said, 'you don't imagine he's just going to walk quietly into some local nick and say, "Surprise, surprise! Look who's here!" do you? The Russians are going to arrange for his first appearance to be as spectacular and public as possible. They know what we'd do if the situation were reversed and they must have many a good belly laugh at the way they can use the West's free press and other media against it. It'll be a long way from London, but it has to be in the West. There'll be a press conference, photographs, printed statements, the full business, then he'll get on a plane to the UK to surrender himself to the authorities. Once he's gone public like that, they know he's safe. For him to die then would almost be better than a trial for the Soviets! All they want is a huge Western scandal. Once this thing hits the headlines, they've got it. No, he's got to be shut up before the press see him and the KGB will be keeping him wrapped up tighter than a nun's knockers.'

She had seated herself in front of the dressing-table mirror and was repairing her face.

'So how do you propose to get to him?' I asked.

I was genuinely curious. I'd almost forgotten we were talking about my father. Reilly's next words reminded me brutally.

'Not me. *You*,' she said. 'By invitation.'

'By invitation!' I laughed. 'Why the hell should he invite me *anywhere* except to jump over the nearest cliff.'

'Because his principal motive for this whole exercise is self-justification,' she said calmly. 'In the eyes of the world in general. But more particularly, if the opportunity presented itself, in the eyes of his dearly beloved son and heir. The only thing that's going to tempt him to bust his security screen is the chance to talk to you.'

'This is stretching things, Reilly,' I said in disgust.

'That's my job. I'm not bad at it,' she said with a grin, spinning round on the dressing-table stool.

'And if we don't know where he is, how do you propose letting him know where I am?' I asked.

'That's a problem we'll work on when we get there,' she answered.

I felt a sudden stabbing pain in my guts. Christ, I thought trying to dampen fear with frivolity, if sex is going to accelerate matters, I know how I'm going to go.

'You OK?' said Reilly.

I burped.

'Fine,' I lied. 'It's just that I don't much care for raw vodka. You said *when we get there*. Get where?'

'Where we think he is, of course,' she replied. 'Rome.'

'*Rome?*' I exclaimed, stomach pains forgotten. 'What makes you say Rome?'

'Just our *understanding*,' she said, eyeing me shrewdly. 'Why, bucko? Is there any particular reason you know why it should or shouldn't be Rome?'

I returned her shrewdness with open-eyed innocence.

'No,' I lied. 'Not a reason in the world.'

. . . we were once very close . . .

There's no place like Rome.

The last time I'd been here I'd been closing the Sam 7 deal with two *consiglieri* of the Red Brigade. They had been sharply-dressed, keen-eyed, fully accredited Italian lawyers. It had surprised me at first just how legally-minded many of these subversive groups were when it came to arms deals! Worst of all were Italians. Oddly, I'd been reassured by the presence of a nervous girl called Monica who wore huge sun-glasses and a University of Rome T-shirt and kept on reaching into her shoulder-bag every time a car hooted in the Via Nazionale, which is about every two seconds. But those two gimlet-eyed lawyers agreed nothing till they were certain one of her nervous twitches was an affirmative nod.

It occurred to me in my taxi from Leonardo da Vinci airport that this was one of the agreements I hadn't honoured and that a lot of very nasty people in this city would be very happy to cause me great pain.

It also occurred to me as we slid across two crowded traffic lanes to make a right-angled left turn at 90 kph that perhaps my taxi-driver was one of them.

I felt as weak-legged and as happy as a round-the-world sailor on his first landfall as I climbed out in the Piazza Barberini and I overtipped out of gratitude. The driver treated me with the contempt I deserved, accelerating away so hard that I hardly had time to let go of the door.

Whatever else was wrong with the Brigadier, you couldn't fault his travel arrangements. I was shown to a comfortable room on the quiet side of the hotel and half an hour later, after I'd unpacked and showered, there was a discreet tap on the door and I was invited to sign for a special delivery package. It contained a million lire in notes of different denominations, plus a little purseful of one-hundred-lire pieces. A nice touch, that. Italian life is impossible without them.

It also contained a Luger automatic. When I examined it closely, I saw it was the same one I'd retrieved from my safe in London. I'd left it and the industrial diamonds in a newly rented deposit box at Coutts. The Brigadier must have decided to combine economy with a reminder of his power.

I lay on the bed and lit a cigarette. I'd given up tobacco years ago, except for the luxury of an occasional after dinner cigar. But in these last few weeks I'd started smoking again. Why not? It's not every man who can have a quiet chuckle whenever he reads the Government Health Warning on a packet of English cigarettes.

I drew deep and thought about my father. An old man now. A has-been in pathetic search of one last dose of limelight. Did that make what they wanted me to do easier or more difficult? I thought about what I'd been told he intended to say about Mama. That would have to be my trigger, more even than the memory of his killing her. But the fury wouldn't come, not here, lying on this soft bed watching the smoke stain the shafts of sunlight like barium meal in a man's gut. Instead I found myself examining those monstrous allegations critically.

At twenty I couldn't have done it. At twenty most boys of my class and upbringing, perhaps of most classes and up-bringings, were innocent, no matter how much experience they'd had. I'd tried buggery at school (Harrow; they didn't charge you extra); paid five quid for the fastest orgasm on record in the back of a London taxi (we got from Curzon Street to Hyde Park Corner); and even balled a girl called May at a May Ball (she was called Marjory in fact, but May made a better story). But I was innocent. I had no compre-hension of debauchery. And as for debauchery involving Mama ... I couldn't even envisage her taking part in the straightforward legitimate act which had produced me!

And yet I thought of her sexually. Oh yes, I could see that now. That flash of relief I'd felt when I'd realized it was Kim writhing beneath my father was based on sexual jealousy as much as filial piety.

Right. I could acknowledge that. Also now, on the edge of middle age (but not about, or *ever*; to fall over that edge) I could look back at my own life and see the strange twists and turns sex, that had once seemed so simple, could lead you through. Not that my tastes had ever been particularly exotic. But for ten years, whatever I'd wanted I'd got, by the simple expedient of paying the piper. And that itself must be a kind of debauchery.

So. Could any fraction of what was going to be alleged about Mama be true? Joe, for instance. Big, black Joe. Big in every sense. We used to go swimming together in the lake at Bessacarr and …

I pushed myself off the bed, ground out my cigarette violently and strode across the room and back, across and back, like a caged tiger, longing for one last furious leap at its enemies before it died. I'd found my fury again. Gone was the middle-aged objectivity of a few moments ago. All I saw now was that it didn't matter whether any of it was true or not.

Truth or lies, the monstrous, unforgivable thing was to offer to speak it in public. Any man who could contemplate that after all these years was indeed a monster.

Such a man deserved to die.

I had to get out and get some exercise. My instructions were strict – remain in the hotel until contacted. But I guessed these instructions were based on ignorance as much as security. The Brigadier wasn't yet certain of when, where or how my father was coming to Rome, though once he had the details I had no doubt an ingenious plan to effect contact between us would be forthcoming. So I must be kept available.

I smiled as I descended the stairs, thinking that I had one large advantage over the Brigadier. I had a strong suspicion I knew at least one of the reasons why Pa had picked Rome. And if I were right, I knew exactly how to make contact with him.

Outside, I guessed I was being watched but it didn't bother me. I strolled slowly down the Via de Tritone, crossed the Corso and paused in the Piazza Colonna to admire the spiralling intricacies of Marcus Aurelius's column. My great-grandmama's Campanian villa was also named after a column, but that was only a weatherworn stump. I had often fantasized about waking one morning to find it had sprung up to its former glories overnight and towered above the villa. There's nothing like a child's mind for imaginative creation.

I continued my walk through crowded little streets in the direction of the Pantheon. I wondered what it would be like to be one of these myriad people about me. Work to do; or, for the tourists, to go back to; bills to pay, families to keep, children to educate, festivals to celebrate, gods to worship; triumphs, tragedies, ecstasies, despairs, pleasures, pains – a man's life, something worth clinging to when the grim reaper started singing harvest home.

Suddenly I felt terror; or rather I had a sense of empathy with them so strong that I felt the terror I would have felt if I had to lose what they had to lose. Then I was indifferent once more. Death meant nothing to me. The first real pain and I was ready to blow myself away. No hesitation. No qualms.

Why then had I left Margarita? I asked myself.

To see my daughter? But why? It would hardly be a meeting likely to do much for her health or happiness.

Or mine for that matter.

The answer came to me as sudden and unexpected as that momentary flash of empathy with the normal, the everyday.

I *wanted* to feel qualms. I wanted that terror to be mine as of right. I wanted to know that death meant loss.

Though this sun on my face, this great arch of unblemished blue overhead, this pleasant anticipation of coming in sight of the Pantheon at any moment and finding a trattoria and sitting outside with a large glass of cold Frascati, all this was much, if not enough, to lose.

Rapt in thought though I'd been, I had let one part of my mind rove in search of the hypothesized Brigadier's man and I soon had him spotted. I checked by going into a newsagent's to buy a two-day-old English paper. I noticed they had an even older *El Universal*, so I got that too. When I came out, he was still there, peering into a shop window a few yards away. Not yet terribly good at his job perhaps, but I gave the Brigadier full marks for his choice in terms of camouflage. He was a slight, dark youth with a black moustache and wearing jeans and T-shirt, indistinguishable from thousands of other young Romans.

I continued and found my café table with a view of the Pantheon, ordered my Frascati and settled down to read the papers. *The Times* was still as dull as it used to be. There was no mention of my name, which was all the news I was interested in. My Frascati arrived. I asked the waiter if there was a telephone. He jerked his head towards the shadowy interior. I went inside, first shading my wine in a tent made out of *El Universal*. When I returned, I sipped the Frascati with a sensuous slowness, then began to read the Venezuelan paper. Again there was no sign of my name as lazily I scanned the pages.

But a name did tug at the corner of my eye the way they often do. I had to go back over three or four columns before I found it.

Ramón Dario.

A body had been found floating in the dock at La Guaira. It had been identified as that of Ramón Dario, a philosophy lecturer at the Central University. Cause of death was a bullet through the spine and the body had been badly mutilated. The police (clever police) were treating it as murder.

Shit! I thought. Bastard Dario the great fixer! So confident of his ability to manipulate the movement. And in the end they had grown suspicious and manipulated *him*, in every sense. I shuddered as I imagined his desperate and ingenious lies. *Swift had escaped. Swift had had a heart attack and been dumped in the sea.* I bet he was convincing. But I knew the kind of people he was double-crossing. One hint of treachery and they'd rather tear the fingernails off a dozen innocent hands than risk letting a traitor get away with it.

So, before he died, Dario would have told them the lot.

Did it make any difference to me?

Hardly. They'd have got the money I paid Dario, that was sure. And they'd probably keep up the pretence a little longer, both to save face and just in case there really was any chance of squeezing some more cash or at least some concession from the authorities in return for my promised safety.

78

Some hope, I thought, laying the paper down and returning to my Frascati. This time it tasted a little sour through the chill and the Pantheon looked more like an overblown tomb than a memorial of some nobler, greater age.

If my shadow had still been visible I think I would have called him over for a chat. I felt like talking to someone. But he had disappeared, probably taking advantage of my apparent immobility to phone through for instructions.

I rose, paid and left. He'd just have to be disappointed when he came back. It would be a useful lesson to him.

But I'd done him an injustice. As I began to retrace my steps, suddenly keen to get under cover again, I saw him ahead of me, approaching.

He stopped about five yards away and smiled uncertainly. I kept going. As I drew alongside him he said, 'Mr Swift?'

The poor sod's been told to fetch me back, I thought.

'Look,' I said, 'I just wanted a walk. I'm on my way back to the hotel now, OK?'

He nodded. I took this for agreement and made to move past him. He struck me lightly in the stomach, not enough to drive me backwards, but enough to wind me.

As I doubled up, the rear door of a light blue Fiat Strada parked alongside the kerb opened. Hands reached out and pulled me in. Behind, my shadow pushed. I didn't resist, thinking if the bastard wanted me that much, he'd better have me.

The shadow got in beside me and the car accelerated violently away.

It was crowded in the back seat despite the slimness of the two young men sandwiching me. They could have been brothers, as could the man in the passenger seat. All I could see of the driver was the back of his head with black hair curling from under a floppy camouflage sun-hat, but he looked much the same type. Dangerous.

I took a couple of deep breaths and got my wind back. No one spoke, but the young man in the passenger seat remained half turned round with his gaze fixed intensely on my face.

'You'll know me again,' I said finally, half jocular, half in irritation. This seemed an absurd example of Italian overkill, quite out of keeping with the Brigadiers' fondness for the understated and elegantly cool threat.

'Shut up,' said the man in the passenger seat.

'Oh for Christ's sake,' I began.

'*Shut up!*' he snapped.

His right hand was resting between the front seats and now it jabbed out and I was struck in the stomach again. I gasped, hesitated between jabbing my fingers into his eyes or up his nostrils, and in the same second realized it wasn't a fist that was poking into my belly.

It was a gun.

A Czech Skorpion machine-pistol with the safety catch off.

I shut up and began to be worried. I got even more worried when we passed my hotel with no diminution of speed and continued up the Via Veneto, through the Porta Pinciana on to the road which skirts the park of the Villa Borghese. Where the road opened out in front of the villa itself, we pulled in to the side. There were one or two other cars around and several people on foot but they didn't make me feel safe.

Next moment I felt even unsafer.

The driver turned round. I had been mistaken. Under the floppy hat wasn't another thin moustachioed male face, but a smooth olive oval. It was a woman, vaguely familiar.

The moment she spoke I knew her. Not that I recognized the voice, but the words made everything fall into place.

'Mr Swift,' she said, 'you owe us a great deal of money.'

Ten years had done a lot for Monica. She was no longer the nervous, jumpy girl I remembered. Perhaps terrorism is a career like everything else. You start with all kinds of anxieties but eventually you become blasé. I didn't feel blasé. I had cheated these people out of several hundred million lire. They were quite happy to blow up people who hadn't cheated them out of anything, so what they had in mind for me didn't bear thinking about.

I said, 'You've made a mistake. My name is Evans ...'

She struck me across the mouth, but very lightly, like a lover's caress, promising pleasure to come.

'We know who you are, Mr Swift,' she said. 'Though you look rather different from when we last met. Did you think that news of your so-called kidnapping would not have been noticed here? And everywhere else you performed your dirty tricks? The brothers everywhere are in close contact now. We asked our comrades in the FALN for a share in you when we read the news. They did not answer for a while but when they did it was strange news. They did not have you. You had left the country. Since then the brothers everywhere have been looking out for you. Finally we heard that a man called Evans en route for Rome might be worth looking at. It seemed too good to be true. But now I see it is true.'

'Monica!' said my shadow urgently.

She looked in the direction he was pointing. A police patrol-car was moving slowly toward us flashing its intention to stop close by.

Monica turned away from me and set the Fiat in motion. In many other countries, such sudden and violent acceleration would have been regarded as most suspicious by an approaching police car, but in Rome it was clearly the norm. The inmates didn't even turn their heads as we passed them.

'Where're we going?' asked the passenger in Italian.

'We'll take him out to the villa,' said Monica.

'The villa?' said the man in a surprised tone. 'Is that wise? It's our only really safe house.'

Monica said, 'So what? He's not coming back.'

We were soon out of the Park and moving at a good lick along the Via Flaminia. It struck me that it wouldn't be long before we were in open countryside. Ahead I saw some traffic lights. As we approached they changed from green and I tensed myself for an assault when we stopped. There might not be another chance. But my captors had the same thought.

My arms were gripped with extra firmness by the two on either side of me and the man with the gun dug it deep into my belly once more.

I relaxed. OK, plan two was to try it at full speed and hope I was the one to survive the crash.

We stopped at the lights. Monica sat with her left hand out of the open window drumming impatiently on the roof.

A pair of motor-scooters drew up alongside. On one of them there was a single rider, on the other, the nearer, a woman was riding pillion, her tight skirt pushed high up on her thighs. The man on my left looked appreciatively at the bare leg which was all I could see and spoke for the first time, expressing his appreciation. The man with the gun didn't take his eyes off me. One of the conscientious kind, I thought. Well, it got him his reward.

The girl on the pillion had a deep duffel-bag crushed between her belly and the driver's back. Casually she reached into it.

But there was nothing casual about the way her hand came out.

In it she held a gun. By an interesting coincidence, which I didn't find very interesting at the time, it too was a Skorpion whose stubby barrel and foldaway wire-stock make it ideal carrying for the lady who prefers a really powerful weapon.

Monica's fingers were still drumming when the first bullet tore into her head. My hands moved like lightning as I grabbed for the passenger's gun. It wasn't so that he couldn't use it in defence but so that he didn't dispatch me with a dying twitch. I rammed my forefingers behind the trigger and felt his finger twitch convulsively as the top of his head joined Monica's on the dashboard.

Now I sat quite still while two more blasts set the men on either side of me writhing bloodily all over the back of the car. Only then did I dive for the door, thrusting the still moving body out of my way. It took no more than a couple of second to fling my leg over the pillion of the second motor-scooter and then we went into a sharp U-turn as the lights changed and tore away back towards the heart of the city.

I didn't look back. A fanfare of horns was already registering the typical Roman protest at the slightest delay. Such impatient music was a fitting elegy for those four young people who'd chosen to take the shortest route possible towards whatever perfect society they envisaged. They'd probably all killed, certainly had no compunction about killing me. But they had been young and vital and I wondered whether a few months more for a cancerous cynical crook could possibly be worth four lifetimes.

No, that's bullshit. I thought it later when I was safely out of the way and at my ease. *Then* I was just delighted to be still alive.

The scooter halted in the Piazza del Popolo. Reilly and I

dismounted. I clapped my driver on the shoulder. He was a man of about thirty with a thin intelligent face and the melancholy introspective expression of one who'd rather have been in a good library rapt in some scholarly project.

'Thanks, mate,' I said with feeling.

He smiled slightly and nodded, then he and the other scooterist took off. Reilly led me to an outrageously parked Alfasud and got into the driver's seat.

'Take your jacket off,' she commanded as I opened the passenger door.

Surprised, I obeyed. Then I saw the shoulders were spattered with blood and something that might have been brain.

'I must be costing the Brigadier a fortune in dry-cleaning,' I said, folding the jacket on my lap.

'And the rest,' she said.

'OK. Save the reproaches. I don't want to hear them twice,' I said. 'And Reilly. Thanks. That was really smooth.'

'All in the day's work, bucko,' she said, adding grudgingly, 'You acted pretty quick yourself.'

I smiled at her and patted the thigh.

'I recognized the leg,' I said. 'We were once very close.'

. . . a good Catholic girl . . .

I was surprised when we headed back to my hotel.

I said, 'Reilly, shouldn't we go somewhere else? Those nasty people know I'm here.'

She said, 'We want *all* the nasty people to know you're here, remember? You'll be quite safe so long as you do what you're told.'

The Brigadier was waiting in my room. He looked more sorrowful than angry, but I got in first anyway saying, *'Mea culpa.'*

'It's of no account,' he said generously. 'I must admit I'd forgotten how many enemies you have in low places, Mr Swift. Perhaps you will now admit the importance of following instructions.'

'You mean sitting around here till you pick up news about my sainted father's intentions?' I said. 'Well, I'm not mad keen on spending my few remaining days hanging around hotel rooms. It's not that I don't think you'll come up with something eventually but I thought I'd see if I could help things along.'

'You mean, simply by parading in public?' said the Brigadier.

'I mean by making contact with what could be my father's contact,' I said.

Reilly who was busy dismantling and cleaning her machine-pistol on a low tiled table stopped her work. The Brigadier raised his eyebrows.

'Perhaps you'd explain?' he said.

'Why not?'

Indeed there was no reason why not. And I felt truly grateful for the care they'd taken of me. (Bullshit.) Also it's always pleasant to feel superior to experts. (Asshole.)

Perhaps the real reason had more to do with the ambiguous human response to independent thought in areas of critical importance. It's a condition more praised than sought after. Free will is one of the pseudonyms of the nameless terrors which send men scuttling to shift responsibility, pass bucks, support football teams, embrace Catholicism, join the Red Brigade. Even the apparent independence of the secret life is mainly illusory. Since my mother's death, I'd enjoyed the freedom of subterfuge and then that other equally illusory freedom of openness which might be called *misère ouvert*. Here I am spread out for all to see. Get lower than this if you can!

The only freedom I'd really had was to be still, to do nothing. Now as the moment of confrontation with my father approached, I was glad to share my knowledge with the Brigadier, glad to put myself back under constraint.

Or perhaps it wasn't that at all.

Reilly, who was rapidly reassembling her gun, said to the magazine she was loading, 'Do you think a bullet up the arse might hurry the cratur along?'

The Brigadier smiled and shook his head slightly, not so much in denial as in affectionate wonderment at the precocity of a favoured child. Some child! I wondered suddenly what the precise relationship between the two was. Perhaps he really was her father.

Some father!

'I think Mr Swift is going to explain without encouragement,' he said.

'But I do like attentiveness,' I said reprovingly.

With a sigh Reilly clicked the magazine home and went into a parody of 'The Boyhood of Raleigh'.

I said, 'The Bessacarrs are an old Roman Catholic family, slightly lapsed of course, but they do say, once a Catholic, always a Catholic. You may recall my father made quite a thing of leaving the Church way back. The ego-trip of publicly renouncing his faith was too attractive for him not to buy a ticket.'

'You're not seriously suggesting,' interrupted the Brigadier, 'that your father wants to be in Rome on his seventieth birthday in order to renew his faith?'

His tone was that of someone addressing an idiot child. Reilly looked more interested. Perhaps at heart she really was a good Catholic girl.

'No, I'm not suggesting that,' I said. 'Though I think he'd like the headlines. What I was going to say was that as well as being an old Catholic family, we are also in some ways an old Roman family. My great-grandmama was Italian. The Contessa Dianti, don't you know? Or perhaps your researches into the Bessacarrs didn't go back that far?'

The Brigadier and Reilly were not yet ready to be surprised.

'Dianti. Francesca Maria Dorotea. Born 1870. Died 1956. Two children. A daughter, Susanna, who married the 4th Viscount Bessacarr, your grandfather. A son, Giulio, who married Emilia Dianti, a half-cousin. One child, a son, also Giulio, died 1976 without increase,' said the Brigadier.

So Uncle Giulio was dead. Ebullient, enthusiastic and totally inept Uncle Giulio!

'End of Italian line,' said Reilly smugly.

I smiled and said, 'Congratulations. To continue. What I imagine my father hates most about growing old in Russia is that, essentially, now that Kim's dead, he's probably alone. No crowds of admiring friends, no adoring wife, no troops of loving children. That's what he'd love to have, I'm sure. A real family, something halfway between English Victorian and Italian peasant. Hordes of grandchildren and great-grandchildren, with himself playing the benevolent, lovable old patriach.'

'And all he has is you and a granddaughter he's never seen,' murmured Reilly. 'He really got sold short, didn't he?'

'Thank you, Miss Reilly,' said the Brigadier. 'So your father has a strong sentimental streak, Mr Swift? What has that got to do with Italy?'

'Who did your research?' I wondered. 'Reilly, I bet it was you. You really should keep her in after school, Brig.'

'Come on, bucko, spit it out,' said Reilly impatiently. 'What is it you're after saying? That Billy Bessacarr is the Pope's old dad?'

'Not quite,' I said. 'But he certainly fathered his firstborn here in Italy. At the age of seventeen.'

They exchanged glances, unable to conceal their surprise.

'He was staying with his maternal grandmother at the time,' I continued. 'It was probably the heat that did it. It gets awfully hot on the Costa Amalfitana in the summer. Great-grandmama Dianti used to spend most of the summer in her villa on the Campanian coast a few miles west of Amalfi. I think it's a hotel now. Ah, the sad change!'

Sad indeed. I remembered nothing but happy days there.

'Do carry on,' said the Brigadier. He spoke soothingly and I realized that I must have been letting some emotion show in my voice and on my face. Perhaps the shooting had affected my nerves more than I'd realized. I suppose I should have been glad to know I wasn't made of stone, but stone's a pretty good building material when you think about it.

'OK. Right.' I said, switching from my Anglo to my American register. 'It was a maid, who else? I mean, a *yes'm, straightaway'm* maid, not a never-had-it maid, though that too, maybe. Anyhow, now she'd had it, and good. There was a child, a girl. No scandal, I mean these old European families really know about these things. The child, Teresa, was brought up decent in my great-grandmama's house till her mother got married. And there the family connection ceased, for the man she married was a young Fascist activist whose one aim in life was to emulate his beloved Duce. Come 1939, that was not the kind of connection, however distant, the Bessacarrs were about to admit to. There was a bit of an anxious moment towards the end of the war when it seemed that hubby was wanted by the War Crimes Commission, but some friendly partisans got to him first and he emulated his beloved Duce in death as in life. His wife did the wifely thing and died of grief or TB a few months later. Teresa, born a bastard, was now an orphan.

I'd moved back to the Anglo mode, I realized. Perhaps I was linguistically schizoid. What could it mean?

'How do you know all this?' enquired the Brigadier.

'You mean, if *you* don't?' I asked sarcastically. 'Well, I was fairly close to the family, you see. And I even met Teresa. I was staying with my great-grandmama in the late forties. She'd gone to work there after her parents' death. She didn't know of her connection with the family, just thought that great-grandmama was very kind. But, hell, my father had to tell her of course. Never missed a cue for a big scene, did good old dad. I eavesdropped. I was seven, I think. I was accustomed to being at the centre of things at the Villa Colonna and I didn't take too kindly to being left to my own devices. So I eavesdropped. Teresa's reaction was very calm. She just repeated the information so that she was sure she'd got it straight. Then ignoring, or perhaps it's truer to say, indifferent to my father's invitation to join him in the big scene, she said a quiet *grazie* and left the house. I followed her. Well, hell, she was the nearest thing to a sister I had. She set off down the road towards Amalfi. When she got there she headed for the Carducci bakehouse and spoke to someone at the door. A few moments later a young man stripped to the waist against the heat came out. His face lit up like a birthday cake when he saw her. She spoke to him. He grabbed her, crushed her, I thought he was trying to kill her, but she didn't seem to mind.

'It turned out he was one of the partisans who had killed her stepfather who she thought was her real father, so she'd been much troubled to find she fancied him like mad and he likewise. But now it was OK. That's the trouble with blood, isn't it? Where there's a blood link, even though you may hate the bastard you're linked with, you can't shrug it off, can you? But now good old dad had set her free.

'She left my great-grandmama's villa that night. Two weeks later she got married. I represented the Bessacarrs at the wedding! End of story. Except . . .'

'Except,' prompted the Brigadier, which was nice of him. Reilly would have let my dramatic pause stretch into bathos.

'Except that the man she married, Bruno Carducci, from being a partisan in the field became a politician in the town, Communist of course, and eventually sought elective office, first at regional level but ultimately as a Deputy, here in Rome. He never made it really big, I gather, and five years ago he died of a heart attack. But his widow, their six children, and their eleven grandchildren still live here in Rome.'

'Well, hello, *Uncle*,' said Reilly.

'So you believe that the presence of a large, ready-made

family might well attract your father to Rome?' said the Brigadier.

'Like honey to a bear,' I said.

'And quite clearly, if he makes contact with his daughter, your half-sister, he would do it *before* he organized the press conference.'

'He won't be able to stir without fifty journalists afterwards,' I said.

'So if what you say is true, then the surest way of letting your father know *you* are in Rome is to let your half-sister know you're in Rome,' he mused. 'You *are* quite sure of your facts, Mr Swift?'

He shot me a sharply interrogative glance.

'Oh yes,' I said. 'You see, I've got this secret source of information. It's called the telephone directory. Which reminds me, if you'll excuse me, I'd better be on my way. I've got a luncheon appointment with Signora Teresa Carducci.'

II

... *et tu, soror* ...

My date with Teresa was for twelve-thirty at the Trattoria
Angelino ai Fori where the Via Cavour joins the Via dei Fori
Imperiali, usually on two wheels at a hundred kilometres per
hour. I arrived early so I could see her coming and get some
idea if she had brought company, but at ten past noon she
was already sitting under the vine-wreathed trellis of the al
fresco section of the restaurant.

'Hello, Teresa,' I said.

She offered her hand. I took it and pulled her to her feet.
There weren't many people here yet and I indicated an empty
table nearer the pavement.

'I like the draught from the passing cars,' I explained.

She followed me without demur. I ordered a Punt e Mes
for her and a Campari-soda for me. I couldn't stand the drink
but I loved the colour. A good-looking boy in his late teens
and a New York Mets T-shirt had been studying the menu
fixed to one of the trellis posts. Now he came and slumped
into a chair at the next table and raised his finger at the
waiter.

I said, 'Is he with you or is he with me?'

Teresa said calmly. 'Vasco, come and meet your uncle.'

Vasco glanced at me sullenly and made much the same
gesture as he'd used to summon the waiter, only this time it
was faintly obscene.

'Cute kid,' I said. 'He should be useful to keep the flies off
the food. How've you been, Teresa?'

I was speaking in English, or rather American. Teresa had
spoken the language perfectly well in the forties and clearly
she'd kept in practice.

'I am well,' she said. 'And you, Tonto? How are you?'

I was taken aback, and taken back too, to hear the old

name. Tonto had been my own infant corruption of Antonio which was the one of my six Christian names my mother preferred. From the start my father had insisted on Lemuel, or Lem in the family circle. I'd gone along with my mother till they sent me away to school and I discovered that 'Lem' was regarded as merely strange whereas 'Tonto' was quite ridiculous. In the holidays I'd even managed to break Mama of the habit, though she still called me Tonio. But the last time I'd seen Teresa at my great-grandmama's Campanian villa in 1949, I'd still been Tonto.

'I'm as well as can be expected,' I said.

'You look well,' she said. 'Fit and brown.'

I quite enjoyed the dramatic irony. A man's got to take his pleasures where he can.

I held up my glass and studied my half-sister over the lucent pink liquor. She was in her early fifties now and her once smooth black hair was grained with grey and the soft clear pallor of her skin had been roughened and ochred by sun and time. But discipline or exercise, or perhaps the Bessacarr genes which like their artefacts to be lean and rangy, had preserved her from that Latin thickening which is frequently the product of too much pasta and too many children.

'You too, Teresa,' I said. 'It's good to see you.'

'Is it?' she said. 'Why?'

I decided a bit of English obliqueness was the best response here so I smiled enigmatically and said, 'Shall we order?'

I waved casually at the waiter, who ignored me. But Vasco waggled his finger again and he came. Teresa confirmed my dietary suspicions by saying that all she wanted was *prosciutto e melone*. I had *saltimbocca* with mushrooms and peppers on the principle that I might as well enjoy it while I had the stomach for it.

'What about him? Is it his feeding time?' I asked, nodding at the youth. Vasco glowered at me and Teresa shook her head. I suppose I was bearing down rather hard on the boy, but I was only reacting to the waves of antagonism emanating from him ever since I arrived. Perhaps he was just being over-protective towards his mother. I made a conciliatory gesture by asking for three glasses when I ordered a bottle of Orvieto. This pleased his mother at least, who sent an admonitory glance along with the glass of wine, which he accepted, albeit grudgingly.

Service was swift and as I tucked into my veal I thought the moment was ripe to touch upon the reasons for my presence.

'What I want to talk about, Teresa,' I said, 'is our father which art in Moscow.'

This produced a small reaction as she worked it out, but possibly all it meant was that her Catholic upbringing had survived her Communist marriage and she didn't care for my frivolity. Or it could mean that she'd heard something.

'Only, he doesn't seem to be in Moscow any more,' I pursued. 'Does that surprise you?'

She shrugged and said, 'You too, Tonto, you are supposed to be tied up in some cellar in Caracas, are you not? Yet here you are, and do I look surprised?'

'No. And *that* surprises me,' I replied.

'I don't think so,' she said. 'You are not a man to be easily surprised, I think. Not like the little boy who followed me everywhere in his great-grandmother's villa, with eyes wide, and with ears wide too, I suspect.'

'I was in love with my great-grandmama's pretty maid,' I joked. 'When I found out she was my sister too, I was even more in love. I didn't know about not loving sisters, not then.'

'You were bored,' she said flatly. 'On the days your father did take you sailing, you did not follow!'

'I'm not sailing now, and I'm not bored,' I said. 'I'm very interested once again in my pretty sister. Shall we get to the point, Teresa? Have you heard anything lately of, or from, my – *our* – father?'

She glanced around. The restaurant was now crowded, every table full. Vasco who was the sole occupant of a table for four was venting his spleen, which seemed plentiful, on the waiter who was trying to dislodge him in favour of some new arrivals. Teresa said something to him, too fast for my rusty Italian, and surlily he rose and came and sat down next to me. The waiter said, '*Grazie, signora,*' and to my surprise, Teresa ordered coffee. I was only two-thirds of the way through my veal and she'd hardly touched her ham. I opened my mouth to speak and she gave me a little warning shake of the head, so I stuffed another forkful of food into it instead. A moment later the coffee arrived. As the waiter set it on the table Teresa grasped my arm and said, 'Come.'

I rose, protesting. Vasco was protesting too and, though another incomprehensibly rapid burst of Italian reduced him to a proper filial silence, he sent expressive looks of hate and anger after me as I allowed Teresa to drag me away.

'Why does that boy dislike me so much?' I asked as we dodged through the Grand Prix traffic on the Via dei Fori Imperiali.

'I told him to take care of the bill,' said Teresa.

It hardly seemed a sufficient explanation. I assumed the suddeness of our departure was to throw any unwanted observers into confusion. It takes a very good man to get away from an Italian waiter without settling his bill!

Across the road, Teresa kept going and led me through the entrance to the Roman Forum. Ungraciously I let her pay. Whatever she was going to tell me would have to be good to compensate for exchanging the shady vines and chilled Orvieto at Angelino's for the high oven temperature of the Forum. The ruins soaked up heat and threw it back like the radiants of a gas fire. Too much of this and I'd either melt, crack, or come out permantly glazed. I tried to head for the nearest shade but she steered me across past the Temple of Vesta into the atrium of the Vestal's house, that central court with its statue-ringed pools round which presumably the Virgins did whatever virgins do when they're off duty. The only other lunatics out in the sun were a party of Germans whose courier was obviously bent on proving the master-race could get round the Forum faster and sweatier than any non-Aryans.

'For God's sake, let's get into the shade,' I begged as she sat down in the full blast of the sun on a fragment of wall close to the statue of the Vestal who had her name scrubbed off the plinth for being naughty. It was possibly Claudia, the scholars say, who got herself converted to Christianity.

I wouldn't be surprised if she'd merely told the head lady she was pissed off with standing out here in the heat.

'In a moment. There are people there,' Teresa answered.

'You can bet your Vestal virginity there's people there,' I replied. 'It's cool. It's healthy.'

'Here is healthy too,' she answered. 'Healthy to talk.'

She had a point. The Germans were moving on. There were a few people lounging in the shade on the other side of the atrium, but apart from the rather Neanderthal silhouette of what was probably a German archæologist poking around beyond the ruined wall towards the three columns of Castor and Pollux, no one else was stirring. Unless Claudia's ears were bugged, we were safe from eavesdroppers.

'Now, little Tonto,' she said, very big sisterly, 'what is it you want?'

I looked into those calm brown eyes, thought rapidly of a dozen good lies with at least three plausible variations on each, then incredibly found that my mental computer was printing out the truth.

I said, 'I want to see my daughter, that is all I want.'

If I'd hoped to take her unawares, I was disappointed.

She nodded calmly and said, 'To see Angelica? Nothing more?'

'That's all,' I said, squeezing her hand. 'I swear it.'

She returned my pressure for a moment, then cried out in protest as it intensified to the edge of pain. I put my face close to hers and murmured, 'And now, dear sister, tell me how you happen to know my daughter's name.'

She glanced around, I thought nervously, then pulled herself free and rose abruptly.

'Please,' she said. 'Let us walk back to the trattoria.'

She set off as she spoke but I wasn't ready to be so easily brushed off. She'd brought me here to talk and I was a long way from being finished. I jumped up and caught her alongside the statue of Claudia. I grasped her arm and jerked her round. She resisted and tried to push me away.

'Please, Tonto,' she said urgently.

There was a slithering sound close to my ear, like silk-stockinged legs being crossed, and some patches of what could have been coarse-grained talc drift across my face.

I looked up. Claudia's slightly bent left knee had a long graze running along it. I looked round. The archæologist

94

with the Piltdown head was leaning across the distant ruined wall as though to steady himself for a photograph. But that was no Leica he was pointing.

Then, heat or no heat, I was off and running. Blood might be thicker than water but I had no intention of giving my half-sister the ocular proof while she held me steady in the sunlight. She was shouting something behind me but all I had to say to her just now was *et tu, soror*.

I overtook the German tourists and plunged into the middle of the party, ignoring their curious glances. American Presidents know that their only real protection against flying bullets is the flesh of fat security men. What was good enough for Ronald Reagan was good enough for me. It was obviously lunch-call for the Germans and they take their food even more seriously than their culture. We moved at a rapid pace towards the southern exit and when we had climbed up to the Arch of Titus, I felt safe enough to break away and look back.

I though I could make out Teresa on the Sacred Way with what could be Piltdown the sharpshooter. They looked to be heading for the Via dei Fori Imperiali. I turned and overtook my Germans. I had no intention of trying to follow a man whose intentions could be so homicidal on such a short acquaintance. All I wanted was to get back to a cool shower in my hotel. But when I chanced straightaway upon a taxi dropping a pair of pale and relieved Americans outside the Forum, I directed him back up the Via dei Fori Imperiali, telling him to take it easy. My notion was to get a closer look at Teresa's friend so that I could avoid him in future. As 'taking it easy' meant only a negligibly minute reduction in speed to my taxi-driver, I doubt if I'd have spotted them if there hadn't been some minor shunt at the junction with Via Cavour which brought the traffic to a brake-squealing halt.

At the other side of the road I saw Teresa and Piltdown, who was a burly middle-aged man looking very hot in a crumpled dark suit. They were standing by a Fiat X1/9 two-seater, bright red and covered with honourable scars and dents. Vasco standing beside the open driver's door was adding to them as he beat on the roof to emphasize whatever point he was angrily making. His mother was replying in kind, but Vasco brought the discussion to an end by sliding into the car and sending it screaming into the traffic, which was still flowing on his side of the road. A moment later, amid a celebration of horns, our side started moving too.

'Piazza Barberini,' I said the my driver. 'And you needn't take it easy any more.'

Naturally he drove me there with all the sedateness of a Victorian landau.

12

. . . ruined for nothing . . .

I entered my hotel with some little circumspection. Even a
dying man begins to feel that two attempts on his life in a
single day are worth taking note of. What I proposed doing
was what Cæsar should have done on the Ides of March – i.e.
take to my bed. He ignored the auspices and look where it got
him.

I felt quite relieved to see Reilly lounging in the lounge but
I didn't stop to talk. She overtook me at the elevator saying,
'Welcome home, Tonto. Kemo Sabe would like a word, I
think.'

The Brigadier was waiting in my room.

'Have a nice lunch?' he asked.

'Very pleasant,' I replied, stripping off my sweat-soaked
shirt.

'*Saltimbocca*,' said Reilly, smacking her lips. 'Scrump-
tious. But you shouldn't bolt your food. Bad for the stomach,
they say. And all those mushrooms. And peppers!'

She shook her head, tut-tutting. Even the Brigadier found
this distasteful and shot her a reproving glance. There was a
knock at the door and the Brigadier opened it and took a tray
from the waiter who stood there.

'I'm glad you enjoyed your meal,' he said. 'Pity you didn't
have time for coffee, though. I've taken the liberty of order-
ing some now.'

They'd obviously been keeping a close eye on me in
Angelino's at least. Reilly busied herself with the coffee in an
untypically housewifely fashion while I dug into my bag for
the bottle of scotch which was what I really needed. This
time it was the Brigadier who tutted and I compromised by
putting a schlurp into my coffee. The Brigadier refused my
offer and I didn't bother with Reilly.

'Tell me, Swift,' he said. 'What happened in the Forum? We rather lost contact with you after you left the restaurant.'

'Not much,' I said. 'It was rather hot.'

They exchanged glances.

'Did Signora Carducci say anything to you?' said the Brigadier.

'Like I say, the temperature wasn't really conducive to conversation,' I replied. My experience with the pursuit of truth in the Forum hadn't recommended it to me. Lying keeps you mentally alert and stops you getting too close to your sister.

'Come on, my bucko!' exclaimed Reilly. 'The signora didn't drag your nose out of the trough just so you could gawk at a heap of old stones. What did she tell you? What does she know?'

'She's particularly interested in the worship of Vesta and has some interesting theories on the symbolism of the Holy Fire,' I said. 'Did you know, for instance, that Ireland's so damp because God decreed that the holy flame of virginity should never burn there?'

The Brigadier sighed and finished his coffee.

'We will talk again later, Mr Swift. But I do beg you to remember that time is of the essence in our contract. For you especially, time is of the essence. Till later, then.'

'Ciao,' I said.

He left. Reilly followed, pausing at the door to say, 'What he means, bucko, is that there's a stop sign ahead for you, and not too far neither. And you'd best bear in mind that you'll start slowing down fast before you get to it, so you'd better look for the action while you can. So be a wise little Indian, Tonto, and tell us what that other Bessacarr bastard told you, eh?'

I said, 'Hi-yo, Silver, away!' and waved dismissively.

She shrugged and went.

She was right, of course. There was precious little I could do myself, especially as every time I entered the streets of Rome there seemed to be someone waiting to be unpleasant towards me. My one consolation was that health-wise I seemed to be enjoying a period of remission and was even beginning to hope that perhaps I had more time than the medicos and the Brigadier realized.

The benevolent deity who created cancer and all things noxious heard my pious hope, smiled, and hurled a very small but very hot thunderbolt into my belly.

'Jesus!' I croaked, collapsing on to the bed.

The thunderbolt hissed and steamed in my pancreatic juices, sending little rivulets of lava dimpling through my midriff. I drew my knees up under my chin, adopting the foetal position which gave me most relief.

I heard the door open and Reilly's voice say, 'And there's another thing you ought to be thinking . . . hey, Swifty, me boyo, that's a lousy shade of make-up you've started using.'

Her tone was alarmed and she came quickly to the bedside and bent over me.

'Are you feeling bad?' she asked idiotically but with what sounded like real concern.

'No, I've just decided I've changed my mind about being born,' I gasped.

'Well, you're certainly getting back to position A,' she answered. 'Where's that stuff the quack made up for you?'

She rustled around in my chest of drawers, then went into the bathroom and returned a moment later with a glass of water and two bi-coloured capsules.

'Take these,' she ordered.

'Orally?' I asked.

'Oh Jesus, Swift, stop being a brave little Indian, dying with your jokes on. Take the tablets and rest in peace.'

I gulped the capsules down. God knows what they contained but after a while the pain eased and I drifted into an uneasy sleep. Not all that uneasy, it seemed, for a little while after waking I realized that my trousers had been removed and a sheet drawn over my body.

'How are you going on?' enquired Reilly's voice.

'Is that an angel?' I asked.

She came to the bedside and leaned over me, heavy breasts pendant beneath her thin cotton T-shirt. I reached up and pulled her down till their warm weight straddled my face. She lay there a moment, then laughed and drew away.

'Quite the little Romulus, isn't it?' she said.

I pushed back the sheet and carefully moved my legs off the edge of the bed. Slowly I sat up, then stood up.

'How do you feel?' she asked.

'All right,' I said cautiously. In fact I felt fine, but I'd done enough deity-baiting for one day.

'You don't look too bad,' she said, examining me critically.

'You neither,' I said. 'Thanks, Reilly,'

I meant it, both parts. The memory of bedding her in London came strong into my mind. In my half-dressed state it showed and she grinned and said, 'Save your strength, Swifty. And don't be eating any more fancy food. We need you fit and well a little while longer, remember?'

It was callous, but I could hardly complain. I'd opted out of empathy years ago.

'Go stick a safety-pin through your tongue, Reilly,' I said.

I got showered and dressed. It was getting to be a habit with Reilly around. I glanced at my watch. It was after six o'clock.

I said, 'What's the word from the Brigadier?'

'No word,' she said. 'I'm off to meet him now.'

'I thought we might have dinner together, Reilly,' I said, part genuine, part probing.

'Sorry, bucko, but I can't and mebbe you shouldn't,' she said. 'At least, stick to the *risotto alla Milanese*.'

She made for the door.

I said, 'Hey, Reilly. What am I supposed to do tonight, then?'

'Don't worry. Whatever it is, we'll keep in touch.'

She was gone. I felt strange, feared for a moment it was a symptom, then realized it was loneliness. I hadn't let myself feel lonely in ten years. Perhaps it was a symptom after all.

I finished dressing and found myself trying to work out ways of leaving the hotel unobserved. For a man who only a few hours earlier had been longing for nothing more than a chance of relaxing in his bed for a day or two this might seem odd. But God had reminded me that in the not too distant future I'd have all the time in, and out of, the world for relaxing. In the end I eschewed ingenuity and went boldly down the stairs and through the great marble lounge which would have made a good mausoleum for a dead hero. A pianist sat in one shady corner playing dirge-like ragtime on a baby grand. A handful of guests sat quiet as mourners on huge sofas beneath erotically religious murals. They regarded my swift passage with what might have been deadly hatred or merely the envious resentment of the bored tourist for the purposeful passer-by.

My purpose at that moment was simply to move quickly enough to make a poor target but by the time I reached the street I was more positive about my plans. Reilly was right, callous but right. I didn't have any time to play around with. God knows, and I didn't, what I was going to do if and when I came face to face with my father, but I couldn't afford to let hours slip by unused, not when I was counting my future in days. I had to act and, unhappy though I was at the thought of Piltdown, my only point of possible contact was my half-sister, Teresa. She had a lot of explaining to do. Perhaps I had been judging her too harshly. Perhaps she had simply contracted to have a bullet put into the half of me she wasn't related to.

I spent the next half-hour dodging in and out of traffic. I had a few near misses, but it seemed the best way of shaking off any tail. No one can cross a busy Roman street and keep his eye on someone he is following without fatal consequences. I didn't spot anyone in close pursuit on foot, but in the Piazza Venezia as I leaned on the bonnet of a taxi which had almost killed me, a Lambretta went buzzing by and I was sure I recognized the slightly perplexed academic features of my scooter-driving friend from that morning. His thin face with its chin slightly out of true reminded me of a scholar of Trinity I'd known vaguely twenty years ealier. Perhaps it was him; perhaps like so many others he'd been recruited into Security at Cambridge!

I silenced the near hysterical taxi-driver by getting into his vehicle and giving him Teresa's address. As we moved away, I kept an eye open for my Trinity scholar, but there was no sign. Coincidence or mistaken identity, I told myself.

I only had a vague notion where Teresa's apartment was situated and had to hope the driver wouldn't seek revenge by taking me via an expensive and circuitous route. We swung round the Colosseum, headed down the Via di S. Gregorio and straight across the Piazza di Porta Capena. After that I lost track except that I glimpsed to my left at one point the blackness of open space with some distant ruins dramatically lit and worked out these must be the baths of Caracalla where opera was performed al fresco during the summer.

My driver confirmed this.

'*Aïda*,' he said enthusiastically, though I couldn't make out whether his enthusiasm was for the music, often inaudible at the back of the ampitheatre, or the spectacle which included great processions, chariots pulled by real horses, and even on occasion a couple of camels.

Our destination proved to be a quiet, rather gloomy side street somewhere between the Terme di Caracalla and the terminus of the electric railway to Ostia. My driver dropped me at the end of the street, took his money, and accelerated away with what looked to me like the unseemly haste of a coachman who has just deposited a passenger outside Count Dracula's castle. I couldn't account for my strange unease but I found myself looking around hopefully for any evidence that my Trinity scholar had indeed stuck to my trail. Naturally there was no sign. Police of any kind are never around when you'd like them.

I checked the address again and set off down the pavement past a line of ruthlessly parked cars. Ahead I could see the block which I'd worked out must house Teresa's apartment. It was an uncompromisingly ugly building. Perhaps Communist deputies were warned to eschew conspicuous expenditure. Or perhaps he'd left all his money to the Party and this was the best that Teresa could afford.

Somewhere behind me I heard a car door slam and suddenly the building didn't look so ugly after all. Its huge black-painted, brass-studded door looked as attractive but as slow-approaching as that swimming pool wall had done all those years ago. I had to shake off a feeling that my limbs were moving as though cleaving a passage through water, but when my fingertips touched the door I was greatly relieved to find it standing slightly ajar. A list of names behind a semi-opaque celluloid strip revealed dimly that the Carducci apartment was on the second floor. I stepped into a poorly lit, stale-smelling entrance hall with one long dark corridor running off to the rear of the building and a rickety staircase rising wearily to the next landing.

I went boldly up it. I could hear vague sounds of human habitation, but muffled and distance and as little comforting as the sound of engines when your dinghy is becalmed in thick fog. I didn't know what kind of welcome Teresa would offer me, but it wouldn't have to be too warm to make a good impression.

I found the door of her flat and rang the bell. When there was no reply, I rang it again, then after half a minute essayed a gentle knock. This was real anti-climax, I hadn't realised how keyed up I'd become in anticipation till this let down. I bent down and squinted at the keyhole. I knew a bit about locks and this didn't look too difficult to me. With the right implements . . . but I didn't have the right implements. I knocked again much more loudly, then started going through my pockets in the hope of finding something I could improvise a pick-lock out of. The best I could come up with was the pocket clip of my rolled-silver pen, a birthday present from Kate which had miraculously survived for fifteen years. I bent it back and stooped to the lock once more, but a few seconds probing told me that my pen had been ruined for nothing.

Behind me a door opened. I looked round. A pair of female eyes gleamed at me through the narrow crack of a door opening on a chain a little way down the corridor. It was shut violently before I could speak. I swore.

There was only one interpretation a suspicious resident would put on the sight of a stranger poking at the lock of a neighbour's door. I could only hope she hadn't a telephone. I crossed over intending to check if I could hear any dialling but another sound intercepted me. A woman's voice, I thought. Some kind of exclamation cut short, no more than a couple of words which I hadn't been able to make out. Yet there had been something familiar.

I waited for more. All that came was a sort of sigh like the last spurt of air from a deflating party balloon, then a diminuendo of what might have been departing footfalls.

I waited another moment, then set off down the stairs,

cautiously at first but suddenly I was running. I slowed down as the hall came into view. Its shadows seemed void of human presence. But when my gaze dropped to ground level, it fell on something which had not been there before. It lay against the wall by the street door, like a bundle of old rags dumped for collection. But these were no rags. I could see pale limbs spidering awkwardly from a slight torso clad in flowered silk. The crazy certainty hit me that I was looking at my dead daughter and I swayed with the pain at it.

Dead, that was certain. I had seen bodies before and knew that there was no room for life in that collapsed parcel of flesh, but I knelt beside her and turned her over as carefully as though I might still cause pain.

My hand beneath the breast touched blood but I didn't flinch as my eyes gave me the good news that this was a woman much older than Angelica. A narrow face, eyes open and staring, nose pinched and white as the blood drained from it.

It was partly the alteration of death and partly of time, but mainly I think the relief at seeing who it was *not* that delayed my recognition of who it was.

Then I cried out in alarm and incomprehension and something of grief too.

Beyond belief, this dead woman I was cradling in my arms was my former wife, Kate.

. . . *through the brightness and into the dark* . . .

I hadn't loved Kate for a long time, perhaps never. And in the end, when even Uncle Percy's diplomatic circumlocutions couldn't disguise the extent of her bitchy obstructionism of my efforts to maintain contact with Angelica, I'd come to resent and even hate her.

But now her empty weight in my arms filled me with grief, and the heavier weight of my awareness that somehow I must be responsible for this squalid, violent end to her life filled me with guilt.

But slowly rising and blanketing all other feelings there came fear. If this had happened to Kate, what did it imply for Angelica?

I laid her down, my concern for my daughter allowing me to look at the body more dispassionately. She had been stabbed cleanly and expertly with that killing blow which sweeps up beneath the ribcage and into the heart. A small black leather handbag was twisted round her right shoulder in the recommended Italian anti-snatch style. I began to remove it, hoping it might contain some clue. Distantly I could hear police sirens, but they were a common night sound in Rome. No one knew about Kate's death yet, except the killer, and he was not likely to have rung the police.

Nevertheless I found myself hurrying. As the handbag came loose, my knee touched a metal object. I picked it up. It was a bloodstained stiletto, that most traditional of Italian weapons.

The sirens were nearer, but not yet near enough to concern me, particularly as I still reckoned they could have nothing to do with me. What I'd forgotten of course was Teresa's neighbour who reckoned she'd seen a burglar in the act of burgling. And what I couldn't foresee was that a motor-bike *carabiniere* would arrive silently in advance of his noisy car-bound colleagues.

The huge black door was flung open. Light spilled in and with it the policeman, looking in his crash helmet and broad goggles like an extra from *Star Wars*. What I looked like to him, crouched over a body with a handbag in one hand and a bloodstained knife in the other, was obvious. He pointed his pistol at my head and screamed at me not to move.

If I'd thought about it I'd have seen it was good advice. Clearly no one in his right mind and a horizontal position would even *think* of attacking an armed Italian policeman, vertical, in a state of considerable excitement.

So I didn't think but kicked the door shut with my outstretched foot. The crash and the renewal of darkness startled him but not as much as the stiletto point which I swung up at his wrist. I missed, but it gouged a deep channel along his knuckles which were tight around the pistol grip, and drove the pistol itself upward a milli-second before he pressed the trigger and sent a bullet ricocheting like a squash ball round that narrow hallway.

I think by this time there was also a thought bouncing around somewhere in the area that this perhaps wasn't such a good idea, but I didn't wait to have it.

I went down that dark passage to the rear with the speed of a man testing Zeno's theory of Achilles and the tortoise. But the expected hail of bullets didn't write their refutation in my back. The cop must have dropped his gun. I hoped his right hand was too painful to pick it up.

On the other hand ... My mind might be eschewing thought but it couldn't get away from bad jokes. This corridor seemed endless and a cop didn't need to be ambidextrous or have night vision to hit a fleeing target in a straight run between narrow walls.

Then the darkness ahead thickened, solidified. I'd reached the end. There was a door. I hit it without any slackening of speed. If it had been locked, I'd have bounced off it nearly all the way back to the *carabiniere*. But Kate's assassin must have come this way too and hadn't paused to turn a key.

The door burst open and I debouched into a narrow paved courtyard. I knew it was paved because I went sprawling and my hands and knees left large deposits on the hard surface. I rolled over and looked up at a narrow strip of velvety sky, *diamanté* with a thousand stars and criss-crossed with cords from which drooped a flag-message of defeat.

They were clothes-lines, I realized, linking the rear of Teresa's apartment building to an identical one at the other side of the courtyard.

And if identical ...

I headed straight across, tried a door, it was locked, tried another, locked also, and was just trying a third when the policeman's pistol opened up behind me.

How close he was I don't know, nor whether the third door was unlocked or not. But I was through it and running down yet another dark corridor with a nightmarish feeling growing on me that at the end of it I was going to find Kate's body once more and the whole ghastly cycle would be run again.

I even looked when I reached the entrance hall, but the floor was mercifully empty. I burst out into the open air with the sobbing relief of one who feels he's reached sanctuary, and for a moment the quiet and stillness of this new street supported the delusion.

Then a police car came planing round the corner, siren pulsating and lights flashing, like a mobile disco.

It hardly seemed worthwhile running, but I ran. For a man with a cancer on his stomach, and a dead wife on his conscience, and a lost daughter on his mind, I suppose I ran very well. But I knew, as Zeno knew all along, that to stop Achilles catching the tortoise you'd need a *deus ex machina*.

He came on cue, not *out of* a machine, but on one, a Lambretta to be precise. He came towards me, swung the scooter round and watched my approach over his shoulder. On his scholarly face was the mild impatience of one who fears he may be late for a tutorial.

He was already moving as I reached him and I leapt on the pillion like an Indian brave mounting his pony in those old westerns they don't make any more.

As far as I was concerned, that was that. If gods on machines couldn't rescue mere earthlings, who could? I clung with my arms tight round my Trinity scholar's waist and my head pressed into his shoulder. I even closed my eyes and enjoyed the rush of air against my head.

Not that it rushed all that fast. The disadvantage of this machine was its relatively low speed, especially with a passenger. The advantage was manœuvrability, especially with a rider who didn't care for the basic laws of traffic or of physics.

There must have been plenty of police cars close to the scene for now they seemed to come dropping out of the sky like seagulls at kitchen-refuse dumping time on the *Queen Elizabeth*. We twisted and turned and used as much sidewalk as road, but still the lights flashed, the sirens wailed.

Then suddenly we were in darkness and moving across grass. My scholar cut his engine and dimmed his lights. For a second, comparatively, the darkness seemed Stygian and the silence complete. But then ahead of us I saw a luminescence against which was etched a range of majestic ruins. And I heard a mingling of voices and music swelling up in glorious harmony.

Heaven, I thought. They got us.

Alas, no, I realized a moment later. It wasn't heaven though as near it as, in the ears of many Italians, you can get.

Verdi.

We were somewhere in the park which houses the ruins of the Baths of Caracalla and over there several thousand people were listening entranced to the famous al fresco performance of *Aïda*.

My straining ears caught the melody now. It was the triumphal chorus '*Gloria all' Egitto*' from Act Two. The victorious Egyptians were returning to their ecstatic reception. And now the trumpets were fanfaring the visual highlight of the production, the entry of Radames in a chariot accompanied by mounted warriors.

It was a moment to savour here in the warm darkness of a perfect Roman evening.

An icicle of white light was suddenly thrust sideways through that balmy air. Its pallor touched and chilled us. There was a confusion of whatever passes in Italian hunting circles for *view halloos!* And my scholar accelerated away with such violence that I was almost dislodged and left sprawling.

We went without lights now so perhaps it was the light ahead that attracted him. Or perhaps beneath that academic brow there had always lurked Italian fantasies of rapturous acclaim at La Scala. Or perhaps I simply dreamt the whole episode.

But it seemed to me that for one long moment we actually found ourselves weaving among the scattering column of Egyptian troops, finally drawing level with a horse-drawn chariot and just pipping him on to a broad floodlit stage before a vast dark amphitheatre. Something like that I saw in my brief open-eyed flashes, though I'm pretty certain the rapturous applause from the thousands of spectators was simply a hysterical delusion. Then, like that allegoric sparrow in Edwin's banqueting-hall, we were through the brightness and out into the dark again.

Perhaps the Pope would work us into his next address.

It was soon after this that the scholar and I parted company. He turned and spoke. I didn't catch what he said but in his movement he loosened my grip round his waist and a violent piece of cornering did the rest. As I sat and watched him disappear, I thought it was a choice between accident and self-interest (his). Then his lights came on and immediately other lights erupted all over the place, and the sirens mingled once more with the soaring cadences of Verdi.

The rest was easy. I got up and brushed myself down. I was going to be tie-dyed with bruises in the morning and my hands were badly grazed. But my clothes had suffered only a couple of minor tears and I was quite passable enough to mingle with the crowds as they spilled out towards the bars at the interval. I bought myself two large scotches worth of receipts and by dint of waving them at the bar-boy in company with the thousand-lire note got immediate service. I poured the two drinks into one plastic glass held it up, muttered my old childish pre-medicine incantation, 'Look out lips, look out gums, look out stomach, here it comes,' and downed it in one.

Most of the crowd began drifting back to the auditorium and I drifted with them. Finding a seat was easy. The first two acts with all their splendid choruses and spectacle play to a full house. But a substantial number of native spectators at

Caracalla opt to spend the second half boozing and talking. They'd have preferred the old days at the Colosseum, where no one ever dreamt of following the gladiators with a team of formation dancers.

I sat in the dark and tried to let the whisky and the music fill my mind to the exclusion of all else. I wanted to think of neither the future nor the past – the future, because I was empty of ideas to make it anything but disastrous, and the past because that was where Kate belonged, now and forever. I'd got into the habit these many years of trying to avoid confrontation with my own emotions. At first it had been because I feared their violence. But at some point, God knows where, I suspected it changed to a fear that they would no longer be there. To think of Kate and find I needed to primp up a proper emotion was something I didn't want to risk finding out about myself. I even half suspected there was something rather contrived about my determination to see Angelica again when I learned I was dying. What the hell did I have to do with a young woman who physically, biologically and mentally must have changed almost beyond recognition from the child I had known? If I'd really thought about it, could I have come?

Perhaps not. But I couldn't have borne finding out I didn't want to come.

And now things had changed. Now it was no longer a case of a lousy father conning himself he had to take a sentimental farewell of an indifferent daughter.

Now Angelica was in trouble, possibly in danger, and needed my help.

I'd been stupid to let myself be side-tracked by the Brigadier and all this talk of my father. What did my father matter any more? He had warped my life for years. I was insane to let him warp my death too. If the world wanted to listen to the malicious paranoiac lies of an elderly egocentric traitor, let it listen. Even killing him wouldn't stop the lies. If the Russians wanted them told, they could find any number of mouths eager to tell them.

All my remaining energies must now be dedicated to finding and protecting Angelica.

And as if this resolution required all my strength and

therefore drew forces away from all those strong barriers my will had set up, suddenly an image of Kate flashed into my mind, Kate as I first knew her, long auburn tresses shaken over her shoulders, restless brown eyes, mobile mouth with lips wryly twisted as she complained humorously about the mandarins of Whitehall; and I surprised my neighbours by my emotional reaction to the entombment of Aïda and Radames, as I buried my face in my hands and sobbed.

. . . covered with faces . . .

I moved out of the Caracalla auditorium on a tide of spectators too deep to be trawled. In any case there was little sign of special police activity at the exits and I guessed this meant that my Trinity scholar had made his escape. Passengerless, once back on the road he'd just be another scooter-rider. I climbed into one of the innumerable coaches waiting to pick up tour parties and drop them at their hotels. A courier counted heads, looked a little puzzled, decided one too many was better than one too few, and we were off.

The first hotel we stopped at was in the Via Cavour. I got out and drifted through the plate glass doors with the crowd. There was a large, comfortably appointed lounge on the ground floor and I settled down in the corner furthest from the door. I wasn't altogether certain what to expect back at my own hotel. It didn't seem likely that the police could have got a line on me unless they'd talked to Teresa and she'd put them on to me. I doubted if she would. But at the very least, my Trinity scholar would have reported back to the Brigadier and there'd be a little reception committee anxiously awaiting my return.

I wanted a moment to relax and also to check through the contents of Kate's handbag to see if there were any clues to her reasons for being in Rome.

It was in my inside pocket. I opened it surreptitiously beneath my jacket and started emptying it out bit by bit.

It didn't take long.

Lipstick, compact; billfold; keyring. There were three keys, one for a car, two Yale type. They could tell a great deal if there were any way to make them speak.

Then there was a cigarette packet, an Italian brand. Ten years ago Kate hadn't smoked. Had she started? There didn't seem to be any lighter. I opened the packet. It was empty. But there was something scribbled on the inside.

It was Teresa's address and telephone number.

There was only one thing more in the bag, a sheet of writing paper folded once.

I opened it and knew at once even before I read the words that this round uncluttered hand was my daughter's.

Dear Mummy, he's in Rome and looking for me so I'm going off somewhere safe. I'll be with friends, so don't worry, and I'll be in touch as soon as I can. Love, Angie.

There were no prizes for guessing who *he* was, and not many for guessing who had got to Angelica with such a picture of a deranged father in mad pursuit of his daughter that she had climbed into that fiery red two-seater and roared off – to where?

The bastard. If I'd had my nephew Vasco within reach at that moment, he'd have found out just how deranged I could be.

What Teresa's part was in all this I couldn't yet fathom and there was no way I was going to be able to ask her till the police activity around her block of flats had abated. My guess was that the cigarette packet address had been scribbled by Vasco and given to Angelica for use in emergencies, that Kate knew nothing about the Carducci connection and, far from reassured by Angelica's brief note, she had headed straight round to the flat when she came across the packet in her daughter's room.

And at the apartment block, she had run into – what?

Speculation had gone as far as it could. One thing was clear to me. Kate and Angelica hadn't picked on Rome as their refuge by accident. The Brigadier had some explaining to do.

I returned Kate's things to my pocket and stood up. It was nearly midnight and I felt weary. It had been a long, demanding day and I had the feeling there was a lot of mileage in it yet.

I went out into the Via Cavour and set off at a brisk pace towards the Piazza Barberini.

There was no sign of any police activity at my hotel, no reason why there should have been. I was Alexander Evans, computer salesman. What link could the Italian police make between me and Kate, Lady Bessacarr? None, without help.

But there was a light on in my bedroom and the sound of voices.

I opened the door with the utmost caution.

Seated on my dressing-table stool was Reilly watching television.

'There you are,' she said, without moving her eyes from the screen. 'Enjoyed your evening, have you?'

'So-so,' I said, heading for the whisky bottle.

'I hear you corpsed your old lady,' she went on as I poured myself a generous measure.

'You hear wrong,' I said.

'Is that right? You just happened to be kneeling over her with a knife in your hand when the police arrived?'

'How do you know that?' I demanded.

'I have it from the highest authority in the land,' she said.

'Not the Pope, surely?'

For answer, she nodded at the TV screen.

'It's made big news,' she said. 'Not the murder, that's pretty run-of-the-mill. But interrupting *Aïda*, that really hit them where it hurts. That was you, wasn't it?'

'It wasn't my idea,' I said. 'You can blame your mad scooterist for that. Not that I wasn't grateful to see him again.'

'I bet,' she said, giving me her full attention now. 'Swifty, are you really saying you didn't do it?'

'Really, Reilly,' I said. 'But I'm not begging to be believed. Where's the Brigadier? There's a couple of questions I need to ask.'

'Oh, he's around,' she said vaguely. 'He'll be keen to talk to you, I've no doubt.'

'Well, you'll do for starters,' I said. 'Tell me, Reilly, why did you decide to bring Kate and Angelica to Rome?'

To my surprise she didn't hesitate about replying.

'Not Rome,' she said. 'Ostia. They were nice and handy there. We put them in a safe house, a little villa near the beach. You weren't likely to run into them unless you decided to spend a day sunbathing.'

'Didn't you have someone watching them?' I demanded.

'Certainly,' she said. 'Your daughter seemed to be happy enough improving her tan on the beach and being chatted up by the local Romeos. Your ex-wife didn't care for that too much, though, the sun-worship, I mean.'

'No,' I said. 'She never did.'

'She got restless, but she rapidly made friends. She spent today cruising around with some of them in a motor yacht.'

'That sounds like Kate. And Angelica?'

'Same routine as always. Sunbathing, swimming, teasing the lads. She went back to the villa in the middle of the afternoon, presumably for a siesta. Our man had his at the same time, it seems. He had no idea she'd gone till your wife came back and started yelling. Then later she went missing too. Well, we know where she went. What we don't know is why. Any ideas, Swifty?'

My instinct was to trust her and pool all my ideas with hers. But to trust someone whose profession was deviousness would be a great foolishness. And besides, whereas previously we had perforce shared the common aim of wanting to get a line on my father, now our paths had parted. Angelica was my only concern, finding her my only object. And I thought I knew how I could do it.

But not with the Brigadier and Reilly in tow.

I passed my hand over my eyes and swayed slightly.

'You OK, Swifty?' she asked, swinging round on the stool to face me.

'Fine, thanks. A bit worn out,' I said. 'God, Reilly, it's a mess, isn't it? Where do we go from here?'

I looked down at her helplessly and reached out my hands.

'It'll be OK, I promise you,' she said sympathetically, taking my hands. 'Don't worry.'

'I'll try not to,' I said and drew her up towards me. She raised her mouth to be kissed and I butted her between the eyes with my forehead.

Even half-numbed with pain, her reflexes nearly caught me. She fell backwards using my own wrist-grips to draw me after her, the whiles swinging her knees upwards to drive into my belly.

I let go, not so easy as it sounds. The natural instinct is to hang on to a falling body. Normally she would have done a simple backward roll, or even a back-flip if she'd felt in the mood, ending on her feet. But this time my head-blow had slowed her down and she exacerbated the damage by allowing her own head to crack sickeningly against the tiled floor.

She lay twisted and still beside the fallen chair. I approached cautiously and then with growing anxiety as I realized this was no ruse to lower my defences. She was out cold. I checked her pulse and raised her lids to peer into her eyes. Then I ran my fingers gently over the back of her skull. I could detect no sign of a fracture and her breathing was deep and regular. I laid her on the bed on her side to lessen the chance of vagal inhibition if she happened to vomit. Why I should feel quite so guilty I didn't know. I shook off the feeling as best I could and swiftly changed my clothes and collected what I wanted – money, passport, my little wallet of keys and instruments, and my pistol. I also wanted to take some spare clothing with me – socks, pants, plus my shaving kit, but I needed something to carry it in. Reilly had a kind of mini duffel-bag with her. I tipped out the contents on the bed. They included a tiny double-shot automatic which looked far too ladylike for Reilly and a set of brass knuckledusters which were far more in keeping. Also a pencil torch which I appropriated. Quickly I stowed my gear in the bag. It was surprisingly capacious and I even managed to get a spare pair of slacks and a T-shirt in.

Reilly stirred as I finished. I checked her eyes again. She looked OK.

Then I was on my way, the parfit gentil knight, accoutred to do doughty deeds to rescue and protect his lady.

At the door I wondered how many knights had looked back longingly at their comfortable bed and wished they were getting into it rather than setting out on the road.

Most of them, I guessed. And left.

An hour later I was back at Teresa's apartment. It had only taken me twenty minutes to get there, but I approached with utmost caution. A black Mercedes moved away from in front of the apartment block as I approached. Probably nothing to do with Teresa, but it had sent me diving into a shadowy doorway like a rabbit down a burrow. There were two people in the car but I couldn't identify their gender let alone their persons. Friend or foe, they'd done me a favour by leaving the main door to the block slightly ajar. Or perhaps it just meant there was a cop on duty at the scene of the crime so it could be examined inviolate by daylight. Well, I was ready to deal with him if necessary.

It wasn't. The hallway was empty. Reilly's torch ran round the angles. The floor where Kate had lain looked as if it had been scrubbed. That would be typically Italian, some house-proud mamma coming out with a bucket as soon as the *pozzi* had gone to scrub out the evidence! But who needs evidence when you've caught your killer in the act?

I shuddered and went up the stairs.

On the dark landing I knelt and began to work on the lock. I'd noted the make when I was there earlier and now tried a selection of possible keys. None of them fitted – that would have been too lucky a strike – but I was getting close with one of them, inserting it, turning till I felt a slight pressure, removing it and modifying the teeth with an instrument like a nail cutter which sliced through the soft metal if not like butter, at least like steak.

One final adjustment and I had it. They key turned. What I feared now was either a chair or bolts. But the door swung open easily and soundlessly.

I stepped inside.

The first thing I did was to check the door with my pencil torch. Yes, there were bolts, two of them, formidably massive. A woman alone in an apartment like this would automatically slip them home before she went to bed. At least, so it seemed to me.

Either – she wasn't in.

Or – she had gone to bed but was expecting someone with a key to appear later. (Vasco?)

Or there was someone else here and *they* didn't want to place any obstacles in the way of illegal entry.

I had drawn my gun.

There *was* someone here, I could sense it. Emptiness feels empty. Building are like bodies, you know before you look if there's any life left in them. Now when I listened I could hear it.

117

Breathing.

Someone was attempting to control it but couldn't. This gave me comfort. Your professional would at least know the art of perfect stillness. I crouched low and made my way towards the one door my little pinpoint of light had shown me to be ajar. When I reached it, I lay down completely flat. An amateur's eyes would be focused at head level.

I counted three to steady myself, then thrust the door open with my shoulder as I rolled into the room. The door went right and I went left, finishing up against the foot of a bed. Here I lay, pressing myself tight against the wooden bed leg. Silence flooded back into the room. Then the breathing started again.

I spoke with my mouth close to the floor to make source-location difficult.

'Say something or I come up shooting. I've got two more men outside. I don't want trouble, just a chance to talk. But I'll shoot if I have to.'

Silence again. Real silence this time. The breath was being held. I decided to risk the torch, cautiously stretching my arm out to full length above my head to distance the target if it brought a hail of bullets.

I flicked it on. Nothing. I could see the edge of the high old-fashioned bed by which I lay. I had a sense that someone was lying on it and I decided to be clever, roll underneath it and come up the other side. One, two, three, go! Only I didn't go far. I was fetched up short by a bulky obstacle.

I turned the torch on it illuminated a pair of wide eyes staring back at me from a distance of about eighteen inches.

I yelled and rolled back.

When I brought the light to bear again, the eyes were still there, still open, still staring. But they weren't seeing me, any more than the gaping mouth was drawing in the life-giving air.

I recognized that jaw now. This was Piltdown, the man who'd fired at me in the Forum. The torchlight picked out a dark stain low in his ribcage. The same blow that had killed Kate. I'd half nominated Piltdown for that crime. It seemed I'd been wrong again.

The breathing had started again, I realized. At least I knew whose it wasn't. I said, 'Teresa?'

'Tonto, is that you?'

The voice was faint and distant but not in terms of space.

I rose slowly and let the little O of torch-light fall like an exclamation on the bed. It was covered with faces; solemn, smiling; in groups alone; young, old. Someone had strewn the counterpane with snapshots for a family album. But among them was one face as still as those photo-printed ones, but touched with an agony it would have taken an artist's brush to convey.

Only an hour ago I'd left one woman lying unconscious on a bed.

Now here was another outstretched before me.

'Teresa!' I cried.

There was a lamp by the bedside. I snapped it on. This one was conscious all right. Her wide brown eyes regarded me unblinkingly but with the sparkle of life.

But unconscious or not I could tell at a glance that Reilly had been better off.

. . . *a romantic violinist* . . .

Teresa's head was resting on a pillow sodden with blood from a huge gash across her left temple. Someone had hit her very hard with a metal club, probably a gun barrel. There was blood trickling from her mouth too and her lips were bruised and puffy. But these were not the injuries which caught my gaze.

Someone had been working on her fingernails. Several were completely detached and the ends of all her fingers were bloody and swollen.

Her legs were tightly bound at the ankles. I swept aside the photographs littering her body and cut the binding. She cried out in new agony as the blood began to circulate into her feet once more. I took that as a good sign – at least she had not progressed beyond that point of no return where pain no longer matters.

I went back into the living-room and dialled the emergency service. I returned to the bedroom with a bowl of warm water and some disinfectant from the bathroom. I washed the head wound but didn't dare touch the fingernails. I felt angry and helpless.

I'd noticed a bottle of *grappa* in the living room and I fetched it. I managed to get a little between Teresa's lips but she quickly gagged and shook her head to show she'd had enough.

I finished the glass myself. It was violent stuff but I was beginning to feel violent.

Teresa was trying to speak.

I said, 'Lie still. There's an ambulance coming.'

She said, 'No time,' very slowly and deliberately.

I thought for a moment she was making a medical prognosis and my alarm must have shown. She shook her head and glanced towards the *grappa*. I gave her another sip and this time it seemed to give her a little strength.

'Tonto,' she said with difficulty. 'You must go.'

I was reassured by the sight of a healthier colour returning to her cheeks.

'Who did this, Teresa?' I asked urgently.

'A man. Russian, I think. Krylov, Vasari called him.'

'Who's Vasari?'

'In the Party. A colleague of my dead husband's. I never liked or trusted him.' Her voice increased in strength as though charged with the energy of hatred. 'A Moscow arse-licker. But I let him in because I knew him. The other followed. Like a violin-player he looked, all Slavic and soulful. But he did this …'

She raised her ruined hands momentarily.

'And the man under the bed, who is he?'

My mind was so full of questions that the lightest and most unnecessary were forcing their way to the top.

'Giuseppe … a friend. I would not have let Vasari in if Giuseppe had not been here …'

Incredibly, even in her own pain, tears for her dead friends were rolling down her cheeks.

'Why did he want to kill me? In the Forum?'

"He was there to protect me … he thought you were attacking me … if he'd wanted to kill … he was a crack shot …'

And a lot of good it had done him, I thought brutally. I could hear the sound of a distant siren. Perhaps I should have been more ruthless and not telephoned for help till I'd tried talking to Teresa. I was sure that Reilly wouldn't have risked being interrupted till she'd squeezed every last drop of information out of the suffering woman. On the other hand, perhaps I should be glad to realize I was staggering back towards the human race.

I tried to collect my scattered thoughts and shuffle them into some kind of order.

'Teresa,' I said urgently. 'Why did they do this to you? What did they want to know?'

I couldn't read the expression in those wide brown eyes for a moment, then I got it. Distrust. She still didn't trust me.

'Listen, Teresa,' I said. 'Like I told you in the Forum, all I want is the chance to see Angelica. I don't know what the hell's going on and I don't really care. I want to see my daughter. I've got cancer. I'm dying. That's why I left Venezuela. I haven't got much time. So if you know anything that can help me ...'

She was regarding me with astonishment.

'Cancer!' she said. 'You, Tonto ...'

'Yes, me. Tonto.'

She turned her head away. Her gaze must have fallen on one of the scattered snapshots for she picked it up, despite the pain the action must have caused her. I could see it was a photograph of a typically unsmiling Vasco.

I said, 'He's with Angelica, isn't he? Where's he taken her, Teresa? I've got to know. Where, Teresa? Where?'

She groaned and shifted slightly. Her colour was very bad and her eyes were half closed. And the siren of the ambulance which would surely end our discussion was clearly audible now.

'I was told they were in Ostia, your wife and daughter,' she said in an almost inaudible voice. 'Asked to talk with the girl ... only the girl ... see how she was. We met her on the beach ... Vasco was with me ... it is easier for young people to talk together. They liked each other ...'

I felt a sudden untimely pang of jealousy. God, she was only sixteen! Then I mocked my hypocrisy as I recalled the ages of some of my annual friends.

'Vasco is impulsive ... he thought it best ... to be safe,' apologized Teresa, looking fondly at the photograph of her son before closing her eyes again.

The siren halted outside.

I said. 'Teresa, for God's sake, where are they?'

She said in a strange, agonized tone, 'I will never tell you!'

Then she opened her eyes wide and after a second registered my face.

'Oh Tonto, it's you ... I thought it was Krylov asking- ... always asking ... I would not speak ... Vasari scattered the photos and said they would kill my grandchildren ... but Krylov said my own pain would work quicker ... but I still did not speak.' She glared at me proudly.

'But where are they?' I asked again.

'Then the phone rang,' she continued 'Krylov answered it. He did not speak. And then they left ... Why did they go, Tonto? .... Perhaps someone else had told them ... You must go after them Tonto ... take my car, little Tonto ... it's in the street.'

'I will, I will Teresa,' I said. 'But where are they?'

It was too late. I'd left the door of the apartment open and now a little posse of ambulance men burst in with a stretcher and Teresa fell back apparently unconscious.

The ambulance men looked aghast when they saw her injuries. One of them muttered something and went into the living-room, I guessed to telephone the police. The others lifted Teresa gently on to the stretcher. I didn't see much point in mentioning Giuseppe at this juncture.

As they bore her through the door her eyes flickered open again.

'The keys,' she breathed.

She meant the car keys, I guessed. They were on the bedside table. I picked them up and thrust them into my pocket and followed the stretcher downstairs. I could tell the ambulance men regarded me a trifle ambiguously but they weren't about to try to detain me. However, if I got into the ambulance with Teresa, it was odds on there'd be a welcoming committee for me at the hospital.

I tried once more as they lifted her into the ambulance, grasping the stretcher to hold it still.

'Where will I find them, Teresa?' I begged. 'Please!'

'She's unconscious,' snapped one of the men. 'We must hurry.'

Teresa's hand moved from under the sheet they'd draped over her. It must have been agony. In her bloody fingers she still grasped the photograph of Vasco. She held it out to me and spoke, but I couldn't catch the words.

I took the photo and said, 'What is it, Teresa?'

'Grandfather,' she said quite clearly. 'Danger.'

Then the ambulance men pushed me unceremoniously aside and next minute the vehicle was on its way, lights flashing, siren screaming. Then the silence and the darkness came rushing back in on me.

I had to get away from here, but I'd no idea where to go. The thought that somewhere in that darkness and silence a man with the face of a romantic violinist and the scruples of Torquemada might be searching for my daughter filled me with an impotent rage which redirected itself against my father. His was the ultimate responsibility for all this. And clearly I'd been right in guessing that he'd make some contact with Teresa. Her final words, *Grandfather. Danger.* must surely refer to him.

She was right. If I got close to him, there'd be plenty of danger.

The thought seemed to release me and I set off down the street in search of Teresa's car which her keys told me was a little Fiat 126. After a couple of bosh shots, I found it.

As I slid into the driving seat, I realized I was still holding the bloodstained photo of Vasco. I tossed it on to the passenger seat and started the engine.

But before I engaged gear, I paused and picked up the photograph again.

Teresa had given it to me at the expense of great pain. What had been going through that almost unconscious mind?

I examined the picture. And I swore at my own stupidity.

So obsessed was I with my own concerns that I interpreted everything to fit them.

Vasco too had a grandfather, old Matteo Carducci, her dead husband's father who had founded and held sway for forty years over the family baking business.

And that was what I could see in the background of the photograph. That sunlit archway, that narrow window with the engraved lintel, these belonged to the Carducci bakery in Amalfi.

Where else would an Italian boy in trouble go but to his grandparents?

It had been the home of my grandparents too and I was certainly in trouble.

As I engaged gear and slowly drew away, I could hear the distant wail of police sirens.

. . . *ring of ripe pineapple* . . .

I was on the Autostrada del Sole, motoring steadily south.

The temptation to burn a furrow in the tarmac all the way to Naples was strong, but for all kinds of reasons I resisted it. For a start, Teresa's tiny car, which fitted me like a thirty 'A' cup fits Sohpia Loren, had eighty thousand doubtless violent kilometres on the clock and gave vibrant hints that too much accelerator would bring the engine off its mounting. And in any case, there's not much point in burning up an autostrada. If the cops don't get you between the toll gates, the bastards checking your time-stamped ticket will often give a handily parked police car a friendly wave if you seem to have been breaking records. So I held steady at the limit.

In fact, so far I'd seen no evidence of police activity. I'd half expected to discover the *carabinieri* were asking *quo vadis, milord*? on all the main roads out of Rome, but now I was buzzing through the Castelli without a sign of them and felt able to relax.

The night was fine but very dark, and after half an hour or so the old hypnosis of night-driving began to lull my already exhausted mind. Time and space ebbed away like a neap tide and the darkness no longer rushed by, but gently stroked and caressed my troubled thoughts, easing away my sense of angry purpose. From time to time petals of light unfolded before me, then drifted by on the slow currents of dark river. Soon, soon, we would all drift into oblivion together. Soon, as I lay here gently rocking in my *chinchorro* watching the fireflies dancing in the dusk, I would fall asleep; soon, the race won, my weary victor's limbs would relax and take their ease; soon Mama would come into the nursery and the darkness would be rich with her perfume as she folded me in her arms ...

Suddenly I was asleep and not asleep; suddenly I was dreaming and not dreaming; suddenly Mama was Numero Siete and my exhaustion was not the clean fatigue of the victorious athlete but the feverish emptiness of the sated lecher ...

Suddenly the dancing fireflies were the tail-lights of a convoy of army vehicles and the little Fiat was astraddle two lanes and almost into the rearmost truck!

I slammed on the brakes and watched the needle plummet towards legality. Fear brought me back to complete wakefulness, but I knew it wouldn't last. And while falling asleep on the autostrada wasn't very clever, at least I'd got a second chance which wasn't at all likely once I reached the Amalfitana.

This is the notorious road snaking along those rugged cliffs which tower above the sea all along the southern shore of the Sorrento Peninsula as far as Salerno. I've been on worse roads in the Alps and it's a four-lane highway compared with some of the tracks I've broken springs on in the Sierra Nevada. But the combination of native machismo and tourist terror make it a dangerous road for a man in a hurry and a fatal one for a man in a torpor.

Ahead was the Casilina service area. I drew in and parked. A couple of turns round the car and a few deep breaths of the exhaust tainted air didn't convince me I was in a fit state to carry on. Only the knowledge that somewhere for some reason a melancholy Russian, with the face of a romantic violinist and the stomach to prise fingernails from living flesh, was searching for my daughter had kept me awake this far. But if Teresa was telling the truth when she said she hadn't talked, he could have no clue to her whereabouts. And what was certain was that I'd be no use to her dead.

Not that I'd ever been much use to her living, I told myself bitterly.

I climbed into the rear of the tiny car, locked the doors and lay down as best I could. I set my mental alarm system for an hour ahead. Then I closed my eyes and for a little while once more travelled back through the past till I reached the warm perfumed darkness of Mama's shadow over my nursery bed. Then I fell asleep.

When I awoke, there was indeed a shadow falling over me but not Mama's. It was cast by a policeman's head which filled the whole of the small rear window. But for the moment it wasn't the presence of the police that alarmed me, it was the source of the shadow.

The sun was clear of the horizon.

I sat up so quickly I bumped my head. Then I looked at my watch and swore. So much for my mental alarm. It was six-thirty a.m.

I climbed out of the car and found I was so stiff I could hardly straighten up. I did a kind of simian shuffle to get the blood circulating and this had the unlooked-for effect of making the *pozzo* laugh.

'You should pick a car your own size.' he said.

It struck me he had taken me for an Italian. It also struck me that his curiousity might quickly be aroused if he realized I was a foreigner in what was pretty clearly not a rented car. So I swore in Italian, swung my foot against one of the Fiat's tyres, pretended to hurt my toe and limped off muttering towards the self-service.

At the cashier's desk I paid for four *caffès* and a dough-nut. I drank the first *caffè* to wash my mouth out, ate the doughnut, and downed the other three in quick succession. The woman behind the counter made a joking comment. I scowled ferociously at her and headed for the lavatory.

The police car had disappeared when I returned to the car park. I got into the Fiat and set off once more.

It would have been nice to discover I felt better after my sleep and breakfast but in fact I didn't. My head was aching and my stomach too, though I tried to ignore that or at least to assure myself it felt no worse than I would have expected after a broken night, four black coffees and a stale doughnut.

There was a lot more traffic on the road now and after I left the autostrada progress became increasingly slow. Tourist buses were on the move and in the end I found I needn't have worried about the Amalfitana. By the time I hit it, I was in the middle of a small convoy of coaches and obliged to crawl along in a miasma of diesel fumes and a carillon of warning horns every time we reached a bend. At least it gave me plenty of time to stare out into the Bay of Salerno and recall those days, now shaded with bitterness as were all my memories of my father, but then aglow with the gold of sunshine and joy, when I crewed for him as he set our sail-boat, the *Ariel* scudding across the Tyrrhenian Sea. In this art as in all that he practised he went beyond self-assurance into an almost godlike arrogance. It took me a long time to realize that gods keep their strength up by feeding on their families.

These were the nostalgic thoughts that burrowed through my mind as I came back to Amalfi.

Already the town was packed. I hadn't been back here since the early 'fifties nearly thirty years ago. Surely, even making allowances for a boy's uncritical memory, it hadn't been like this then? The place seemed riddled with tourists and every inch of space on the sea-front was packed with cars. I drove into the Piazza Duomo and parked by the cathedral steps. The last time I had climbed that splendid flight, which looked as if it could have been designed for a Busby Berkely set, I had been following great-grandmama Dianti's coffin. It had been hard to feel sad. The sun had been shining as brightly then as now and the gilded mosaic front of the Duomo had sparkled more like an entrance to Disney-land than to the Other World. Afterwards I would be returning to the Villa Colonna perched on the edge of the cliffs on the road to Positano. Later in the day perhaps, changed out of these stiff formal clothes, I would climb down the cliff-face with Pa to run up sail on *Ariel* and go in search of a breeze. Nothing seemed more certain.

I've learned a lot since then. Joy is to be trusted like a politician's mail – it can always blow up in your face. No wonder the majority of the human race finds such consolation in the banalities of certain repetition – spring after winter, dawn after darkness, Saturday after Friday! But I was young enough to be quite devasted when I found myself an hour after the funeral heading for Naples and home with no prospect of ever returning to the Villa Colonna. It was now the property, by right of male primogeniture, of Pa's cousin, Giulio Dianti. Great-grandmama didn't care for him much, but as the only son of her only son, he had an inalienable right of inheritance. It was Giulio's intention, Pa told me with distaste, to turn the villa into a hotel. Giulio was a notoriously unlucky speculator and Pa derived some consolation from the certainty that any such commercial enterprise was doomed to failure. But such consolations are balm only to adult wounds. All I knew was that a joyous sunlit area of my life had been blacked out without warning.

I shook my head free of the memory and got out of the car. The Carducci bakery was quite close, but I contented myself with observing it from a distance. The family did not live on the premises and I doubted if Vasco and Angelica would be here. Through the open door I glimpsed work in progress. It suited my book very well that I should find the young people alone. Vasco himself would be bad enough to deal with, but the rest of the Carducci family was a complication I could do without. .

I had only a vague idea where the family house was, but a telephone directory soon solved that problem. I headed back for the car but on re-entering the Piazza, I saw a uniformed figure standing at the foot of the Cathedral steps. I guessed I'd broken one of the very few parking laws which were enforced in the town and as I'd no desire to be asked to produce documents, I just kept on walking.

In fact the Carducci house wasn't all that far, though I increased the distance by getting lost a couple of times. It stood in the middle of a whitewashed terrace. The windows were shuttered aginst the opposing sun, but on the top floor there was an open balcony and here I glimpsed the head of a seated man. He had a fine mop of snow-white hair. I guessed this would be old Matteo Carducci, Teresa's father-in-law, who must be in his eighties now and had wisely decided that the heat of the bakery was no place for a man with two daughters and a son to run the business.

I paused to light a cigarette. There were a couple of cars parked in the vicinity but none with Roman number plates. I felt suddenly uneasy. Suppose Teresa had been wrong and Vasco had not headed south? Or, worse, suppose the phone calls which had interrupted her torturers had been news that Vasco and Angelica had been traced and taken?

Perhaps they were being held in this very house. It didn't seem likely but I made sure the automatic tucked into my waistband was ready for a rapid emergence and crossed the road.

There was an open archway which led into a small outer hall. It was cool and dark in there after the blaze of the mid-morning sun. I stood for a moment to let my eyes grow accustomed to the change of light. I let my instinct run loose and it told me there was no one on this floor, but I checked anyway. Instinct was right. I went up a narrow stone staircase to the next floor. Quickly, and quietly too so I thought, I checked the rooms here, but as I peered into the last empty bedroom, a male voice called in a strained hesitant tone, 'Anna? Is that you?'

I went cautiously towards the balcony, suspicious that this tone might indicate constraint. But the old man was alone and it took only a moment to spot the source of the constraint. Some time recently he must have suffered from a stroke. In repose, with his head cocked on one side watching my approach as a cage-bird might watch the approach of a cat, he looked perfectly well, his sun and presumably oven-baked skin and white hair giving him a splendidly patriarchal appearance. But when he shifted his position and spoke again, asking who I was, the effects of his stroke became apparent. The right side of his body and of his face seemed almost completely paralysed.

I quickly introduced myself. He nodded and made a gesture which might have been an invitation to sit. I took it as such. He nodded again and smiled and spoke, but the combination of his physical difficulty in articulation and the stroke sufferer's typical mental difficulty in getting the right word out made it hard for me to understand him outside the most obvious phrases. He repeated *poco Inglese* several times before I grasped he was referring to me as I had been all those years ago.

I nodded and, pointing to myself with a laugh, echoed, 'The little English boy.'

I asked him about Vasco and again he nodded and said, 'Yes, yes, Vasco.'

When I asked him if Vasco was here, this seemed to cause considerable trouble as he sought for the words.

'Vasco,' he said several times. Then something I couldn't

make out at all. Then finally and most hopefully of all, 'Little English girl.'

'With Vasco?' I asked. 'Was the English girl with Vasco? Are they still here?'

Again the difficulties of expression, again the difficulties of understanding. He was growing most frustrated by this time, banging his usable hand on the arm of his chair.

Finally he said two words which came out loud and clear.

'Villa Colonna.'

Then as if exhausted by his efforts and their frustration, he sank back in his chair, breathing hard, and closed his eyes.

At the same moment a woman's voice yelled loud in my ear, 'Who are you? What do you want? What have you done to my grandfather?'

I looked round. A woman of about thirty stood behind me. She had rather thin, undistinguished features but they were lit up with a splendid rage. Only in the woman of Southern Italy is anger a beautifying emotion.

This I guessed was Anna. I stood up to explain myself and she shouldered me aside to get to the old man, who certainly didn't look all that healthy.

Once more I started to explain who I was, but this time as soon as I mentioned my name she began to scream at me in terms of virulent abuse. There was no way of switching her off, and I guessed by the time she had run out of steam an audience would have collected below, possibly including a local cop or two. So I left her raging richly and tactically withdrew. She leaned over the balcony and matched the rhythms of her abusive rhetoric to my retreating steps.

My only consolation was that at least I was certain Vasco and Angelica were here somewhere. I toyed with the idea of going back to the Carducci bakery and continuing my enquiries there, but no doubt they would be as uncooperatively antagonistic as Anna. No, the clue I decided to follow had been given by old Matteo. Of course, when he said Villa Colonna, he might have been merely continuing the reminiscent theme of 'the little English boy', but I didn't think so.

I got back to the Piazza Duomo. The car was still there at the foot of the steps but the traffic warden had been joined now by two large policemen, so I walked right through the square to the sea front, where a row of taxis stood while their drivers argued football in the shade.

I climbed into the leading one and waited. No one came so I leaned forward and blasted the horn. The drivers looked, then continued their discussion. I sighed, leaned forward again, switched on the headlights, windscreen wipers and radio.

He was with me in two seconds.

I didn't give him a chance to start an argument but held up a twenty-thousand lire note and said, 'Villa Colonna.'

He switched everything off and said, '*Hotel* Colonna?'

I nodded sadly. 'Si.'

He took the note and started the engine.

As we left the town by the rising road which climbs back up the cliff out of the ravine in which Amalfi lies, he began to chatter away, assuring me that his knowledge of the country-side and the antiquities around Amalfi was second to none, that he could arrange anything from a live performance of Wagnerian arias at Ravello to a moolit trip to the Grotta dello Smeraldo. And if I preferred a knowledgable female courier on the latter, he could fix that too.

I told him to shut up and closed my eyes. I was feeling this journey sinking the claws of the past into me more than anything I'd done since leaving Margarita. This was a jour-ney back to a time when I'd been completely happy. No, that's wrong. Not even happy children are happy all the time. But certainly to a time when the state of complete happiness was a daily probability. Nothing after Mama's death, not even Angelica's birth, had been lit with that pure dazzling white light of joy which casts no shade.

Once more, as always, the memory of that very last joy-lit moment shone perfect in my mind. My limbs supple, strong, and godlike even in their exhaustion, cleaving through the water. My fingers touching. The cheers of the crowd. The congratulations of the team. And then Mama, oblivious of the protesting officials and of the rivulets of water still running down my body, embracing me with joy and pride and love.

The happiness I had felt in my victory had seemed immortal. There was no friendly voice in my ear saying, '*Mira, chico*, that's it. *Finito*. There is no more. The rest is anti-climax.' My heart sang. The singing it seemed would never end.

Three months later Mama was dead, Pa was justifying himself in Moscow, and I was miming to someone else's record, the someone else who those few months earlier had still been capable of perfect happiness.

A discord of horns brought me back to the present as my taxi and an oncoming coach exchanged opinions. I was grateful. This was where I had to be for the little time that remained to me. The one real thing to come of that old mimic life was Angelica, and she might be in danger.

We were almost there. Soon we would turn off the winding road and bump down the rutted drive to the rocky plateau on which the Villa Colonna stood overlooking the sea. Or perhaps that wasn't such a clever move. I saw the turning ahead and said to the driver, 'That's fine. I'll get out here.'

At the entrance to the drive, I saw a sign had been erected. It read *Hotel Colonna* but it looked to me as if it would be commercially counter-productive. The paint had been stripped off by the blow-lamp of the sun leaving the words scarcely legible, and one of the posts on which it was nailed had rotted away so that it listed like a railway signal ready to drop next time that violent wind known as the *Tramontana* blasted down the mountains from the north and set the boats rocking at their storm-anchorage in the middle of the bay.

I started to walk down the drive. The villa was built against the face of the cliff with the roof not far below the level of the road. The drive-way was an elbow doubling back on itself to form a hairpin which Pa had claimed did more for religion in Amalfi than all the relics of St Andrew preserved in the Duomo. The drive ran through a lemon grove clinging in a series of terraces to the cliff-face. It looked as if it had been sadly neglected in recent years, but there were some people working in it now. They looked like a family or perhaps two families, and they regarded me, men, women and children alike, with the blank inimical stare of the true peasant. As I reached the corner I met three or four hens picking at the dusty track and their reaction was even less welcoming, scuttering away clucking a loud warning to whatever lay ahead.

At the point of the elbow I paused and looked down. From here you got a magnificent view of the rocky cove above which the villa was built. In the 'twenties a lift had been installed and I could see its shaft still clinging like a Meccano structure to the cliff face. It had been pretty unreliable even in the early fifties and I wouldn't fancy using it now. I looked past it far below to the little cove where in good weather we had kept *Ariel* moored to the concrete landing platform from which you could dive into fifteen feet of water. There was a boat there now, no *Ariel* this, but a broad tub with a sad stump of a mast, wallowing in the gentle swell.

I resumed my approach to the villa but not before I had become aware that two men had emerged from the lemon grove and were standing watching me on the drive behind me.

I was on the same level now as the main terrace whose white wall was almost invisible under a cascade of scarlet bougainvillæa. The driveway ran down to the third or bottommost level which housed the kitchen, the cellar and the garage. I kept straight on along a little dusty track which would take me direct to the terrace.

There were signs here both of neglect and of habitation. The pink walls of the villa were badly weather-stained, some tiles had come off the roof and a quick repair job had been done with what looked like a black polythene sheet. A shutter hung loose from its window by a single hinge. Over the rail of the balcony which ran the whole length of the top floor above the terrace were draped sheets, and from a line stretched above the rail hung a variety of washing.

But to me the most surprising, indeed shocking, sight was the stump of the old column from which the villa derived its name. Thought to be the remains of one of the pillars of a Greek temple on whose foundations the villa itself was built, it stood in a little patch of grass with a few olive trees to the side of the building. Now someone had erected a makeshift chicken-wire fence around the column and in this pen a family of tiny pink piglets were rooting and basking in the sun.

I had no right to be indignant, but indignation was what I felt. Obviously the hotel had failed, probably because of it difficulty of access, and the place had been left to the deprivation of squatters.

With difficulty I shook myself free of this distracting emotion. I had more important matters in hand. At least I hoped I did. But I was beginning to wonder what possible reason Vasco could have for bringing Angelica up here.

I climbed on to the tarmac. Signs of occupation multiplied. From the kitchen below came drifting a smell of hot oil and garlic accompanied by a tuneless peasant singing. On a table on the fine marble floor of the terraces were glasses and some soft drink cans.

A sound behind me made me turn. The two peasants I'd noticed before were at the foot of the three stairs which lead up to the terrace. One of them was in his fifties with a deeply-lined, leathery face full of shrewdness and distrust. The other was younger, gipsy-like in English terms, with the surly, dark good-looks of a Heathcliff. In his right hand he carried a broad and vicious-looking billhook. Slowly, as I watched, they mounted the stairs and came towards me.

I undid the button on my thin linen jacket and slid my hand inside till it rested on the comforting solidity of my pistol-butt.

'Who are you? What do you want?' I asked.

They stopped.

Then another voice, a young female voice repeated my words in hesitant Italian.

'Who are you? What do you want?'

I turned to the speaker. She must have just emerged on to the terrace from one of the rooms which lay behind it. She was quite tall, very slender, with long dark hair and a lively, pretty face. She was clad in the skimpiest of bikinies and there was no suggestion that the deep brown of her flawless skin diluted to modest pallor beneath the flimsy cloth. She stood there so young, so unself-conscious, that for a moment I could only admire her. Then my hormones got to work and desire set in.

But it was short-lived.

'Who are you?' she repeated, but this time in English.

I heard the truth in her voice for there I caught a rising inflexion of Kate's which came back to me now after so many years. Even then I hesitated belief. The last snapshot I'd received via Uncle Percy had shown me a round-faced, uniformed schoolgirl, not this nubile nymphet. I suppose there was an element of defence-mechanism in all this. A man doesn't care to find that his long-sought reunion with his little daughter had touched his groin before it touched his heart.

'Angelica?' I said stupidly.

She nodded uncertainly.

I took a step towards her. I don't expect I looked a very appetizing sight and at the best of times my soulful express-ion tends to look like acid indigestion.

She let out a little cry of alarm and retreated, half stumb-ling against a canvas chair. I reached forward to help her. There was a noise of running feet. I looked up. Heathcliff was descending on me swinging his billhook with the easy vigour of a man who has no doubt but that he can remove the top of a man's head like a ring of ripe pineapple. Even when I pulled out my gun, he kept coming.

Angelica's cry of alarm swelled into a full-blooded scream of terror which drew my glance towards her once again. I'd still have had plenty of time to return my attention to Heathcliff and pick a spot in his muscular body to put my bullet into, but over Angelica's shoulder, just emerging from the shadows of the terrace-lounge, I saw a man.

Tall, round-shouldered, grey-haired; a patrician head wearing at this moment an expression of mixed surprise and disapproval, but without the slightest trace of concern or uncertainty.

He spoke. I had my gun on his breastbone but I froze. Perhaps it was amazement, perhaps doubt. Perhaps I just wanted to savour the moment.

'Lem,' he said reprovingly. 'Oh, Lem.'

And then I couldn't fire because Angelica had run into his arms which went protectively about her. But oh! how that sight whetted my blunted purpose!

I'd forgotten Heathcliff, of course.

And now he was on me.

Everyone yelled at once including me. But yelling was all I had time for.

Fortunately, instead of slices he settled for chunks and at the last moment turned his wrist so that I got the flat instead of the edge of the blade full against my right ear.

The immediate result was just the same.

Like some wayward asteroid, I had travelled thousands of dangerous miles through the bright air for this encounter.

And now as I touched their atmosphere, my daughter's and my father's, I felt my substance dissolve and I went sputtering into darkness.

. . . *a matching pair* . . .

Waking was like coming out of one of the cellar dives in downtown Caracas. My head seemed full of noise and smoke, my belly awash with rotten liquor, and at first even this dim light and musty air hit me like a squirt of caustic. I'd have rolled back into the dive if I could, except that black memories were now stirring, like recollections of having been taken for every *bolivar* in your wallet.

I sat upright, regretted it, collapsed again, but the memories had been shaken loose. It wasn't money I'd lost, but everything. Now he'd taken everything from me. He was up there with Angelica, holding her, comforting her, persuading her that I'd broken into the villa to harm her ...

Up there. I opened my eyes again. Above my head a single-bulb, grime-encrusted to near opacity, spilled just enough light to paint shapes. It was sufficient. My subconscious had been right. I recognized where I was. Far from emerging from a cellar dive, I was actually languishing *in* a cellar, the wine-cellar of the Villa Colonna. Here I'd come as a boy, fascinated and frightened by this cave of cool darkness carved in the rock behind the bright sunlit house, moving among the racks of bottles peeping like cannons from their ports, broadside upon broadside at the ready.

I sat upright again, slowly this time, and let my eyes grow accustomed to the light. I was lying on an old mattress, thin, lumpy and stained with God knows what, but at least it indicated some slight concern for my comfort, which was hopeful. I touched my right ear and winced. It felt big enough for Dumbo. Perhaps if I belted the other one equally hard, I could fly out of here. My head ached, but that apart, I suppose I didn't feel too bad for a dying forty-year-old.

I got to my feet and tried a few steps. It felt like a novel form of locomotion and I didn't reckon it would catch on, so I sat down again and resumed my examination of the cellar. It seemed to have weathered the years as badly as I had. The racks were still there but the only bottles in sight were a pile of empties in a corner. Odd bits of broken furniture littered the floor. It had degenerated to a junk-room. I should have felt at home but all I wanted to do was get out. I stood up once more and found I was beginning to master the new fashion. This time I made it to the door.

Why I bothered, I didn't know. They weren't going to dump me in here and leave the door open. Still, I had to try it before I started digging my tunnel through about half a mile of solid rock.

I tried it. It was locked. Disappointment has nothing to do with expectation. I was disappointed. I had decided to postpone my excavations for a while and return to my mattress for a ponder when I heard a key being turned in the lock. I dug deep into my mind, hoping to find some reserves of strength with which to launch an attack but when the door swung up it caught my shoulder a glancing blow and I immediately fell down.

I felt myself picked up and returned to the mattress. There were two of them and they spoke together in Italian in the strong accent of Avellino. One of them moved away and I wondered if this might not be my best chance, but when I opened my eyes, I saw the Heathcliffian face of the man who had hit me and in his hand the billhook he had hit me with, and I changed my mind. The other man couldn't have gone very far for he was back in a moment with a tray. On it was a jug full of black steaming coffee, from the smell of it liberally laced with *grappa*, and a plateful of coarse brown bread, mozzarella cheese and a handful of juicy olives. He set it down a few feet away, the other made a permissive gesture and I sat up and began to drink and eat.

They waited till I had finished, then took the tray and dishes away and locked the door behind them. I listened for a while but was unable to determine how far they had moved away from the door. But presumably this meant that my own movements would be as difficult to follow. I rose once more and began to investigate.

The food and drink, or at least its *grappa* content, had reinvigorated me. Obviously this little hive of Communists had no immediate plans to sting me to death. Indeed, if I had a fair notion of how my father's mind worked, he would already be examining the possible propaganda contribution my sudden appearance could make to his own little schemes. Perhaps I would be pulled out of a hat at an international press conference. Or sub-poena'd to appear as a witness at his trial. What could I say? That I'd been blackmailed by M16 to assassinate him? What a spendid reinforcement of his own case against British security! Angelica too. My own daughter describing how she'd fled in fear while I was back in Rome, murdering her mother.

Oh Jesus. I'd almost forgotten about Kate. Did Angelica know yet? I had to get out of here and see her and speak to her and convince her that among all her bad memories of me that one at least should never figure.

I took off my clothes and started searching among the debris in the cellar.

They came back an hour later.

When they opened the door, they had the sense to remain cautiously a couple of feet back from the threshold. Then came a gasp of horror at what they saw silhouetted against the dim glow of the bulb. A body, dangling from one of the hooks in the ceiling and slowly turning as if the last shallow breath of life were still ebbing out.

Caution was forgotten.

'Holy Mary, mother of us all!' rasped Heathcliff and they rushed forward to save this demented foreigner from self-destruction.

I pushed myself off from the wall beside the door and hit the nearest of them with a bottle which had once held a Gragnano that I hadn't tasted for thirty years. It didn't suit this peasant's palate and he collapsed to his knees, groaning. It was Heathcliff, I was glad to see, not out of any particular animosity but because he struck me as the more dangerous of the two.

I was right. The other backed away from me in terror. It was time the KGB gave him a refresher course. Finally he came up against the dangling dummy. The poor sod can't really have imagined I'd dug up a genuine corpse from somewhere but he shrieked as if it was cold flesh he'd touched rather than my pants and shirt stuffed with straw. I kicked him in the balls. By this time Heathcliff, who obviously had a better head for red wine than I'd thought, was back on his feet and casting around for his billhook. I spotted it first and scooped it up, but he in the meanwhile had got hold of a solid baton of wood from one of the dismembered wine-racks. I computed the odds. At the moment, slightly in my favour, but not enough by a long chalk.

I hurled the still unbroken bottle at him and, as he ducked, I turned and ran. He hit the door behind me just as I turned the key, and then began to beat it with his baton. I felt the weathered wood vibrate as I leaned against it, panting like an overworked satyr.

I couldn't hang around here, not with that noise drumming all over the villa. It seemed to be beating inside my head too and I had a dreadful suspicion that if I tracked that sinister throbbing through the labyrinth of my body it would prove to emanate from my guts. I didn't make the journey. There were too many things to do before I faced up to the monster in that cave.

I set off at an unsteady lope.

The cellar was set behind the kitchen at the end of a narrow corridor with store cupboards on either side. The way back to the upper storeys of the villa led through the kitchen. I pushed the door open.

After the gloom of the cellar, it was like stepping into the radiance of Heaven. The windows gave out a stupendous view over the sea and the pure blue light hit my eyes as though thrown from a bucket. When the dazzle settled down, I realized there was a woman working at the kitchen table. She was chopping tomatoes with a fierce-looking knife. Already she must have been disturbed by the noise from the cellar. Now she stood stock still and viewed this strange apparition with curious but unfrightened eyes. She stood between me and the door which led to the stairs. I smiled and wished her good-day, but she replied in neither mode, merely adjusting the broad blade in her strong brown fingers.

I decided to forget about the stairs.

Another door led out of the kitchen on to a small terrace where in the lee of a low white wall generations of cooks at the Villa Colonna had cultivated their herbs. I stepped out into the warm air. It tasted good. The herb garden had been allowed to go to ruin, not in the riotous luxuriance that is produced by neglect in the British climate, but in a dry, baked dying, despite the protection of the wall. Only a few sprigs of marjoram showed that someone was making an effort at restoration. Perhaps my friend with the knife.

I looked over the wall.

Below, the cliff fell almost sheer to the tiny rocky cover where *Ariel* had once been moored. Yet again I felt a desperate longing for the years to peel back and give me once more the untroubled and untroubling days of childhood when the loss of an afternoon's sailing might seem like the end of the world, but every hour was capable of creating a dozen new worlds to take its place.

I pushed the feeling aside and turned my eyes upward. Above me hung the villa with its lemon groves on either side where the cliff eased back from the precipitous to the merely very steep. The main terrace was on the step above the kitchen. I could see the fluted balcony rails intertwined with hibiscus and bougainvillæa and I thought I could hear voices.

The woman with the knife had come to the kitchen door and was watching me. Soon she must surely go to see why there was so much noise coming from the cellar. I realized I was still holding the key. I tossed it out over the cliff and watched it disappear without any visible splash into the water far below.

Now I walked along the little kitchen terrace to the edge of the building. Here the path diverged. Ahead was the old lift down to the sea. Even if it were still working, I didn't fancy getting caught in it. There was the alternative of a rudimentary stairway hacked in the rock face, almost as dangerous as the third route which Father and I had taken on one occasion, abseiling down the cliff at its sheerest alongside the lift chute. Great-grandmama had caught us at it and hurled abuse at my father in the patois of back-street Naples, but this only provoked the exhibitionist in him and he had finished his descent with a series of rapid pendulum runs which took him through an arc of near one hundred and eighty degrees.

With an effort, I thrust the insistent past out of my mind. There was no going back. Nor, I decided, was there any going down. Even if I could escape on the old tub moored below, where was I escaping too? Everything important left for me to do in my life was waiting for me up there in the villa. That's where I needed to be.

To my right a flight of steps ran up alongside the kitchen to the main terrace.

I went up these as quietly as I could, slowing down to second-class mail pace as my head reached terrace level, and stopping when I could get a good view through the bright blossoms round the rails.

There were two figures on the terrace. One was Vasco Carducci. He was kneeling alongside Angelica. Her face was invisible as it rested on his shoulder, but I recognized the long black hair and the slender athletic body even though I had only seen them once, and that briefly. She was wearing a sundress over her bikini now. I regarded her with pride and residual lust and incipient jealousy, not the traditional paternal emotions, I know, but in the circumstances the best I could manage. Vasco's hands were on her shoulder-blades, caressing. I didn't know how far he was planning to go out here on the open terrace, but I wasn't about to become an incestuous voyeur. I rose and vaulted lightly over the rail. At least that was my intention, but I wasn't in top condition for light vaulting and my heel caught the rail and I went sprawling on to the tiled floor.

The couple jumped in alarm. Now I could see Angelica's face and I realized I'd been wrong about Vasco's intentions. What I'd taken for a licentious caress had been more of a comforting pat, for her features were taut with grief and stained with tears.

And I'd also been wrong about my appearance causing female panic. The woman in the kitchen had merely regarded me with puzzled suspicion. And what now twisted Angelica's face out of its mask of grief was not terror but rage and hate.

She came running at me, screaming, 'You filthy sodding bastard!'

The billhook had fallen from my hands and she snatched it up and would have brought it swinging down on my head if Vasco hadn't grabbed her upraised arm. I was grateful, even though I could see it wasn't concern for me that had caused his intervention.

I pushed myself to my knees.

'Angelica!' I said urgently. 'Listen to me.'

'You bastard!' she sobbed. 'You murdering bastard!'

Then I understood. She must have heard about Kate. I shook my head and said, 'No, no, Angelica, please, believe me ...' but I could see that my words had no chance of penetrating that fury of sobbing.

Vasco had taken the billhook from the girl's unresisting hand and as I moved forward, purposing comfort, he raised it threateningly, purposing decapitation, and spat out a stream of very unpleasant judgements, not all of which were true.

'Vasco!' I yelled, deciding that he at least was within voice-contact. 'Have you been in touch with your mother?'

The mention of Teresa gave him pause. I pressed my advantage.

'You telephone her,' I urged. 'You ask her what these people have done to her.'

'Mama?' he said incredulously. 'What has happened to her? Which people?'

'These people, you moron!' I yelled, making a gesture which took in the whole of the villa. The only people actually in sight were a few working among the lemons. Their status to me was still rather ambiguous except that I didn't reckon they were on my side. I could see heads turning at the sound of my upraised voice and I didn't doubt it had penetrated the villa too. But all that mattered to me was that somehow I should use this, perhaps my last opportunity, to get through to my daughter.

'They hurt her,' I said. 'She'll be OK, but they tortured her to find out where you'd gone with Angelica.'

I had his full attention though he had not relaxed his aggressive stance with the billhook.

'Who?' he demanded. 'Who has done this?'

'I keep telling you!' I screamed. 'My father's people, that's who. Oh Jesus, what do I have to do to make you understand?'

'But why?' he said. 'Why should your father need to do this when it was to Amalfi that we were coming anyway?'

I had the feeling this was getting me nowhere. Angelica's sobbing had slackened from a torrent to a fordable flood. I switched to English and said, 'I didn't kill Kate. I didn't kill Kate. I didn't kill your mother!'

She looked up at me with tear-reddened, disbelieving eyes. I looked down at her helplessly. It was hopeless. Not so much convincing her that I hadn't murdered her mother, though that wasn't going to be easy. No, what was hopeless in the time available was convincing myself that this lovely young woman was my sixteen-year-old daughter.

'I didn't. Honestly, I didn't,' I said almost petulantly. The sound of upraised voices came from the house and I guessed that finally the alarm had been raised. It occurred to me then that the important thing was not what Angelica thought of me but her immediate safety and I didn't know if that was guaranteeable in the villa. Pa's egotistical sentimentality might keep her under his protection so long as she didn't get in the way of his plans, but Pa's mates wouldn't be much inclined to leave witnesses wandering around. Witnesses to what? Probably to my killing for a start!

Vasco had relaxed his attention for a moment as he too listened to the sounds in the villa. It was easy to poke him lightly in the stomach and remove the billhook from his hand. Terror filled both their faces and to the boy's eternal credit he thrust himself in front of Angelica to ward off my expected attack.

'Don't be so bloody stupid!' I said wearily. 'If you want to protect her, take her down to the town, back to your uncle's bakery. Contact your mother. Do it now. Don't go back into the villa. Walk, run, catch a bus, but just take her away. Please, Vasco, I beg you. I am your uncle too, remember, and Angelica's father. Would I want to see you harmed?'

It was the familial appeal that did it, as well as the fact that I was urging them to take off when I could very easily have been chopping them up if that was what I fancied.

He grabbed Angelica's arm with one hand and scooped up their pile of clothes and possessions with the other. Angelica looked set to resist. There was a stubbornness on her face which reminded me of young pictures of myself. Suddenly in that second she became my daughter. Fortunately there was Bessacarr blood in the young Italian too and his mind was made up.

He dragged her after him. I could hear footsteps slapping on the tiles from within the house. A group of people were approaching rapidly.

'Hurry!' I urged.

There was enough Latin in Angelica for her to know when to resist and when to give in. Suddenly she moved ahead of Vasco and together the two of them raced off the terrace and up through the garden towards the road. I watched their brown young bodies dappled with sun and shadow from the lemon leaves till they were out of sight. The untypical fancy struck me that so must Adam and Eve have looked as they roamed through Eden in pre-lapsarian innocence.

The serpent entered on cue.

He held a Beretta 70 single shot automatic in his hand with the easy assurance of one who could have represented his country in almost any shooting category, had he felt it a talent worth displaying. I have seen him break fifty clay pigeons in a row at maximum scatter, and place five shafts in the gold with a longbow at eighty yards, but the target pistol was always his favourite weapon.

There were three men with him, though I was sure he didn't feel the need for their support. One of them was the same breed as Heathcliff, with a secretive peasant face and in his gnarled hands a double-barrelled shotgun of the kind Italians like to destroy birdlife with. I think it was a Bernadelli Roma 4.

But it was the other two men that my eyes were drawn to, or rather one of them. I recognized that thin, worried, academic face! It was my Trinity scholar, the Brigadier's man who had rescued me twice on his scooter. He smiled shyly at me, then shrugged as if to say third time unlucky, and that shrug rearranged the group for me. This was not a united party, but my scholar and his companion, a stout

146

middle-aged Italian sweating profusely in a crumpled dark business suit, were being propelled ahead at the business end of those two contrasting weapons.

Pa spoke.

'Good day, Lemuel. How nice to see you out and enjoying the sun. It will do you good. You really do look a little peaky. I hope you can assure these gentlemen that the cellar was not too uncomfortable. They are going to be resting there for a while.'

I suppose the sensible thing to do was to assume that the Brigadier would have some notion where his operatives had got to, and to spin things out till reinforcements arrived. But that voice, that air of complete assurance, that expression of ironic amusement at the odd way in which God had arranged the world, all these things here in this place where once I had worshipped him before I saw behind the mask stabbed my heart like angina and I ran at him with a shriek more like pain than rage. All I could see was Mama's body, crumpled at the foot of the stairs with a ribbon of blood coiling across the floorboards from her black gleaming hair.

What he could see I don't know. Perhaps a small boy running to embrace him. Or perhaps age had simply dulled his reflexes. But I was on him before the pistol could swing into line with my body and the force of my assault sent us both crashing to the floor.

Heathcliff 2 swore violently in a rough peasant dialect, but he knew well enough that you can't be selective with a shotgun when two bodies are locked as closely together as ours. We rolled over and over, scattering chairs and tables as we thrashed from one end of the terrace to the other. Pa's strength surprised me. If this was what he was like old and sick, no wonder his stamina had seemed endless when he was in his prime. Our faces were pressed close as lovers' and I heard him gasp, 'Lem! for God's sake ...' but the note of appeal triggered no compassionate response, only an awareness that he must be weakening. I had not relaxed my hold on the billhook all this time, which initially disadvantaged me as he had dropped his pistol and was able to use both hands to grapple with. But as I gained the ascendancy, some still calm, still cold part of my mind told me why I was hanging on to the weapon. Despite everything, killing him with my bare hands was not possible. Even now, even as I felt his skinny old man's throat in my grasp, I could feel my fingers relaxing as those eyes bulged out at me and those lips funnelled wide in a desperate search for air.

But the billhook made what would have been a murder into an execution. I felt his body go limp beneath me. I let go of his throat and knelt over him, raising the billhook high in both hands. Thus had overweening, treacherous aristocrats always died throughout the ages. He lay quite still except for the rise and fall of his chest and looked up at me unblinkingly. Incredibly there was a faint, almost pitying smile on his thin, pallid, blue lips.

'Lem,' he said hoarsely. 'I didn't kill your mother.'

The words rang like a familiar but meaningless incantation in my ear. The mention of Mama only confirmed my purpose. I knew I could execute him now. My muscles were tensed for the down-driving blow.

Then a hand plucked the billhook from my grasp like taking a rattle from a baby.

'Please, Mr Swift, it will make such a mess on the terrace. Your task is over now. Leave the rest to experts.'

I looked round, ready to conceal my relief beneath anger. My Trinity scholar stood there with Pa's pistol in one hand, the billhook in the other. Behind him, his fat companion had the ancient shotgun trained on the ancient peasant.

I pushed myself upright.

'I think when you see the Brigadier you'll find you've exceeded your orders,' I said.

'The Brigadier?' he said, a faintly puzzled look on his sad, intellectual face.

'Yes. He wanted this anthology of lies closed for ever,' I snapped, pointing at Pa who was sitting slowly upright, feeling his limbs in search of broken bones.

'Ah, the Brigadier,' said the scholar. 'Of course.'

He seemed amused, as a don might seem amused at some nice piece of academic wit in a footnote.

Pa had pushed himself upright, irritatedly elbowing aside his old peasant retainer who was kneeling beside him checking for damage and clucking like an old hen. Two decades of comradeship hadn't diluted his blue blood all that much.

He looked at me with his old you've-got-things-wrong-but-it's-best-if-you-can-work-it-out-for-yourself expression.

'Lem,' he said kindly, feeling his head, 'I begin to suspect that, not for the first time, you are the victim of a mis-apprehension. In a way, I'm glad of it. I gives me hope that other aspects of your extraordinary behaviour can be explained as acts of folly rather than criminality.'

I looked at him in disgust. I didn't want to kill him any more, just be rid of him for ever.

'For God's sake take him away,' I said wearily and began to move towards the interior of the villa.

But I was prevented by the fat man who thrust the ancient shotgun into my belly.

I turned angrily to my Trinity scholar.

'Come on!' I said. 'I've kept my share of the deal. Now I'd like to get after my daughter, OK?'

'Don't worry. I've arranged for your daughter to return here,' he replied. 'Meanwhile I should avoid disturbing Signore Vasari's equilibrium if I were you. He's had a hard day and is not in the best of moods, I fear.'

Vasari. I glanced at the stout and sweating Italian. The name meant something, but my mind wasn't working too well.

Then gradually two mental images began to merge together. Only they didn't make any kind of sense.

Pa said, 'I recognize that look of dawning enlightenment, Lem. Bravo! Let me complete the process. I'm not certain who you imagine this gentleman to be but may I make a formal, and accurate, introduction. Lem, I'd like you to meet Major Vassily Krylov of the KGB.'

Krylov! I looked at him stupidly. And now the mental images overlay each other perfectly.

To me those high-boned, hollow-cheeked, sad-eyed and pallid features had suggested a scholarly Cambridge academic.

To Teresa they had suggested a romantic Slav violinist.

But now I saw that my friend from British Intelligence who had twice come riding to my rescue on his scooter was neither scholar nor musician but a KGB officer who had mutilated my sister's hands in his efforts to get her to talk. And in the end he hadn't needed to. Warned on the telephone of my return to the apartment, he had merely retreated and waited till I took off down the autostrada, then followed me.

Something else connected in my mind.

'Kate too?' I cried. 'That's how you were so handy!'

'I'm sorry,' he said. 'She walked into me in the hallway. Unfortunately she recognized me. It did not suit me to have her talk to you after that, but she would not be persuaded. So ...'

My reaction was instinctive too, but my tired and unresponsive muscles were past reacting with the lethal speed which must have sent Krylov's knife driving up under Kate's ribcage.

I pushed Vasari's gun barrel aside and lunged desperately at Krylov, who had all the time in the world to decide where to hit me. I think that basically he had the political extremist's orderly mind and perhaps it was his sense of symmetry as much as anything that made him choose my left ear so that I would have a matching pair.

The Beretta's barrel was cracked against it with expert force and for the second time that day I did my falling star act into the cosmic night.

. . . look for the laugh . . .

This time when I awoke, I'd gone far back beyond adult debauchery in Caracas clubs. I was nine and *Ariel*'s boom had come swinging across as the wind shifted and caught me unawares, cracking me across the temple and lifting me into the sea. There had been a sensation of drowning, then Pa's arms around me in the water and the knowledge that I was safe. I had remembered little more till I awoke in my narrow bed in my narrow room with its whitewashed walls and the purple evening sky pressed like a bishop's vest against my window. Then as now I had a splitting headache, and now as then Pa was sitting at the end of the bed reading a book and making occasional notes in the margin.

'There you are then,' he said cheerfully. 'I thought you would like to be in here. Krylov would have preferred the cellar, but Giorgio and Piero had just about shattered the door in their efforts to get out, so that wasn't much use, was it?'

For a second the names were meaningless, then I jumped thirty years and I was back in the present.

I sat up, tried to resist the temptation to touch either ear, failed, and winced.

'Yes, you've got a matching pair there,' said Pa, showing that, like Krylov, he too had an orderly mind. 'Though I don't think the shading's quite right. There's a trifle too much royal blue in the left one, I would say.'

I said, 'Father, can we cut this crap?'

I was lying on the bed, not in it, and now I swung my legs over the side. I was still clad in nothing more than my Y-fronts but there were some clothes draped over the brass bed-head. I reached for them but my father made a familiar admonitory gesture with his index finger.

'I would recommend a shower first,' he said.

I looked down. He was right. All that wrestling, first in the cellar, then on the terrace, had left me considerably besmirched with dust adhering to sweat.

I went to the door and paused, uncertain whether I might not find myself confronting a shotgun muzzle when I opened it. I glanced at father, but he had returned to his book. The old way, I thought bitterly. Little Lem must be left to his own decisions until he himself decided he'd made the wrong ones. I'd been right about the shotgun. Vasari was sitting on a wooden stool a few yards down the corridor. He levelled the gun at my chest and I indicated the open door of the bathroom straight opposite. Gloomily he nodded. I got the impression that he hadn't banked on letting himself in for all this when he did his Russian friends a couple of favours. But that didn't mean he wasn't ready, willing and able to shoot me.

As I luxuriated under the shower, I tried to come to grips with the situation. Why had Krylov been following me and rescued me from the police? Why had my father been pointing a gun at Krylov? What the hell was he doing in the villa anyway! And who were Giorgio Heathcliff and all *his* mates?

I gave up. The clearer my mind became under the healing jets, the clearer it grew that I wasn't going to reach any solutions via rational discourse.

I towelled myself dry and, just as I would have done thirty years ago, I went to admit defeat and ask my father to explain.

He put his book down as I entered the room, as if he had been anticipating this moment.

I began to pull on the clothes. They didn't quite fit, but I wasn't posing for any fashion plate.

'You're even bigger than I remembered, Lem,' said Pa.

I laced up the sneakers provided. Fortunately they were the right size.

I said, 'Pa, before I was rudely interrupted out on the terrace, I was about to chop your head off. What gives with all this *sang-froid?* I mean, what makes you think that as soon as I finish tying these laces I won't carry on where I left off?'

He said, 'Lem, whenever there was something you didn't

want to do, you used to be more expert than anyone I've met at finding little procrastinating jobs. Like tying up your shoes. For the moment at least, the murdering mood has departed from you.'

He was right, of course. He frequently was.

I replied, 'Don't bet on it lasting.'

He said, 'While it does last, can I ask what brought it on in the first place?'

There were things I wanted him to explain to me, but I knew from old experience that this kind of exchange would be done to his blueprint or not at all.

Besides, there were things I wanted to say to him. I didn't know whether I'd work myself up into a killing mood again, but this chance of confrontation was one I'd long dreamt of.

I told him that I'd come back to England to see Angelica – I didn't tell him why, merely leaving it as a sudden upsurge of parental love. I told him about the Brigadier and what had happened in Rome.

'So you really came down to Amalfi in search of Angelica, not in pursuit of me?' he said.

'You've got it,' I said. 'Face it, Pa. You don't mean enough to me to make a tuppenny bus-ride worth while.'

He fingered his neck thoughtfully. 'I got a different impression earlier.'

'What did you expect? A big hug?' I asked incredulously.

He shook his head. 'No. Of course not. But I had hoped that my letters might have sown a seed of doubt ...'

'Letter! I read one! The others I tore up. For God's sake, don't you think I'd had enough of your eternal *rightness*? Your self-justification?'

My anger blazed up again, not a killing anger this time, but one which was not going to be denied. I had one enormous advantage over those bastards with the guns out there. In the end, they cared about their lives. I had no life to care about.

I went on, standing now and towering over my father who suddenly looked a frail old man easily to be brushed aside, 'Listen, Pa, my first concern is to get out of here and make sure Angelica's safe. As for stopping you pouring out your poison about Mama, there are plenty of people waiting out there ready and eager to put an end to you, so I may not even have to save a bit of energy for that task. But rest assured, I've got the stomach for it!'

This macabre double-entendre tickled my fancy and I laughed, perhaps a trifle crazily, for my father seemed to experience a moment's unease, though typically he tried to express it as concern for my well-being.

'Are you all right, Lem?' he said.

'Never better,' I said almost gaily. 'Never better. Now if you'll excuse me . . .'

He seized my arm and said fiercely, 'Then if you're feeling so well, for God's sake use your head! How do you imagine you're going to get out of here for a start?'

'You're not going to stop me, are you?' I asked curiously. '*You?*'

He held on to my arm and said with passionate intensity, 'Lem, I did not kill your mother! Believe me!'

'Why the hell should I believe that?' I shouted. 'What else would you say? There's too much evidence, Pa! Too much by half!'

'I would say, from what I've heard, that there's just about the same amount of evidence that you killed Kate,' he said judiciously. 'Why should Angelica believe that you're innocent?'

I froze and stared down at him. It was queer, but this was the first time this obvious parallel had occurred. Father and son, both fleeing guiltily from houses where their wives lay brutally done to death.

I said, 'She'll believe. I'll explain.'

He said, 'I hope she gives you the chance, Lem. That's all you'll need, isn't it?'

He was at it again. Not pleading. Oh no, the great Billy Bessacarr would never plead! But forcing me to confront my own decisions in the light of my own experience.

I was older and wiser now; or cleverer, at least.

I turned his own device on him and said, 'She'll have to give me that chance or kill me. There's no other way I'll be stopped. And, believing what she does, I wouldn't blame her if in her grief and rage she killed me. But I'll take that risk. We have to choose our own risks, isn't that right, Pa?'

There it was, threat and warning, leaving the choice with

him. He smiled faintly as if in appreciation of my table-turning skill, but his first words reduced me to my old pupillary status.

'To state the obvious, in case you are still bent on not seeing it, I am not in control here. Not since your dramatic intervention, that is, though you musn't feel too badly about that. Your misinterpretation of the situation is one which many reasonably intelligent minds would have arrived at. The story which this Brigadier has told you is well constructed, with enough of the truth in it to provide a pretty solid foundation. Your own unreasoning prejudices have supplied the rest.'

'Oh come on!' I burst out. 'What are you trying to say – that you haven't been an honoured guest in Moscow these twenty years? That the Brigadier and all his people are double agents?'

'I wish you would listen, Lem,' he reproved me. 'Use your brain! You imagined Major Krylov was one of the Brigadier's men. Why?'

'Because I saw him working with someone I knew for certain was,' I replied, resenting but not resisting this catechism.

'Now what does that suggest?' said Pa.

'Either that someone's fooling someone else. Or that they've got an interest in common.'

'Yes. Yes. Come along. Come along,' he said impatiently. 'And what would that interest seem to be?'

It was amazing. Even after all this time I still felt ashamed that my slowness was disappointing him. But the conclusion he was driving me to seemed too ludicrous to be worth saying. Yet there was no other.

'They're *both* interested in stopping you from getting back to the UK,' I said. 'But I thought it was the Russians' idea, a great Soviet propaganda exercise ...'

'So your precious Brigadier told you, no doubt. Lem, when will you learn that in all your life there's only been one person who never told you anything but the truth. And that has been me. Listen now, and believe. The last thing the Russians want is for me to go back to Britain.'

'You mean you're too valuable to them!' I jeered.

'On the contrary, I have little positive value,' he said. 'I have not been too well of late and it's a long time since I've been up to much in the way of original research. I had a moderate pension, a comparatively young wife. It must have looked to my Russian hosts as if I could be allowed to drift into senility without much expenditure of money or concern on their part. But Kim died, you see.'

An uncharacteristically bitter smile touched his lips.

'Strange how the death of a wife has always signalled a radical change of direction in my life.'

The reference to Mama stung my fury to life once more but before I could even speak he raised his hand and said wearily,' You must listen, Lem. For your own peace of mind. First, let me tell you about Angelica, my Angelica, I mean. We met, we fell in love, we married, we drifted apart, we fell out of love. But we never fell out of friendship, that's for certain. We led our own lives to a great extent, but still met, partly for your sake, but most for the mutual solace, advice, and simple pleasure we derived from each other's company.

'I had my own concerns, the Trust, my scientific work, my political work too. There was a growing campaign against me. It was a neurotic time, of course. "Lord Moscow", the Yellow Press cartoonists called me. And I was under active investigation. Not that there was anything to find, but it was a source of irritation.

'Angelica, now, Angelica was a creature of high society. Not that she hadn't worked as hard as anyone during and immediately after the war. But later she began to take some of the rewards. She moved in the highest circles. She was, you must understand, in her morality, like an eighteenth-century *grande dame*. Whatever you did should be judged in terms of style, taste and, above all, discretion. She was the true aristocrat.'

'You mean, it was all right as long as you didn't do it in the street and frighten the horses?' I jibed.

'If you prefer to be coarse, Lem,' he reproved. 'I'm merely trying to explain. If this interferes with some nursery notion you still retain of your mother as some warm, kind, cuddly, walking doll created entirely for your service and your comfort, then I'm sorry for you. If on the other hand you merely feel that it contradicts your knowledge of her as a beautiful, intelligent, humane and lovable woman, then be assured it doesn't. I had hoped you would have known her well enough to know that.

'To proceed: she had begun to find, however, that taste and discretion were not as easy to maintain in the twentieth century as in the eighteenth. To move in the highest circles could also mean to have contact with the lowest. The Profumo business proved that.'

'You're not trying to tell me she was mixed up with that gang of pimps and prostitutes,' I said dangerously.

'Oh, Lem, if I offered you a list of those who were mixed up with them, the snob in you could hardly resist envy at the chance of being in such company. No, the public side of that affair was but the beast's rump. The cover-up which took place made poor Nixon's efforts after Watergate seem a very shoddy, amateurish affair. But your mother had begun to be sickened by it all long before the scandal. And the rather too timely death of Stephen Ward as he waited for the verdict at his trial completed her disillusion.'

'Too timely? What the hell does that mean?' I demanded.

'Dr Ward, you will recall, was being tried for living off immoral earnings. He it was who effected introductions between some of his lady friends and members of the Establishment. And also between them and Captain Ivanov, the Soviet naval attaché. The social Establishment hates sexual scandal, the political hates security scandal. Poor Ward was one of those creatures high society depends on, with one foot in the *beau monde* and one in the *demi*. Pathetic and dispensable. And he was dispensed with.'

'But not literally. He committed suicide,' I protested.

'He attempted suicide,' corrected Pa. 'But he was recovering sufficiently rapidly to be expected back in court in a few days when he died. But this is beside the point. All I'm trying to do is to explain Angelica's position. She was in a very unhappy state of mind that summer and autumn, even you may have noticed that.'

'I put it down to you,' I retorted.

'Consistent in that at least,' he applauded. 'No, nothing I

was doing worried your mother. She knew all about Kim, so even if she had discovered us in bed, it would have caused her no more than a slight embarrassment. But she didn't, Lem. She didn't. In fact I never saw Angelica at all that night.'

'But you must have done!' I protested. 'You were in the house. I saw you!'

'Yes, I'm sorry about that. But this is what happened afterwards. Kim and I were having a quiet drink when the phone rang downstairs. Kim went down to answer while I had a shower. She came back rather worried to tell me it was Percy Nostrand wanting to have an urgent word with me. I asked Kim if she'd start packing my things. We were flying to Paris later that evening to attend a Peace Rally the following day. When I got on the phone, Percy told me that he'd heard on the Home Office grapevine that a security team was being sent round to talk to me that same evening, 'talk' being a euphemism for interrogate. They'd probably have a search warrant, possibly even an arrest warrant in case it was needed. It was absurd, of course, I had nothing to hide. But I knew they were quite capable of sitting on me till I missed my plane and I didn't care to have my plans disarranged. So I grabbed my ticket and passport and headed off, leaving Kim to put the rest of my things together and bring them to the airport.

'When Kim joined me at Heathrow, what she told me disturbed me. She'd just finished packing when Angelica arrived. Kim thought she'd been drinking a bit. Kim explained what she was doing and Angelica helped her finish off the packing. According to Kim, she was talking rather wildly about packing up herself and catching the first flight to Venezuela. She was sick of this country, its hypocrisies, its lies. She assured Kim she could tell her things which would make her set off back to South Korea in disgust. And she said she was in the mood before she went to let the Great British public know what kind of people were running their country.

'Kim was concerned. She'd never seen your mother like this before. But they were interrupted by a ringing at the doorbell. It might have been Special Branch or perhaps SIS, though Kim got the impression that Angelica was expecting someone too. Anyway, your mother said she'd take care of it and Kim slipped out of the back entrance and joined me at the airport.

'I tried ringing the house but got no reply. I was half inclined to go back, but Kim dissuaded me. Angelica was far from incapable in any sense of the word. My flight had been called already, so I left, telling myself that Paris was only a couple of hours from London in any case. I remember regretting it almost as soon as we took off and I must have appeared very nervous and very anxious during the flight, which didn't help me later.

'We took a taxi from Orly to the house of the people we were staying with. My host was a member of the French CP. He was a friend of long standing, one I trusted implicitly. What he told me was quite horrifying. He had just been telephoned by a London contact, someone who knew where I was going, with the news that Angelica was dead.

'Naturally after the initial shock, my first instinct was to head back home. But they persuaded me to wait for more news. Officially there was very little, but by dint of using all possible contacts, mainly a chap in the Venezuelan Embassy and Percy Nostrand, the story was pieced together. Every piece was more horrifying. At an early stage I was taken to another house in case the trail was picked up. I could see no cause to run and hide, but my friends overruled me and for once I was in no fit mental state to go my own way. But even then I just wanted to make sure I had all the facts before I returned.

'Well, as you know, *all* the facts added up to something pretty formidable. All the circumstantial evidence pointed to me. Fingerprints, times, my demeanour on the plane. And above all, your evidence which suggested Angelica might very well have found me in bed with Kim. Added to this was the news that the crime had been discovered by a group of Special Branch men calling on me to 'invite' me to go with them for questioning on some security matters. This rapidly became the equivalent of an arrest warrant. And certainly the following morning there was no doubt that an arrest warrant for me on a murder charge had been sworn out.

'I still wanted to go back, Lem, but everyone argued against it. This was no accident, I was assured. This was a carefully organized plot to discredit me and to silence your mother at the same time. A man I knew from the Soviet Embassy in Paris was brought to see me. He offered me the security of his own country as a base from which to conduct my defence. No strings attached. I would be there merely as a visitor, not as a defector. I took a lot of persuading. But in the end I was persuaded.'

'Bravo!' I applauded. 'That took a lot of guts, Pa. Running like that against your will. I must learn that trick of persuading you to do something you don't want to do. How did it go again? Oh, I'm sorry. I'm interrupting. Do carry on with your interesting tale.'

It was childish stuff, but in my father's presence, I always felt a child.

'I'm not sure it's worth the effort, Lem,' he said. 'But as we're not doing anything else, either of us, just for the moment, I'll persevere. I went to Moscow, I called a press conference, I proclaimed my innocence. All those newspaper jackals wanted to know was whether I was applying for Soviet citizenship and whether I intended to marry Kim. I got angry, I'm afraid, and I recall letting them know at some length just what sort of monsters held the so-called free world in chains.

'In the end I gave up in disgust. The choice had become very simple. Return to face a false but superbly orchestrated accusation which would almost certainly get me locked up for twenty years, or stay in Moscow where I was honoured and respected and offered every facility to work. The logic was inescapable. I had to stay. Anything else would have been an emotionally self-indulgent gesture.'

I said, 'I know the feeling, Pa. I decided much the same about my initial impulse to go under with *Vita 3*. It was inescapable logic that made me decide to run with the money.'

He said icily, 'The cases are scarcely parallel.'

But almost immediately he relaxed and added, 'Though perhaps the psychologies are. And you too will naturally resist the truth which has made a mockery of so many years of your life as I resisted the truth that made a mockery of mine. Though, curiously, the circumstances of our learning it are not dissimilar. What odd parallels of experience seem to exist between us, Lem!'

'You mean you were in captivity in an Italian villa when you found out the truth?' I implied, still attempting mockery.

'No,' he said. 'I was in a hospital ward. I was listening to my wife, Kim. She was unburdening herself. You see, she was dying of a cervical cancer.'

The word shocked the frivolity out of me, reminding me of what I was, what I must expect.

I said, 'And Kim told you …?'

He sighed and said, 'Kim told me what should have been utterly clear all those years ago, that I had indeed been the victim of a plot, but not an imperfect plot which I'd been able in part at least to thwart. No, this plot had succeeded perfectly, for its ends had been to silence Angelica and to get me to Moscow. It had been laid by the KGB.'

I was reduced to silence. Curiously, it was not the shock of what he was telling me that had this effect, but something else, something implied …

I said, 'And Kim knew this all the time and had never thought to mention it? I mean, you married her, you shared her bed!'

'A quaint phrase.' He laughed. 'Yes, I shared her bed all those years and she never said a word. Though, ironically, since she told me, I have shared her bed again and her words have never been out of my mind. Oh, don't judge Kim too harshly, Lem. Yes, you've surely guessed, she was a KGB agent, and she may have kept quiet in the first place because of her political loyalties. But I loved her and she loved me and in the end she kept quiet for love. To speak of such things especially in an official apartment would have been far too dangerous for either of us. Even in a hospital or a death-bed it was scarcely safe.'

I cut in on him, for now it had come to me. Two things he had said with implications I could not ignore.

I said, 'Pa, when you said these circumstances were not dissimilar and then that crack about sharing her bed after you'd heard her confession …'

He nodded approvingly.

'How sharp of you, Lem. I was going to tell, not out of any wish for sympathy, but because I should like you to know, in the remote contingency of your feeling impelled to take any risk on my behalf, that there's no need to bother. By one of life's little ironies, during my visits to Kim I began to feel unwell myself. I was in the right place for a swift diagnosis. It had more of tragic inevitability than tragic shock when I was told that I too was suffering from cancer.'

I have not often startled my father but now I startled him. I let out a great whoop of laughter. It had as much of outrage and protest and savagery in it as humour, but it was still a laugh. He stared at me, amazed.

'Forgive me, Pa,' I said with a kind of desperate gaiety. 'These odd parallels you talk about just keep on going on and on. Still, it's nice after all these years to find we have so much in common!'

Now it was his turn to work things out. I could see he was finding it hard to let himself get there.

I nodded. 'Right, Pa,' I said. 'Me too. In the gut. I'm not making any plans for Christmas.'

To my horror I saw his face contort with distress and those sharp blue eyes of his go hazy as though at the approach of tears.

That would have been unbearable.

I jumped up and grabbed his shoulders and began to shake.

'Laugh, Pa! It's a joke, isn't it? Grisly but clever, eh? You taught me that there's a laugh in nearly everything if you look for it! So look for the laugh, Pa! look for the laugh!'

I set an example by throwing back my head in an unconvincing bellow. Suddenly he joined in. For a moment our combined efforts were merely cacophonous and near-hysterical. Then all at once the rhythms of real laughter took over. We giggled and chortled and guffawed; we exploded, holding on to each other as the peals of amusement sent us rocking round the room. I don't know about Pa, but I hadn't laughed like this for twenty years. And the laughter allowed our faces to be stained with those tears that our psyches needed but our sensibilities did not dare to show.

After a while the door opened and Major Krylov came into

the room, his automatic at the ready. The sight of his face set us off again and another couple of minutes elapsed before it was worth his while trying to speak. But he waited patiently with the sad, knowing expression of a serious man who could put a stop to this misplaced jollity whenever he liked.

He was right.

He said finally, 'I have visitors for you.'

And the laughter stopped as he waved Vasco and Angelica into the room.

. . . all good friends together . . .

I went towards my daughter and said, 'Angelica ...'

'My name's Angie,' she interrupted angrily. '*Angie,* you hear?'

She was strung out to breaking-point. Vasco put his arms around her and drew her down on to the floor in the corner. I stood over them feeling helpless. We were back to square one. Their world had been invaded by strange, violent, old men and they trusted only each other now. I couldn't blame them. Krylov must have whistled up reinforcements from somewhere and had them intercepted on their way in to Amalfi. Now on their return to the villa they found armed men in control and, more bewilderingly still, these two strange creatures, so recently at each other's throats, now embraced in helpless laughter.

It struck me with a shock that in my daughter's eyes, standing before her were the men who between them had murdered both her mother and her grandmother.

I wanted to speak, but no words came. Pa grasped my arm and drew me back to the bed. He shook his head slightly but commandingly as I opened my mouth, and he resumed his narrative as though we had been uninterrupted.

'I had an exploratory operation in the small intestine,' he said as if he were talking of a visit to the dentist. 'They cut away, but the prognosis was bad. A few months, a year at the most. Everyone was very kind. They are kind people, the Russians. Most of them. I dare say even Krylov loves dogs and his old grandmother. He was very decent when we talked just before my operation.'

'You knew Krylov in Moscow?' I said.

'Just vaguely. But I put in a request for a chat with someone in the KGB before I went into hospital and he came along. You see, it had occurred to me that it was very likely my last conversation with Kim had been bugged. Or, even if it wasn't, that the KGB would simply assume Kim had told me all. In either case, it would be very convenient for them if I died under the anæsthetic. So I saw Krylov and repeated to him exactly what Kim had told me.

'For God's sake, why?' I exploded.

'To save my life, of course,' said Pa patiently. 'In fact it was quite clear that the KGB knew exactly what Kim had told me. I think Krylov had been put on the case because he'd actually been in London for a time at the start of his career and knew many of the people concerned. He made no effort to deny what Kim had told me. Why should he? An old man, full of cancer, shortly to be operated on. I must have seemed a good security risk! He was all smiles, but the smiles stopped when I told him I'd prepared a full transcript of what Kim had told me and arranged for it to be smuggled to the West to be delivered in the event of my death.'

'Delivered? Who to?'

He looked almost apologetic as he said, 'To you, of course, Lem. Who else? Though naturally I didn't tell them that. I had no desire to involve you in any unnecessary risk. Krylov pretended not to believe me, but I could see he knew I was telling the truth. He also knew that I had advertised my imminent operation widely among my acquaintances in the foreign embassies. News of my death would be impossible to conceal or even contain. So I survived the operation. But they can't have been happy when the surgeon revealed that my life expectation was severely limited.'

'Pa,' I said, 'what the hell is it that Kim told you that still worries them so much after all these years? And who's got this transcript now?'

I got the old exasperated look again. He pulled his left ear lobe and his eyes flickered towards the youngsters. He was telling me that we might well be bugged even now as we spoke and the less that Vasco and Angie knew of things, the better their chances of survival.

I said, 'How did you get out?'

'It was surprisingly easy,' he answered. 'I made an excellent and rapid recovery from my operation. It's not unusual,

I gather. A short Indian Summer before the Fall. But I let on that I was a weak and decrepit old man. They sent me to convalesce in a sanatorium near Odessa on the Black Sea. They were glad to get me out of Moscow, I suspect, while they did everything in their power to track the exit route of Kim's confession. I meanwhile was planning my own exit route. To cut a long story short, I got into Jugoslavia via Romania. I have many old friends in Jugoslavia from the war. Communists, of course, but with no great love of the Soviets. They kept me under cover till they could arrange my passage. I was ferried in a fishing boat across the Adriatic from Split to Manfredonia. The next stop was to be Rome.'

'For the press conference?'

He looked at me in puzzlement and said, 'There was to be no press conference. It was merely to be a staging-post on my way back to England. I had someone I could trust there.'

'Teresa,' I said.

He nodded. I glanced across at Vasco whose defensive posture had relaxed considerably. As for Angie, the tension had almost vanished from her face and she was listening raptly.

'But you hadn't seen her for twenty years!' I said.

'Not so long,' he said. 'She came to Moscow twice with Carducci who was on various delegations. We met the first time by accident at an official reception. It was strange. She'd always kept very quiet about the Bessacarr connection. Noble bastardy is usually something the Italians are quite happy to boast about. Even when we met, she gave no sign of recognition. Well, we met again privately and we talked. If we aroused suspicion it was only that the lecherous old Englishman was trying to seduce the signora. As I say, she came to Moscow twice. And she wrote. I had a friend at the … at one of the foreign embassies who let me use their bag for any incoming or outgoing mail I wanted to keep private.'

'So you were actually in Rome?' I said.

He shook his head.

'I never got there. Perhaps fortunately, as I found out later that my plans were leaked in Manfredonia and Krylov would have been waiting for me along the road. The strain of all the journeys had been too much and I was taken ill. I needed somewhere completely safe and preferably a bit remote to recuperate. So I came here.'

'But why *here*, for God's sake?' I cried.

He smiled. 'Didn't you know, Lem? You remember dear old Cousin Giulio with his plans for a hotel? Well, he tried it, eventually went bankrupt, of course – he could have bankrupted King Solomon's mines, given a free hand for a week – and lived alone in a corner of the place till he died ten years ago. He would have sold the villa, obviously, but under the terms of Grandmama's will, he only had a life interest in it which passed to me after his death. When I go, it will pass to you.'

'Bets?' I said jocularly. I wished I hadn't. As he remembered, an expression of weary pain crossed his face.

'I'm sorry,' he said.

'But all these people, Heathcliff, that is to say, Giorgio and his mates, who the hell are they?'

'They're refugees from the earthquake in the mountains last year,' he said. 'I hadn't been here, of course, but I'd arranged through an agent – an estate agent I mean! – in the town to have a caretaker living in the villa. When I read about the devastation of the earthquake, not to mention the administrative chaos that followed, I sent instructions for the property to be made available to the refugees. During the winter I gather there were about sixty here. Most of them went back to their villages in the spring, but about a dozen stayed on. They're good people, tight-lipped, hating authority but tremendously loyal. When my Jugoslav friends brought me here and explained that I was the villa's owner and that all that I wanted from them was a place to stay in peace and quiet, they asked no questions but took me in and cared for me and kept their mouths shut. And when they saw that I was in some kind of danger, they rallied round to help, unasked. I hope to God none of them has been hurt!'

There he goes! I thought, half irritated, half admiring. The big humanitarian gesture even from Moscow, and that aristocratic inspiration of loyalty even, or perhaps inevitably, to the point of discomfort and danger.

'For once in your life, Pa, begin your charity at home,' I

said. 'We're all family in here. Let's take care of our own.'

I may have sounded more reproachful than I intended. He responded by saying, 'It's not my fault they're here, Lem. I let Teresa know why I hadn't turned up. A couple of weeks later I had a reply via the Carduccis saying that she'd learned through various CP contacts of her own that the Soviets had known I was heading for Rome and that one of their safe houses at Ostia was now occupied by a couple of English-women called Swift. I asked her to find out more about them, especially the younger. She turned Vasco loose on the beach, I gather, and he soon came up with their identity and background. I'm afraid that Angie didn't paint a very promising picture of you, and when you turned up, he played safe and got her out.'

'Bringing me and Krylov with him,' I said bitterly.

'You weren't to know the Russians and British were hand in hand on this one,' said Pa consolingly.

And I still didn't really understand why. But what was quite clear was that I could abandon any hope of the Brigadier and Reilly busting in mobhanded to do a US cavalry rescue act.

But looking on the positive side, at least I now had the chance to achieve the goal which had drawn me from the lotus-life on Isla da Margarita after all those years.

I went across to Angie. Vasco regarded me with suspicion. I said in Italian, 'Please, I would like to talk with my daughter.' He still didn't move, but Pa joined me and took him by the arm and led him to the other side of the room.

Angie was leaning back against the wall, her long legs crossed in a half-lotus position. She didn't look at me.

I squatted beside her, bones and muscles protesting.

I said, 'Angie, I'm bitterly sorry for what I did to your mother.'

She looked at me now in alarm and pain and said, 'You said it wasn't you!'

So she wanted to believe me. That was good.

'It wasn't,' I hastened to assure her. 'I didn't harm her, I swear. But it was because of me she was there.'

'Yes,' she said fiercely. 'Why did you have to come back?'

She had to be told, though I felt a great reluctance to do so.

Partly because I did not want to pain her – but also partly because I feared to see that it did not pain her enough. My usual reasonings – the bullshit and the asshole – only this time they both happened to be true.

I compromised a little and said, 'I've been ill, very ill. I got to worrying I might die without seeing you again. So I came back to talk with you, which I'm now doing.'

'So I'd have a happy memory to cherish when I was old and grey?' she said.

She had a sharp tongue and a lot of spirit. I liked that. If I wasn't doing anything else, at least I was provoking her out of depression.

I said, 'I'm not so optimistic nor so sentimental. But I didn't think I could leave you with a worse memory than running off and abandoning you when you were only six.'

'Didn't you? You've come pretty close,' she said.

'I know. I'm sorry.' I sighed deeply, feeling myself close to floundering. 'Listen. Memories are … memories. Good or bad, they have no substance, mustn't be allowed to have substance …'

She looked at me blankly.

I pressed on, like a man lost in deep snow.

'Once you let them become substantial, they accrete more and more … substance … and in the end they can become- … cancerous.'

'What do you mean?' she said.

'I've got a couple of memories,' I said. 'One of them is about a swimming competition. I used to be pretty hot stuff in the water, did anyone ever tell you that?'

'I think Uncle Percy mentioned it,' she said slowly. 'He often told me … nice things about you.'

Good old Percy. It must have been like trying to oppose tanks with a sling-shot.

'This memory is of the summer of 1963. I swam for England – well, for an England team,' I went on. 'I was a last-minute substitute. No one imagined I could be anything but a respectable last, least of all me. But Mama – your grandmother – came to watch, and I wanted so desperately to do well that somehow I excelled myself. I won. Everyone was delighted, of course, but it was Mama's delight that mattered. She was so happy. So proud. So beautiful.'

I fell silent.

'That sounds like a good memory,' said Angie softly.

'And then there's another,' I said, almost to myself now. 'The same year. Mama with blood streaming from her head. So still, so pale. The last time I ever saw her.'

Angie said nothing now, but I could guess who she was thinking of.

'Listen, darling,' I said urgently. 'The point is, they're both just memories. But I let them root themselves in my mind and grow and gain substance, so that one became the last good thing that ever happened to me and the other a bad thing that would keep on happening for ever.'

She made a raft of her fingers between her legs and stared down at it.

'The last good thing,' she echoed. Again I felt I could read her thought.

'There were other good things,' I tried to explain. 'I was married and that was good for a while. And you were born. That was always good. But those two dominant memories made these other good things seem like some kind of betrayal. The memories were always making demands on me, urging me on ...'

I tailed off feeling that this was hopeless. These incoherent babblings could only be convincing her that she had been fathered by the dangerous lunatic the Brigadier had warned against. I had to be absolutely explicit with no subtle shades of meaning to hide myself in.

I said very distinctly, 'I wanted to hurt my father. It was the most important thing in my life. I couldn't get at him direct, so without thinking almost, instinctively, intuitively, I set out to hurt the things he loved. I destroyed what he had laboured to create. And myself also; I destroyed myself.'

I looked across the room. Pa's eyes were fixed on me. I couldn't read the emotion in his face. I said slowly, 'I suppose I feared or suspected or recognized that he loved me. And that was what I set out to destroy, above all. His love for me as I thought he had destroyed mine for him.'

Angie said quietly, 'And Mummy and I were just ... unimportant.'

'No!' I said fiercely. 'Kate and I were far apart, I admit that. We both drifted, *both* of us. But you were never unimportant.'

'Less important then,' she said. 'You felt you could sacrifice us for a greater good.'

She spoke in a cool, objective voice like some aged philosophy don pursuing a point in a seminar. I looked at my father once more in despair. To my surprise, I had no difficulty now interpreting his expression. It was angry exasperation, the look he always wore when he felt I was missing what lay right under my nose.

I looked back to Angie. Her face was a blank, but not her eyes. And suddenly it dawned on me that this measured, impersonal manner wasn't just a way of distancing events, nor even of simply grasping them. No, in a mad way she was trying to please me. I was conscientiously talking to her as though she were a self-possessed adult, and she was trying to live up to my apparent expectations! Yet everything that had happened to her that day must be making her long to be encouraged to react as a terrified and comfortless child.

Awkwardly I put my arms around her. For a moment she was stiff and unyielding. Then, as though through some violent chemical change her substances had deliquesced in a second, she slumped against me and sobbed against my chest as if every sorrow of her neglected childhood were fighting for passage through her slender throat.

This time I made no attempt to change tears into laughter.

We were still clinging together a few minutes later when Krylov came into the room.

'I hadn't realized what emotional depths the British conceal,' he remarked. 'I'm sorry, Mr Swift, but I must ask you and your father to come with me.'

I glanced round at him. He was smiling with that melancholy, sympathetic smile of his, but there was nothing sympathetic about the way he was holding the pistol. Angie's sobs died away, but she clung to me even more tightly and I had to exert my strength to break her grip.

'Listen,' I said urgently. 'Eventually there will be money for you. Whether you take it or not must be your decision. But understand, it came from my arms deals. It came from all kinds of governments and all kinds of political persuasions. What you feel about that is up to you. But whatever was said at the time or has been said since, not a penny of it came from donations to the Bessacarr Trust. Every penny of every charitable donation was spent in the way proposed. Believe that.'

'What do you mean?' she cried. 'Why are you talking about money? I'll see you again, won't I? What's going to happen to you?'

'Nothing,' I said. 'Nothing. Believe me. I just wanted you to know, that's all. Of course I'll see you soon, back in Rome probably. Right, Major?'

'Of course, Mr Swift,' he said courteously. 'We just have one or two small business matters to sort out. So if you will step this way, gentlemen.'

I rose, pulling Angie with me, and led her across to Vasco.

'Take care of her, nephew,' I said.

For the first time ever he looked at me with something other than aggressive distrust and nodded. I kissed Angie and she clung to me once more. That disturbing eroticism of my first impressions had disappeared entirely. Psychologically we were in our proper relationship at last.

'Goodbye, love,' I said. 'I'll see you soon.'

Pa kissed her next, a grandfatherly peck. He did this kind of thing so much better than me. It was impossible to believe he regarded this as anything more than a brief, inconsequential separation.

'*Ciao*,' he said.

He went out. I followed him, I glanced back and gave what I hoped was a reassuring smile to Angie, but the look of tragic loss on her face did not change and I would have gone back inside. But Krylov pulled the door to and locked it and handed the key to Vasari who was standing in the corridor with the shotgun at the port.

'Please to walk, Mr Swift,' the Major said. 'But do not stop smiling, either of you. We are all good friends together, for a little while longer at least. Now *move!*'

. . . a bit of rope . . .

What he meant by being good friends was made clear to us in a few graphic sentences as we walked towards the stairs. The peasants (as Krylov contemptuously referred to them) needed reassurance that all was well. Pa was to give them that reassurance. With his customary incisiveness, Pa got the matter absolutely clear.

'You mean there are too many of them to dispose of?'

'Not necessarily. But it would be inconvenient.'

'And if I refuse?'

'Then your granddaughter and grandson will suffer.'

'And if they won't believe me?'

'They'll believe you,' Krylov said, laughing. 'It's a good set-up they have here. The last thing they want is policemen and officials all over the place. They'll believe you because they *want* to believe you.'

'And what happens after that?'

'To whom?'

'My grandchildren.'

'They go free,' said Krylov. 'They keep quiet because you reassure them all is well, and also because they know we have the two of you.'

'Ah yes,' said Pa. 'The two of us. And what will you do with the two of us?'

Krylov's face expressed a kind of pedantic puzzlement.

'But surely it is understood? Nothing. We merely have to keep you a little while and do nothing, isn't that the situation?'

Pa wasn't the only one with an instinct for clarity.

The meeting took place in the villa's main room, a long cool salon lying behind the terrace on which I had so ill-advisedly attempted to kill my father. The refugees were represented by five men including my old friends from the cellar, Giorgio and Piero. Krylov had tucked his pistol out of sight and entered the room with his hands resting familiarly on our shoulders like a friendly host escorting a couple of honoured guests in to supper.

I felt a great impulse to take his arm and break it slowly in several places. Though if I broke it quickly in only one place, perhaps I could get to the goon (a new face this) outside the door before he could use his machine-pistol or raise the alarm. And having done that, perhaps I could make it upstairs and blow away Vasari. Of course, I'd no idea how many more reinforcements were hanging around the villa, but none the less it was a matter for serious consideration.

In the event it took less than a second for me to decide.

For as I stepped into the salon, I realized that the peasants were not alone.

With his back to me, seated on a hard chair before the standing group, was a grey-haired figure. He was speaking in a rapid but highly anglicized Italian. I recognized the clipped tones and the clipped hair at the same moment.

It was the Brigadier.

And there, looking soulfully out of an open window across the Tyrrhenian Sea like a fairy-tale princess waiting to be rescued, except that not many fairy-tale princesses wear Gucci jeans and a string vest, was Reilly.

The odds had lengthened. Krylov's arm was safe for a little longer.

The Brigadier looked round, stood up and came towards us, hand outstretched, official smile creasing his Empire tan.

'Lord Bessacarr! Mr Swift! How nice to see you both. How are you?'

He shook our hands energetically, talking all the while in a mixture of English and Italian, the former being used to tell us that in the eyes of the peasants he was a representative of the British Consul in Naples, the latter to assure the peasants that Her Gracious Majesty, the Queen of England, would be glad to learn her subjects were in such good health after the little series of misunderstandings. His audience received these ramblings with the stoic indifference they deserved. There was only one man they wanted to hear.

Pa did his job perfectly. There had been trouble. It was now sorted out. Soon they would all be leaving and life at the Villa Colonna would become normal again. He was grateful for their help and their loyalty. He hoped they would continue as his honoured guests in the villa as long as they wished.

A bottle of *grappa* was produced, glasses filled. We all toasted each other solemnly. Reilly, who had been studiously ignoring the proceedings, came wandering across when the scent of booze hit her broad-flared nostrils.

'Here's looking at you, Reilly,' I said.

'Motherfucker,' she replied, taking me aback till I recalled that last time we'd met I'd had to thump her.

'Don't be a bad loser, Reilly,' I said.

'You look terrible,' she said, examining my swollen ears critically. 'I'm glad to see someone's started what I hope to finish.'

'I rather think you've lost your place in the queue,' I said. 'Besides, you've had your own back. It was you who rang Krylov at Teresa's apartment to say I was probably on my way, wasn't it?'

She nodded.

I said. 'Don't feel too bad about it, Reilly. At least it stopped him pulling her fingers off their joints.'

It was strange, she was as much my enemy as anyone else here, but the sight of those squashed up features beneath that lurid hair, not to mention those swelling breasts straining against her string vest like the fresh pink piglets against the chicken wire round the column stump, moved me like a friendly face in a jury-box.

I said, 'Reilly, listen. You know they've got my daughter upstairs? Keep an eye on her for me, will you?'

She looked at me uneasily but didn't speak. The Italians were being ushered out of the room, each solemnly shaking Pa's hand in turn. The rest of us they ignored.

I said to Krylov, 'You certainly know how to relate to the workers, comrade.'

He smiled and said, 'The class characteristics of the peasantry are just as dangerous to the revolution as those of the bourgeoisie or the aristocracy.'

'Hell,' I said, 'As an aristocratic peasant with bourgeois tastes, that makes me a pretty dangerous creature, don't you think?'

'Hard to breed in captivity, certainly,' he replied.

The door closed behind the last of the peasants. The guy with the machine-pistol was now inside the room, I noticed.

'Well, that seemed to go pretty well, I thought,' said the Brigadier with the satisfaction of one who has just presided over a rather delicate social occasion.

'Awfully well,' I agreed. 'So, what now, friends? A rubber of bridge?'

The Brigadier looked at me with faint distaste. Frivolity should be reserved for the Mess, after the loyal toast. Here we were on the field of battle.

'I think you can leave the rest safely with us,' said Krylov. 'Goodbye, Brigadier. Safe journey home.'

'And you,' said the Brigadier. 'Come along, Miss Reilly.'

I coughed and interrupted their progress to the door.

'Aren't you forgetting something?' I asked.

'I don't think so.'

'I'm your responsibility,' I suggested. 'We had a deal.'

'So we did,' said the Brigadier. 'Something about – you kill your father and we'll let you see your daughter, wasn't it? Well, you've seen your daughter, I understand, though you don't seem to have killed your father. So on the whole I reckon you've done rather well out of it, wouldn't you say?'

They left. Reilly didn't even look back at me. That's the payment you get for kindness. I wished I'd broken her head open when I knocked her out in Rome!

During these exchanges Pa had seated himself at a table by a window and was once more deeply immersed in his book. Krylov went and stood behind him and peered over his shoulder. They made a perfect study for a picture of the comtemplative life. Pa with his white hair and patrician face was the Father Superior guiding some devout young theologian through the intricacies of an ancient text.

'What now?' I demanded, strangely irritated by the pacific scene.

'In a little while we will depart,' said Krylov. 'In Naples

harbour is a Bulgarian freighter, discharging its cargo. We join the ship and enjoy a pleasant summer cruise through the Mediterranean and into the Black Sea. There your father will resume his interrupted convalescent holiday, this time accompanied and attended by his devoted son. Is that not a pleasing prospect?'

'And meanwhile?'

'Meanwhile we remain here quietly under the same constraints as before.'

He smiled in a displeasingly self-satisfied manner. I felt a strong urge once more to do his arm some large damage, but he was right. The constraints remained. A machine-pistol at my back and Angie helpless upstairs.

Then to my horror I saw Pa's body tense. He sent out more signals than Nelson's flagship. But what the attack lacked in physical surprise, it certainly made up in sheer unlikelihood and for a second the disbelieving Major hesitated as Pa made his kamikaze approach, chopping at his head with the book he held. Then the inevitable reaction set in. One deep-driven punch to the stomach was enough to send Pa crashing to the floor. Even then he didn't give up, but came wriggling back like some cumbersome snake across the polished marble, shouting in rage and pain till Krylov leaned down and stunned him with a chop across the neck.

I was meanwhile standing helpless with the other man's pistol rammed hard against my spine.

Krylov rubbed the side of his head where the weighty volume had fittingly raised a patch of angry red.

'I see we must use other more physical constraints!' he said. 'It will be more convenient anyway. Come!'

Pa was dragged to his feet and given into my care which effectively neutralized me. We were waved to the terrace door with pistols. Krylov whistled softly and yet another goon emerged from the darkness. He murmured something to the Major, assuring him (I presumed) that the peasants were quiet, and the next thing we were bundled down the stairs, through the kitchen and into the corridor which led to the cellar. The damaged cellar door hung from its hinges, but that was not our destination. One of the store rooms was unlocked and we were thrust inside. Here all the sailing gear had once been kept and in the dim light I could see that some of it still remained. There was certainly a great variety and length of rope and under Krylov's supervision we were firmly bound and finally gagged with strips of sail-cloth.

Then our captors retreated without saying a word, locking the door behind them and leaving us in pitch blackness.

I lay there in helpless fury, aimed in equal parts at the Brigadier for callously abandoning us, at Krylov for ruthlessly mishandling us, and at my father for his stupidity in provoking this reaction. At least before, we had freedom of movement, and though it seemed that a wise passivity might in the end have proven the best policy, I'd rather be passive in comfort than passive because I was trussed like a Christmas goose. And God knew what stuffing the Major had in mind for us!

I tried to shift first my bonds and then my gag, but rapidly abandoned both efforts, the one threatening to shut off circulation of blood completely and the other of air.

Then to my amazement out of the darkness came Pa's voice.

'That's better,' he said, breathing noisily. 'Ah, what memories the smell of this place brings back, eh Lem?' I managed a convulsive wriggle and he said contritely, 'I'm sorry, old chap. It must be terribly irritating to be addressed without the power of reply. An old man's mouth is a curiously elastic thing and I took the precaution of achieving maximum inflation as they gagged me, so I haven't had to do much more than collapse my cheeks to get this confounded gag to slip. I dare say if you had the power of speech you would be inclined to reprimand me for having so precipitously drawn down the wrath of our captors upon us. All I can do is remind you of the fine old tale of Brer Rabbit and the bramble bush which I am sure I must have told you in your angel infancy.'

There I lay, bound, gagged, locked up in Stygian gloom, and my blessed father was *still* prodding me to work things out for myself!

'Yes, you're quite right, Lem,' he resumed after a longish pause (a shorter one might have been more flattering, but he was probably making allowances for circumstances). '*This* is where I want to be. Or somewhere like it, out of their immediate supervision. But *this* will do perfectly. As long as we remained in Krylov's company on apparently friendly terms, there would be doubt. We had to get ourselves separated from him in the most unfriendly way possible.'

Another pause.

'How would they know we were separated, you ask? Well, firstly, you do not watch a Campanian peasant without him knowing he is watched. And *that* provokes both his resentment and his curiosity. So he watches back. Shortly someone will be dispatched to investigate.'

An hour later, no one had come and it's a curious comment on the human mind that even though my personal survival was involved, the bonds having reduced the flow of my blood to a barely sufficient trickle, I was still able to feel a certain gleeful delight that at last he was going to be proved wrong! It was premature, of course. I should have known. He was always bloody well right!

There was a muffled noise outside and the sound of a key being cautiously turned in the lock. Then the door swung open and a pale cone of torchlight drifted over us.

It was Giorgio. He untied Pa first and waited till he got an affirmative nod before untying me. He and Pa whispered together as he performed this task. Finally, with a show of some reluctance, Giorgio retreated. What the whispering was about, I didn't catch. I was too busy listening to my own internalized shrieking as the blood forced its way back through my blocked veins.

Pa seemed much less affected than me. Perhaps he'd inflated his limbs too or perhaps at his age the veins are already narrowed beyond further restriction. He knelt beside me and massaged my legs while I flexed my upraised hands in the classic strip-cartoon gesture of barely repressed hatred. It was aimed at restoring the circulation but it was also a very adequate expression of my current state of mind.

'Where's Giorgio gone?' I asked when at last I felt able to open my mouth without shrieking.

Any hopes I'd had of leading a peasants' revolt against Krylov and his friends disappeared when Pa replied, 'I've told him to go back to his family and stay there. This isn't their fight.'

'Not their fight? Jesus, Pa, this is a hell of a time to rediscover your aristocratic principles! What's happened to the good old working-class struggle?'

'I will not be party to setting up women and children against machine-pistols in the hands of ruthless men,' he said coldly.

'You won't? Aren't you forgetting that there's already a couple up there, one a woman, both scarcely more than children, being held by those same fucking men!'

I felt rather than saw him wince in æsthetic pain at my language. Americanisms he deplored, obscenities he plain hated.

'It's still not their fight,' he said. 'They have suffered enough already. Besides, what could they do against experts with guns?'

'More than us alone,' I retorted. 'But let's get to it.'

He gripped my arm as I moved towards the door.

'No,' he said. 'We can't go up against them, Lem.'

'Not go against them? They've got Angie and Vasco!'

'That's precisely why it would be no contest, don't you see? If we attack, which in any case would be suicidal, all they'll do is bring out the children and threaten to shoot them before our eyes.'

'Then why the hell go to all this trouble to set us free?' I demanded. 'You've just made a good argument for taking Krylov's deal and going along quietly.'

He released me and was searching around the storeroom. In the dim light from the open door I saw him pick up a heavy coil of rope.

'You don't really believe that'll guarantee their safety?' he asked. 'I know the KGB mind, Lem. The moment we're safely on our way to Mother Russia, those youngsters will be silenced. No witnesses. Believe me!'

I stared at him in horror.

'No witnesses? But what about all these peasants?'

'What do they know? In any case they're by nature a stolid, quiet lot when the Law's around. But Vasco and Angie are different. There'll probably be an accident.'

'Accident?' I said stupidly.

'Yes. Bathing perhaps. Or more likely on the road. There are some very nasty bends up there, Lem. An inexperienced and reckless young driver could easily put a car over the edge.'

'But if we escape,' I protested, 'surely Krylov ...'

'Will do nothing till he has us back. Their value then to him is *alive*.'

'They're still witnesses,' I objected.

'With us loose, who's worried about witnesses?' replied Pa. As always, his reasoning overwhelmed me. But I wasn't happy.

He slung the coil of rope over my shoulder and beckoned me to follow him.

'What's this for?' I asked savagely. 'Are you planning to challenge them to a tug-of-war?'

'You never know when a bit of rope'll come in handy,' he replied.

We moved out quietly and found the kitchen deserted. The lingering cooking smells made me recall that I'd had nothing to eat since my stale doughnut at breakfast. My stomach was tight and aching. I hope it was just hunger. I picked up a hunk of bread from the table and began to gnaw it. When Pa looked at me impatiently, I said, 'Man cannot live by rope alone.'

We set off up the stairs that led to the salon level, but the sound of voices on the landing sent us into hasty retreat. We went back through the kitchen and out on to the small kitchen terrace. For the moment a low moon was flooding the cliff-face with light but a menacing tide of black cloud was blowing up from the south and though the sea looked calm enough from our height, I could see the old fishing tub at its moorings below begin to rock in the swell. The thought crossed my mind that it really ought to be taken out into the little bay and anchored before the winds started rattling it against the landing platform.

But the voices were still pursuing us and I put the weather out of my mind. If the people coming downstairs into the kitchen checked the storeroom, the hunt would be up immediately. Keeping low, we ran along the kitchen terrace and across the drive. Standing in front of the garage was a large black Mercedes, probably the same one that I'd seen departing from the front of Teresa's apartment.

I looked interrogatively at Pa but he shook his head. He was right. Given time, I'd no doubt I could start it without keys, but time we did not have. We kept on going down the narrow flagged track which led to the lift. The door was open and we took shelter inside.

We could see the kitchen terrace quite clearly in the moonlight. Through the doorway came a group of people. I felt Pa's hand grasp my wrist tightly as we saw Vasco and Angie in their midst.

Between them, hands familiarly on their shoulders, was Krylov. He seemed to be talking in a friendly, reassuring fashion. When they reached the Mercedes, he gallantly opened the rear door and ushered the youngsters inside.

After what Pa had just said, the sight of the children getting into the car filled me with alarm. I glanced at Pa who looked worried too, but shook his head. I thought I followed his reasoning. They were hardly like to stage an accident in the Mercedes which was, first, not Vasco's car, and, secondly, would be needed to take us to Naples. Perhaps they were merely transferring them to a safer place, down in the town maybe.

One of the other men had got into the driving seat and a moment later the lights came on and the car moved off towards the road. We couldn't see it from this angle below, but its curving line was clearly marked by the headlights still sweeping along it even at this late hour.

As its tail lights disappeared, the garage door was opened. One of the remaining men went inside and a moment later a red Fiat X1/9 emerged. It had Roman number plates and Roman dents. I watched in puzzlement as it followed the Mercedes up the driveway to the road. I felt Pa's fingers tighten on my arm and I think that the pressure alerted me more than my own ratiocinative powers.

This was Vasco's car, just the kind of vehicle a foolish young man might try to impress his girl-friend in. It would surprise no one if such a car were involved in an accident on the Amalfitano. Somewhere along the road, the X1/9 and the

Mercedes would rendezvous, the children would be transferred to the sports car, there would be a lull in the traffic, and then Krylov would have left no loose ends.

I turned to Pa again, got confirmation from his expression, and sprang from the lift-shaft screaming, 'No! You bastards. No!'

Two ideas motivated me. Once was that perhaps Pa had been right about one thing and if Krylov knew we were free, he would somehow contrive to countermand his orders.

The other was a mad desire to be among those bastards, killing them.

Not that there was much chance of that.

There were only four of them now, Krylov, Vasari, and two others. But they were all armed and any one of them would have been able to turn and cut me to ribbons before I got within five yards.

Two things saved me. One was the clouds which had just reached the moon and now gobbled it up in a second. It was like switching off a light.

The other was Pa, who flung himself after me and with the dexterity of a Rugby League defender tapped my ankle and brought me crashing to the ground.

There was a single burst of fire which stopped as Krylov shouted out angrily. He probably still didn't want to disturb the peasants and could see no reason why he shouldn't be able to recapture a pair of unarmed and cancer-eaten English aristocrats trapped on a sheer cliff-face.

Pa dragged me back into the lift. I didn't resist. Common sense had set in and I knew now that I had to live long enough to get to a phone and alert the police to stop every Merc and X1/9 along the Amalfitana.

I fell over the coil of rope which I'd dropped on the lift floor. Pa was pulling the door shut behind us and hitting the controls. For a moment nothing happened. Why should it? I thought. This contraption must have been defunct for years.

Then slowly, with a nerve-searing grating noise as though it was being dragged by a huge hand against the cliff-face, the lift began to move.

'Well done!' I said to Pa.

I should have kept my mouth shut.

The noise changed for the worse. It was as if someone had thrust a huge bar of metal into the works. Perhaps that was precisely what Krylov had done. Or perhaps it was simply that the old mechanism was suffering like its passengers from the ravages of decay and fatigue.

Whatever the cause about twenty feet down the cliff-face we stopped. We hadn't been going fast enough for the halt to feel violent.

But it certainly felt permanent.

I looked out of the window at the still visible headlights on the winding road high above and knew at last what it felt like to be defeated beyond all hope of recovery.

. . . do you believe in fairies? . . .

Pa was pushing me aside and examining the broad plate-glass window which gave lift-users a panoramic ocean view through the open-grid shaft and doubled as an emergency exit.

'What the hell are you going to do, Pa?' I demanded. 'Fly?'

'Come now, Lem. Surely you remember how to abseil?'

Oh yes! I remembered. How I remembered!

Scared shitless, but even more scared of letting his father know how scared, a small boy walking down a vertical cliff, paying out rope with hands that seemed so far removed from the frozen brain commanding them that every year-long second they felt as if they might flap away from his body like frightened gulls.

'Pa,' I said. 'You can't. For God's sake, in your condition at your age!'

He looked at me in amazement. I suppose it was a significant moment, the first time I'd ever had the temerity to suggest that something might be beyond *his* scope.

'What do *you* suggest?' he asked with calm curiosity, working away at one of the rusted wing nuts which held the window in position. 'Here, help me with this.'

There was nothing to add. The window creaked open on ancient hinges and suddenly there was nothing between us and Sicily. I had to nerve myself to peer downwards. The landing platform and the gently swelling sea can't have been more than a hundred feet below, but in the rich darkness which the rising wind seems to stir like an old velvet curtain, it looked more like a mile.

'What's the point, Pa?' I demanded. 'What are we going to do when we get down there? Sail off into the wild blue yonder in that stinking old tub? It's probably only her mooring line that's keeping her afloat.'

Pa gave me a rather curious smile.

'Here,' he said. 'You go first.'

He was already slipping the rope around me. I opened my mouth to protest again but didn't bother. Protesting to Pa was like making a speech from the gallows. He'd listen patiently till you stopped talking, then open the trap. In the circumstances, perhaps not the best of similes, I realized as I grasped the rope.

'Ready?' said Pa. 'Don't hang about, will you? Once they spot us, speed, I think, may be of the essence.'

He was right. I'd hardly begun my descent when a beam of light shot down from the terrace and picked me out. Dazzled, I missed my footing and swung sideways against the cliff-face knocking the breath out of me, and when I tried to right myself I got temporarily snarled up with the scaffolding of the lift-shaft. If Krylov had cared to use his gun, I'd have been a sitting target, but he must have still reckoned that there were good odds on getting us back to sunny Moscow alive and without fuss. Probably he'd already given assurances and wasn't going to lose face if he didn't have to.

There were shouts from away to my right. They'd found the steps cut in the rock, I guessed. Well, good luck to them. For fifty feet or so they were all right, with a not too rickety wooden balustrade on the outside. Then they began to deteriorate as they reached a stratum of soft, crumbling rock. Suddenly the balustrade was a death-trap, hanging out at a crazy angle. Then it disappeared altogether and the sharp angles of the steps became progressively more round till finally they were merely a series of undulations in a one-in-two descent.

At least that's what it had been like thirty years ago. I could only hope that good old Italian *dolce far niente* had resisted any repairs.

Meanwhile I'd got my rhythm going and was moving down the cliff-face in a series of plunges and runs. Suddenly I was no longer a frightened little boy but a Marine commando who was used to making far worse descents than this, often quite literally before breakfast. Half way down I paused on a ledge. If my memory served me right I would be just about on the same level as the worst part of the old path. The wind was loud in my ears, pressing me to the cliff-face, but I thought I could hear voices in it and the scuffling of shoes on stone. I prised a large chunk of rock loose, set my feet against the side of the lift-shaft and thrust myself off, penduluming towards the pathway. At my outermost point, I hurled the rock upwards and inwards. I had no target to aim at but on those rotten steps even the slightest distraction could be fatal.

The rock hit the cliff and loosened a shower of small flakes which accompanied it in a mini-avalanche. I heard a cry of alarm, a babble of Russian voices, then a long descending scream of terror which competed with the wind's sobs for a few seconds.

There was a sound like a ripe melon bursting as it rolled off a table on to the kitchen floor, and the wind had won.

'Lem! Lem!'

I could hear Pa's piercingly alarmed cry from the lift. Maliciously I waited a moment before giving the rope a jerk and resuming my descent.

When I reached the platform, I jerked twice in signal of success and rushed to where I could see a crumpled figure lying half on the rocks, half in the sea. There was no element of humanitarianism in my haste. I had two hopes; one, that it would be Krylov; two, that there would be a weapon lying close.

I was disappointed in both. It was the stout out-of-condition Italian, Vasari, the least (I suspected) of our adversaries. And if he'd had a gun when he fell, it must have bounced into the sea.

I glanced up. I could hear nothing, but I could see the dark shape of Pa descending the cliff. Even at seventy, he made it look easy.

I turned my attention to the boat, stepping carefully on board for fear of putting my foot through rotten planks.

She was not as bad as I'd thought, but a bloody sight worse. From above I'd merely got the impression of a wallowing tub. Now I realized that she was much narrower in the beam than I'd imagined, but that someone (probably those land-grubbing peasants in the villa who fancied doing a bit of fishing but knew nothing of boats) had attempted to give her more stability by nailing four or five planks across the foredeck and lashing an oil-drum under the bows on either side. Everything about that pathetic botch-up of a boat had the mark not of the amateur, but of the pig-ignorant. The mast was broken off above the forestay. Sailing had obviously proven too difficult. The gooseneck fitting on the mast was bent as if someone had dragged the boom off by main force in order to get rid of this dangerous lump of redundant wood. The foresail halyard was attached and what looked like a spitfire jib was lying creased and sodden across the foredeck. But a couple of oars in the well showed what the principle method of locomotion was, and it looked as if the rudimentary rowlocks had been carved in the gunwale with a hatchet.

The wind was still on shore and rising and every blast sent this ugly duckling of a boat slamming against the landing platform. Elementary fenders in the shape of a couple of plastic bags stuffed with God knows what were absorbing some of the impact, but eventually she'd just be dumped unceremoniously and probably upside down on to the platform surface.

Pa arrived and leapt lightly aboard.

'Time to be on our way,' he said, picking up one of the oars. 'Cast off.'

That proved easier said than done. The stern was made fast by a loop of thin wire hawser dropped over the jut of rock which acted as a bollard and I lifted this off and tossed it into the boat. But the bow was attached by a length of line drawn tight in a sodden and amateurish knot. I could hear voices now and a sudden scatter of small stones. The pursuit was close. Suddenly, as I struggled with the line, it parted behind me, almost precipating me into the sea. Pa had produced a small penknife and cut it at the bow. I fell rather than jumped into the boat, sprawling in inches of foul water and fish scales. The peasants must have met with some success. Pa was pushing us off with one of the oars. I seized the other and dropped it into its crude rowlock. A moment later Pa joined me on the thwart and cried, 'Pull!'

We strained at the oars, fighting against the strong swell which was strengthening by the second and threatening to drive us back against the platform. For a moment it seemed impossible that we could win. We strained at a standstill, then we slid down into the trough of the swell and when we rose up again the gap had widened. Another few strokes and we were out of the greatest turbulence, where water met land.

'Well, Lem,' said Pa in my ear. 'On such a night as this we once sailed to hear the Sirens, remember.'

Again, memory flooded back. It hadn't been such a wild night but wild enough. We had sailed to Positano in the evening and the sudden bad weather had penned us there till late. On the way home with the sea still rough we had diverted to the Isole Galli, those rocky islets which are the traditional home of the Sirens. There we had strained our ears, Pa pretending to hear wild music and enchanted singing, I hearing nothing but the slap of water and the sough of wind. Pa told me laughingly that, like Ulysses' sailors, my ears were full of wax.

I said, 'I wish to God it was *Ariel* we had under us now.'

He laughed quietly and replied, 'I thought you hadn't twigged. It is, boy. It is!'

For a moment I couldn't believe him. Then the truth of what he said hit me and rattled round my mind like a golf ball sliced into a car park. This poor maltreated boat was indeed all that remained of my beloved *Ariel*! How could I have missed it before? I suppose I shouldn't have had anger to spare for such a trivial matter, but anger I felt, strong and hot, as I recalled the times in those golden days when we had slipped away from our mooring like a dolphin racing for the open sea.

I began to speak but Pa shushed me imperatively. The clouds had eaten up the entire sky and only the violence of their movement distinguished them from the looming bulk of the cliff. Darkness so complete was now on the face of the waters that though the distance we'd covered was short, the landing-stage was completely invisible. Except that now the beam of a flashlight bobbed there to show us that Krylov and his men had at last reached the foot of the cliff.

Pa leaned forward to cut down on his silhouette and hide the whiteness of his face. I followed suit and we held the boat steady with our oars. It seemed impossible that they would not spot us at this distance but I reminded myself how small a patch of darkness we were against the shifting shadowy sea, and there are few things blacker than the ocean when it has no sky light to give back again.

Light there was from the torch and this slipped over the waves like Tinker Bell in *Peter Pan*. I felt an insane desire to cry *do you believe in fairies?* at the silent watchers on the shore. But I guessed my answer would come in a hail of bullets. Any inhibition Krylov had about causing a disturbance wasn't going to extend to letting us escape, and besides, as the wind rose now it was unlikely that the noise of their weapons would be audible beyond fifty yards or so.

But if the wind was our enemy as far as noise went, it was becoming our friend for direction. The southerly swell which had been trying to push us inshore began to die away. The wind was veering sharply into the opposite quarter and now we laid our blades flat on the water to preserve stability while minimizing resistance as every second drifted *Ariel* further away from the searching torch.

Pa put an end to my brief delight by pressing his mouth to my ear and murmuring, '*Tramontana*'. I took his point at once. With the wind veering to the north it would soon be coming straight down the steep mountain gorges behind us and exploding out over the sea in one of those violent squalls the local fishermen so feared. Thirty years before we had safely run through one of the worst of these, but those thirty years had not left any of us unscathed, not Pa, or me, and least of all, *Ariel*. I realized with dismay that my feet were already ankle deep in water. One big sea and she would be swamped beyond redemption. The oil drums might keep her afloat but she'd be completely at the mercy of the waves.

Our only hope was to make a landfall in one of the neighbouring coves before the violence of the storm made that impossible.

We rose upright once more and laid ourselves into our oars with all our strength. I thought I heard a cry from the shore and looking back I could see the flashlight waving madly. Well, let them see us! Bobbing around on waves like these, we must present a more difficult target than a pingpong ball on a water-jet at a fairground.

I dipped and pulled, dipped and pulled, till the blood throbbing in my ears almost obliterated the sound of wind and water. Something plucked at my arm. A gust of wind, I thought. Then again. I looked. It was Pa, resting now on his oar. I thought at first he was telling me he was exhausted. But then he pointed.

I looked back once more. The throbbing in my ears had not all been the pulse of my blood. We were no longer alone on the water. Not more than fifty yards away I could see the lights of another vessel. It was hard to tell in the circumstances, but it looked and sounded like a small motorcruiser, probably no more than ten metres away. Our rescuer, I thought optimistically. But sent by whom? And why was it edging closer and closer to the Villa Colonna landing, urged on by the flashlight which was waving as enticingly and seductively as any ever held by a Cornish wrecker?

Then the more likely explanation came to me. No rescue boat, this, but our transport to the Bulgarian freighter. Why risk the road journey and the dock police when they could lift us by boat and transfer us outside the limit?

But we might be safe yet. The men on the motor-cruiser could have no way of knowing that we were loose and at sea. And it seemed to me that only a lunatic would attempt a landing in these conditions. And it was doubtful if they would even get within decent communicating distance and be put on our scent.

As I watched, it looked as if my picture of a Cornish wrecking might come to life.

The launch had got within a dozen metres of the landing-stage, far too close for safety, and the helmsman had decided he'd had enough. The bow was coming round to the open sea when suddenly a huge surge of wind and water picked them up and thrust them landwards. It seemed impossible that they would not be smashed against the concrete platform. Certainly they must have come within a couple of feet. I heard a confusion of cries both from the launch and the shore. Then she was running out to sea again as the gust temporarily abated.

I found myself letting out my breath which I did not know I'd been holding. Oddly, it was in relief. I hate to see any vessel wrecked. But the relief didn't last.

Pa shouted in my ear, 'Krylov!'

'What?'

'Krylov jumped. I saw him.'

I looked at him in doubt and amazement, doubt that he could have seen anything in these conditions, amazement that anyone would have behaved so suicidally.

Then I looked back at the launch. If indeed Krylov had got on board, that's where the evidence would come from.

It came as if I'd given a cue. A white light suddenly exploded outwards from the cruiser's deck. No flashlight, this, but a broad, dazzling, sharp-edged beam which sliced through the darkness towards us with a most un-Tinker-Bell-ish purpose and menace.

'Row!' cried Pa. 'Row for your life.'

And we flung ourselves against the oars as the light broke like a wave over our stern and the shooting began.

22

. . . grasp my reaching hand . . .

The Cambridge Eight on a good day with the wind at their backs and the tide running beneath them might have struck a couple of dozen times before that motor-cruiser caught them.

The Bessacarr Coxless Pair, on the other hand, had less scope for manœuvre. Indeed, all I managed was one decent stroke and one complete air shot before the cruiser's bows reared above us. Krylov was up there somewhere, rattling out a *feu de joie*. I heard something thud into the gunwale close to me and instinctively ducked sideways. A huge finger of water curled around my oar and flicked it away as a fastidious father might remove the dirty twig a child has picked up in the garden. The loss seemed of little consequence, as did the bullets. A thirty-foot motor-cruiser is not exactly your *Titanic*, but when it's about to fall on top of you, you start straining your ears for the Palm Court orchestra. I suspect that if Krylov could have contrived to be at the helm as well as firing his gun, that would have been the end of us. But fortunately this craft's skipper had other ideas. Probably he reckoned his contract was for a simple picking-up job.

The bow swung away and the wave created by its passage drove us apart. It could only be a momentary respite. Even if the cruiser lost us, the ocean wouldn't. The wind was more intermittent now, but in its gusts it seemed to have aspirations to becoming a full-blooded gale. I had no doubt whose full blood it would be. With only one oar, we had lost all control of movement or direction. The open sea held little prospect of safety and the only way we were going to make a landfall was from a great height and with almost certain fatal results. We didn't even have the option of a nice sandy little beach to run around in. There was nothing close by but solid rock-face, as hard and unyielding as state charity.

The launch was coming at us again, its one bright eye gleaming, like a lustful Cyclops hot from Sicily in search of a mate. If anyone were watching from the shore, this light must be tracing such an erratic pattern of movement that surely they'd contact the coastguard. At least, they would in England. Here, I doubted it and could only hope that nothing in its oscillations could be taken as a confirming signal to the yo-yos in charge of Angie's accident.

That was the only thing which held me back from surrender. Our case was hopeless. We had no means of evasion nor of defence, and least of all of counter-attack. I don't know about Pa, but my own death meant nothing. Even if I wasn't dying already, it meant nothing. But as long as my life kept Angie alive, I was going to go on fighting.

Now in typical Tyrrhenian Sea style, the weather was definitely changing. The wind's fury was diminishing as it veered into the southern quarter once more, but I didn't see this as being particularly advantageous. What I didn't like at all was the improvement in visibility. The cloud was thinning fast and in the east a hazy moon, low-hanging like a pale breast glimpsed through black chiffon, was making our pursuers' task easier. I could see Pa's face by its light. He yelled something at me. At first I thought it was simply a fond farewell, but I could see nothing of paternal sentimentality on his face, only the familiar exasperation. Now he rose and turned so that he was facing the bows and reached forward.

I watched with an amazement that did not diminish as I caught his purpose.

He was untying the oil drums lashed to the side of the boat.

At first I thought he'd simply opted for a rather strange form of suicide. *Ariel* had no built-in buoyancy apparatus and we'd taken on so much water I was sure that the oil drums were the only things keeping us up. Then I saw that just the opposite applied. Pa's finger stabbed out a line of bullet holes running clear across the bows. Both drums must be badly punctured. Once full of water and they'd drag us down like tubs of concrete.

I joined him at his task. My pinched and sodden fingers

made little impression on the water-tightened knots. I looked at Pa who passed me his small penknife with a sigh which not even the wailing wind could conceal from my mental ear. I sawed away and a moment later the oil drums were released simultaneously. We tore at the planks which had held them, ripping their nails out by main force, and hurled them into the ocean. For a moment the only change seemed to be the expected one in our stability. We were lying across the wind and we almost turned turtle. Then Pa grabbed at his oar and using it both for momentum and stability turned us down-wind. And now the incredible happened. As she moved forward on the swell, I could feel that ancient, leaky, rotten tub trying to gather her strength beneath me, like an old fighter after fourteen rounds. I reached forward and grasped the foresail halyard. I had no real hope that the peasant butchers who'd been using the boat would have left her properly rigged, but presumably that spitfire jib was there for a purpose. It was. It came up almost smoothly and though it was the smallest, scruffiest bit of sail I've ever seen, it caught the strong south wind, every plank in the old boat creaked, and suddenly she was under sail and our *Ariel* once more.

Pa and I looked at each other and laughed like madmen. He pushed his oar over the side and sprang to the helm. The rudder, hitherto useless and unusable, was now operative again. A feeling of such tangible vitality ran down the whole length of the boat that I experienced the crazy certainty that if we wanted we could sail beyond the sunset and the western stars. Pa shared it with me, I knew that. Our gazes met and locked. In that moment we were completely united, loving equals in a great adventure.

It was all we had. In another moment we were back in the sordid world of squalid deceit and violent death. The launch was back upon us, its light holding us steady in the calming seas. I could hear bullets chomping at the woodwork and I felt a violent burning sensation down my right side. I sat heavily on the thwart. Pa seemed to be untouched and was holding a course directly towards the huge bulk of the cliff whose rim was marked by a set of car headlights which seemed to be pointing directly out to sea. My hand was exploring my wound reluctantly and even more reluctantly my mind explored those lights. Revelation was simultaneous. I felt the hot pulse of blood beneath my shirt in the same instant as those headlights came over the cliff. For a second I could see no car, just the lights. Then a third of the way down it hit, bounced, hit again and burst into flames.

And now for the rest of its descent, which seemed as long and as slow as that fabled for the rebelling angels thrown from the ramparts of Heaven, I could see the bulk of the car clearly in the middle of those defining flames till it hit the sea not a furlong from us and left a blackness which began at my soul.

If I'd thought that the events of this night hitherto had been nightmarish, I now realized that by contrast with what followed they were gentle as a waking dream.

I don't know who did it. Perhaps Pa, exhausted or wounded, collapsed across the helm and inadvertently brought us round. Or perhaps the cruiser's skipper, cowed by Krylov's KGB authority or simply desperate to get things done with and be away, deliberately ran us down.

Or perhaps it was simply old Triton deciding that these insects had disturbed his rest for long enough and flinging them together to bring an end to it.

Whatever the cause, the motor-cruiser passed through us like a blunt hatchet through a rotten log and *Ariel*'s brief taste of her former glory was gone. Well, she died as she deserved to die, under sail on the open sea, with the emblems of her recent degradation stripped from her elegant frame.

God send us all such a death! Not that it seemed to be what he had in mind for me. *Ariel* folded up like a book and I was flung with great violence against the mast, cracking my nose and loosening a couple of teeth, mere trifles to a man about to drown. For a second I clung like some silent-comedy figure to the mast and had a brief glimpse of Pa going over the stern, his old fingers grasping at the wire hawser as if in hope of keeping contact with the dinghy. But there was nothing left to keep contact with except matchwood. I lost my grip and went deep, deep down, and found I didn't much care if I never came up. But even the sea is choosey and up I rose, almost as fast as I'd sunk, and as I re-emerged into the air, I cracked my head against something solid.

It was the mast, determined to get me coming or going. I clung to it once more and looked around for Pa. There was no sign of him, but I could see the launch quite clearly and something very interesting was happening to it. I doubted if the impact could have seriously damaged its hull, but it was quite clear that something was fouling the screw. The engine was spluttering and sparking as the propeller tried to free itself from the obstruction. But it must have been something very strong, the wire hawser perhaps, and finally the engine fell silent and the launch drifted away on the long swell. I could imagine what was going through its skipper's mind. Being powerless on a lee-shore is the sailor's nightmare, especially when the shore's as unwelcoming as this one.

But I had neither time nor inclination for sympathy as I desperately scanned the surface for a glimpse of Pa.

It seemed a hopeless task. In these seas we could already be fifty yards apart, assuming he was still afloat. And at water level, fifty yards meant out of sight.

Then I saw him. The moon came momentarily into a break of open sky and its beams glanced off the distinguished grey of his patrician head. I took a few strokes in his direction but the effort pained my wounded side so much that I had to grab my piece of flotsam once more and try to proceed by dint of a one-handed dog-paddle.

Progress was slow. The launch was still drifting out of control and I felt able to risk a shout. At my second yell, the head turned and he saw me.

I got quite close. He looked to be in a bad way, but I could see his mouth working though I couldn't make out any words. He must have become aware of this for I saw for the last time that old look of contained exasperation at my slowness, then he spoke again with a visible effort at clarity of articulation. All I caught was a few broken syllables and I wasn't sure even of those. One combination sounded like *emerald* but that made no sense. Another, more typically, could have been still *persevere!*! Anyway, I smiled and nodded as if I'd got the message.

We were within five feet of each other. I reached out my hand.

The exasperation had vanished from his face. He regarded me with unqualified affection and, I like to believe, something of pride. Then he raised his arms from the water, to grasp my reaching hand I at first believed.

Then with the numb horror of one who has gone into nightmare far past the shrieking point, I saw that both his arms ended in bloody stumps and became aware of the colour of the water all around him.

He slipped down out of sight as I helplessly watched, deep deep down, as he must have dived clutching the wire hawser. Did he deliberately set out to foul the launch's propeller, or was he sucked into it despite his effort? God knows. I wouldn't put it past him. All I knew was that this time he did not reappear.

I dived once and I think I saw his body turning slowly in the deep currents a little way away. I made no effort to go after it. He was as likely to lie at peace here with his beloved *Ariel* beneath these familiar seas as anywhere else in the world.

I looked around for the cruiser. It had been carried in against the cliff-face with incredible speed and the huge swell was thrusting it at the rock again and again. I began to swim slowly towards it. The pain in my side seemed to have been numbed by immersion in the water and my stroke was long and strong.

The motor-cruiser was breaking up. I saw two or three figures go over the side. God would be good, I was certain of that. He had taken everything I ever cared for ... Mama ... Angie ... Pa too. He could afford to toss me a crumb surely ...

He tossed. The crumb came floating by. Krylov, his narrow intellectual face contorted with the effort to breathe, to keep alive. He didn't look a very expert swimmer. I moved steadily towards him. He saw my form approaching and shouted in Russian. Perhaps he thought I was going to save him.

Then he recognized me.

I had got within a couple of yards, when he raised his arms

in the air and sank without a struggle. I screamed in rage at being deprived of my active vengeance and dived and dived again, eager to drag him back to the air so that I could drown him! But he was gone deep, far beyond my reach.

And with these violent efforts my strength was gone too.

The currents were in charge now. It was all I could do to keep afloat. They whirled me away from the wreck of the cruiser, dragging me down the coast, toying with me by bringing me close to the cliff-face, then hurling me back just before impact. There was no break in the cliff, no hope of a safe landing. I didn't care. I listened to the thunder of the water breaking on the rock and surrendered myself completely to the ocean's driving force.

This time there was going to be no last-second pulling back. The sea hurled me forwards. There was no sense of impact, just a plunge into great darkness. A brief intuitive struggle. Then blackness, total blackness, within and without.

Later, if time still meant anything, the blackness broke up into a strange shifting green light. *Emerald.* I remembered Pa's voice. *Emerald.*

Voices, not Pa's. Pain. Blackness again.

And much, much later, white, white, white.

. . . nothing but my continental breakfast . . .

I really thought I was dead.

And in hell, of course. Where else? If God exists, and he's not as stupid as some of His creation suggests, there has to be a special circle of the Inferno for English peers who went bad. A dress circle, of course.

That was what alerted me; the dress. I was in a sort of nightshirt which might have passed for Other Wordly wear in a medieval mural, but felt neither paradisal nor penitential enough to me.

I pulled back the white sheet which I'd contrived to drag up over my face and looked at the white ceiling and my nose told me before my eyes that I was in hospital.

The door opened and for a moment I almost revised my conclusion as a woman entered wearing unequivocally religious garb, and medieval at that.

Then she was followed by Reilly and the Brigadier and, knowing angels by the company they keep, I realized she must merely be a member of the religious nursing order which ran this hospital.

'Good day, Mr Swift,' said the Brigadier. 'How are you feeling?'

'Like death warmed up, I think is the phrase,' I replied. 'To coin a cliché, where are we?'

'A hospital,' he said. 'Quite close to Sorrento. We had you brought here.'

'Well, thanks,' I said. 'From where?'

'From Amalfi. After you'd been found in the Grotta dello Smeraldo by the first party of tourists that morning. It was quite dramatic, I believe. The lighting was switched on to demonstrate the interesting green light, and there you were, draped over a stalagmite.'

'The Emerald Grotto,' I said. 'So that's what Pa meant!'

'Your father?' said the Brigadier alertly. 'What precisely did he say?'

'Before he died, you mean?'

Reilly and her master exchanged glances.

'Oh yes,' I said softly. 'You can rest content, you and all the bastards like you. He's dead all right.'

'I'm sorry. For your sake, I mean,' said the Brigadier. 'You seem to have had some kind of reconciliation. We'll need to know everything he said to you after you left the villa.'

'Meaning you've got a record of everything we said to each other in the villa, I suppose?' I said bitterly. 'Then you heard it all, Brig. Afterwards, we were too busy working on ways to keep me alive. His last instructions to me were *emerald*, meaning head for the Emerald Grotto, and *still persevere*. He just wanted me to keep going.'

I felt tears stinging my eyes.

'What about the launch?' I said to occupy my mind.

'No survivors. You did a good job there, bucko,' said Reilly.

I shot her a glance of pure hatred.

'They have recovered Major Krylov's body,' added the Brigadier. 'A sad loss. We must send flowers.'

'And my daughter and nephew, will you be sending flowers to their funeral too?' I exploded rising in the bed.

The Brigadier looked uncomfortable, which I suppose was to his credit. Reilly, who had no credit to increase or diminish, said jocularly. 'It'll need to be a floating wreath, me boy.'

'You mean they haven't found them yet?' I asked, suddenly touched with a crazy hope.

The Brigadier said with that combination of military crispness and commanding officer's sympathy which was his hallmark, 'The car seems to have exploded and broken up. It's in a couple of fathoms. They've sent a diver down, but so far, nothing. I'm very sorry about this, Swift. A terrible accident.'

'Accident, shit!' I said. 'It was Krylov's way of getting rid of a couple of witnesses. And don't let's have any babes-in-the-wood act from you two. You know exactly what happened. All I've got to decide is whether you knew about it in advance!'

They exchanged glances.

Reilly shrugged indifferently and turned away.

The Brigadier said, 'You're quite right, Mr Swift. We did guess that it was probably no accident. But I assure you that we had no idea in advance what Krylov's intentions were with regard to the young people. It was our understanding that they would be released safely after your father had been returned to Russia.'

I didn't know whether to believe him or not. On the whole I was willing to give him the benefit of the doubt, but perhaps that was just my bullshit reason for not wanting to kill him. My asshole reason was that with a bit of luck the Russians would blame the fiasco at Amalfi on a British double-cross and take out the Brigadier and Reilly at their earliest convenience.

But for once the real reason was neither obscure nor far to seek.

Revenge was meaningless. I had destroyed my own life and the lives of others in its pursuit. A whole acre of bodies couldn't begin to balance my losses. Deaths were meaningless now. Except one. My own.

And I didn't intend sitting around waiting for it to come either from the sleeping dragon in my gut or from some brainless yo-yo paid by one side or the other to remove my embarrassing presence.

The Brigadier was on his feet and making for the door.

'They tell us your wound is not too serious,' he said. 'You should be fit to travel in a couple of days. You shouldn't be troubled by an official interest. I've pulled a few strings and now we'll head back to Rome and make a few more soothing noises. I'll arrange to have you join us there. Goodbye, Mr Swift.'

He went out.

Reilly came to the bedside and leaned over me.

'You look terrible,' she said.

'What's this, Reilly?' I asked. 'The usual technique? The

Brig goes and you hop into bed for a quick screw and a friendly chat? You're out of luck, girl. Both ways.'

'Like to bet,' she said lightly.

Suddenly to my surprise she leaned down and kissed me, a pleasant sisterly kiss, not the open-mouthed, tongue-prodding erotic version I'd have expected.

'Listen. You take care,' she said.

'I intend to,' I answered. My new resolve made me feel easy with the world, even with Reilly. And her kiss, though doubtless carefully measured, helped also.

She had left the bedside but seemed reluctant to leave the room. The door opened again and a nurse came in announcing that she had to change my dressing.

'Stay and watch if you like, Reilly,' I invited.

A faint smile touched her lips and she shook her head.

'Take care, bucko,' she repeated. 'And I'll see you soon.'

'Bets?' I said under my breath as she went through the door.

But I waved my hand languorously. A dying man needs someone to say goodbye to and Reilly was all I'd got.

I looked at my gunshot wound with interest as the nurse removed the dressing. The bullet had pierced my right side. A little lower and it would have shattered my hip. A little more central and it would have bust my gut. A little higher and it would have punctured my lung. As it was it hadn't done me a great deal of harm and the major damage had been the vast amount of blood I had lost before being discovered.

The nurse chattered away as she went about her work. I don't know what explanation had been given for the presence here in a private room of a gunshot Englishman, but it's been my experience that nuns and priests take most things in their stride. I wondered idly what her reaction would be if I told her that a few inches away from this wound she was helping to heal was a cancerous growth programmed to shake me off the tree while my new scar was still in full blossom.

Probably nothing except regret and prayer. Though if she'd guessed I was planning to put myself in a state of mortal sin by suicide, she might have become a little agitated.

I was supposed to lie in bed but I persuaded her to let me sit in a wheelchair by the window. From here I had a fabulous view right across the Bay of Naples. It was a day of sparkling clarity. To my right, the chopped-off cone of Vesuvius looked to be within grasping distance and, straining my eyes straight ahead, I thought I could make out the heat haze above the water the shape of Castel dell 'Ovo over the harbour of Santa Lucia, but it probably owed more to imagination and memory than farsightedness.

I turned my gaze closer and looked downwards. I was on the second floor and though there was a concrete terrace below, it wasn't far enough below to make death certain. To die of cancer with all your limbs in plaster would really be gilding the lily, I thought. No, jumping was out.

Still, if you're going to kill yourself, surely a hospital must be one of the easiest places to do it?

I tried a few tentative steps. My legs were weak as a satyr's after a hard day chasing woodnymphs. I got back into my chair and went for a little ride, partly to get the lie of the land, partly to flush out any watchers. My nurse came out of a room only two doors away from mine as I passed and with a great show of anger wheeled me back and commanded me to bed. But I'd noted that the room she came out of was lined with medical cabinets.

I asked for a sleeping tablet that night. She went out leaving my door open. I counted her steps. Just enough for the room I'd seen. She returned with a brown capsule. I studied the name on it before taking it.

The following day I felt much stronger but my mental state was just the same and all that the returning strength meant to me was that death was much more easily accessible.

I timed my move for after the doctor had examined me that morning. He pronounced himself very satisfied with my progress and then went out with his little crowd of acolytes, my nurse among them. The moment the door closed, I got out of bed and went and opened it a fraction. The procession was disappearing round the furthermost corner of the corridor. I moved as swiftly as I could to the medical store room. It was empty. Locating the cabinet which contained the sleeping capsules took only a moment. It was locked but I'd brought with me a spoke removed from the wheels of my wheelchair earlier that morning and bent into a useful pick-lock shape. Two minutes later I was back in my room with a couple of hundred capsules, congratulating myself on a perfect crime.

I was mad, of course. Not for planning to kill myself – that's an area of ethical vagueness which I'll leave to the philosophers – but for planning to do it in a hospital. There I was, telling myself it's the best place on earth to use as a launching-pad for the next world, and ignoring the fact that its full of instruments and expertise for keeping you in this. Even if I'd got hold of some fast-acting poison, it would have made poor enough sense. But sleeping tablets! Jesus!

Well, perhaps it's like the shrinks say, just a cry for help. If so, it was heard with commendable speed. Perhaps I'd been spotted going into the store-room. I don't know. But I hadn't even started taking the damn things when my nurse and a couple of muscular orderlies came rushing in. They wouldn't listen to my protestations of emptiness which in any case are hard to maintain at a high level of coherence when someone is shoving a tube down your throat. I hoped they felt sorry when they pumped up nothing but my continental breakfast, but I doubted it.

The doctor returned, very Italian, very angry. *He* decided which of his patients lived or died, nobody else. *He* alone was responsible.

He was also curious. Why had I done it? My wound was minor. There was a mystery surrounding my presence here, it was true, but I had official standing and as there were no armed guards sitting at the foot of my bed, I could hardly be a dangerous criminal intended for trial as soon as I'd recovered.

I couldn't resist the chance of sneering at his professional competence.

Hadn't the Brigadier mentioned to the authorities that I was a sick man? Obviously not. But surely any properly trained doctor would have observed the signs? Surely they took X-rays of my abdomen to assess the full extent of the bullet wound? Or, failing that, if he cared to take a more than cursory glance at the goo they'd just trawled from my stomach, he might spot something to my disadvantage.

He listened carefully, ignoring my heavy sarcasm. He

asked for details of diagnosis and symptoms. They he spoke to my nurse. I caught something about X-rays.

'You mean you *did* take X-rays?' I demanded in mock amazement.

'Of course. But not such that would necessarily show anything of this cancer. On the other hand, if it has the hold that your previous doctor's prognosis suggests ... you say that it was confirmed?'

'Yes. Dr Quintero diagnosed it in Venezuela and it was confirmed independently in a London hospital ...'

'Independently?' he echoed.

'Yes, that's what I bloody well said!' I snarled.

Then it struck me that I was getting angry with this man because he was apparently doubting the very worst news I'd ever been given.

No, I corrected myself. It was *myself*. I was getting angry with. It was my own fear of hope, my own terror of being disappointed once more. I had been absolute for death and now, suddenly, incredibly ...

They performed tests. I begged him to let no one know they were performing them, suggesting that it would be unkind to raise false hopes in my many loving friends and relations!

Early that evening, he came back to see me. His face was expressionless, but I could read the answer in my nurse's eyes.

He made his announcement like an official bulletin being read at the palace gates.

'Signore,' he said. 'We have carried out all the conventional tests and so far as the evidence provided by these goes, it has not emerged that a cancerous condition is presently affecting any part of your alimentary tract.'

He said this in Italian. Then he said it in English. It sounded too convoluted to be true in either language.

I said slowly, 'No cancer?'

He sighed, more in puzzlement than disappointment, I think.

'No cancer.'

Even then it was my nurse's face that was my real confirmation of the news.

I don't know what they do to you in hell for kissing a nun, but I've got it waiting for me. She didn't seem to mind, so perhaps she'll be there too, looking for more.

'No cancer!' I cried. 'No bloody cancer!'

Now at last the doctor smiled and shook his head.

'No, signore. Definitely no cancer. Not now. Not ever.'

That pulled me up short. There were huge and very unpleasant suspicions swirling round my mind and I had to be sure.

'You mean there never was any cancer?' I asked. 'I couldn't have had it and then had some kind of miraculous cure?'

The nurse's eyes lit up again, this time at the prospect of being privy to a case of miraculous healing, but the doctor was too jealous of the skills of his profession to allow that possibility.

He made a dismissive gesture and shook his head again.

'It was Tyrrenhian water you were full of, signore, not Lourdes. No, the initial diagnosis was mistaken. And the confirmatory diagnosis in London too.'

Mistaken!

Oh no, far from it, I thought grimly. I thought of Quintero's embarrassed uneasiness which I'd put down to the emotional strain of having to tell an old acquaintance such bad news! I remembered Hunnicut's equal uneasiness in the London hospital which I'd ascribed to much the same causes. At least old Honey would have been forced to play along "in the national interest" or some such phrase, but that greasy little abortionist Quintero must have done it solely for hard cash. And no doubt the assurance that I'd never return.

And the symptoms – the stomach pains, the blood on the toilet-paper – these too must have been arranged probably via bribery in Margarita; and since then, I now worked out, every time I'd suffered a bout of gut-ache, I'd recently taken something provided by Reilly's fair hands!

'So,' concluded the doctor. 'No more thoughts of death. You will be robbing yourself not of a few painful weeks as you thought, but many happy years. Agreed?'

I smiled and nodded and wept a little and clasped his hand. It was a highly charged emotional Latin moment. But deep down inside of me, there was a hard Nothern coldness which was as resistant to joy as permafrost is resistant to the sun.

Pa had been finally proven right in his sublime egotism. What a vast importance he must have had for such steps to be taken in his pursuit! I had been deceived out of my exile and put on his trail. It must have been a complicated and expensive operation, but by Christ it had worked! I had led them to him as surely as any hound-dog. And now he was dead, and Kate was dead, and Angie was dead, and Vasco was dead, and for all I knew, Teresa might be dead also.

The previous day I had decided that all these deaths were meaningless and that the deaths of those who might be responsible would be meaningless also. But I hadn't been thinking straight. My so called 'real' reason had been as fallacious as both my bullshit and my asshole reasons.

Now I felt the life-force running strong through my veins once more.

And it was telling me to kill.

24

. . . *the staircase to Paradise* . . .

A driver called for me the following day with papers authorizing my transfer to the Policlinico in Rome.

I took a genuinely fond farewell of my nurse. Every sick man should fall in love with his nurse, especially if she's a nun and can't take advantage. The doctor assured me he had put full details of the cancer tests they'd run on me into my file, plus a recommendation that they double-checked in Rome. I thanked him, but I didn't feel it would be necessary.

I was wheeled carefully down to the car park and transferred to a luxurious Mercedes estate-wagon ambulance. The Brigadier was doing things in style.

I was lightly strapped down on a well-cushioned bed, but I still groaned a couple of times as the suspension absorbed some minute unevenness in the road surface.

'Take it easy, will you?' I begged the driver, who glanced down at my haggard, pale face and grunted indifferently.

A couple of miles later while we were still a little way from the autostrada I cried out in pain and managed to pierce his indifference. What came was irritation rather than concern, but it was a step in the right direction and after another long juddering cry, he drew in to the side and came back to look at me.

'I think I'm bleeding,' I gasped.

He undid the strap to have a look. Up to this point I'd had rather mixed feelings about this fellow who might after all just simply be a genuine ambulance driver with mortgage worries. But as he leaned over me I saw a familiar outline under the left armpit of his white linen jacket, so when I chopped him below the ear, I didn't feel the need to go too easy.

It was a 9mm Makarov he was carrying, which is really a

nothing weapon except that it's better than nothing. I took it and the holster, plus his trousers, shoes and jacket. Traffic was heavy along the road but the opaque windows gave me protection and I just had to hope that no Good Samaritan or nosey cop stopped to offer a hand.

Whatever the status of my driver, the ambulance was genuine enough and I bound his wrists and ankles with a roll of surgical tape before covering him with a blanket and strapping him down as tight as I could manage. Finally I inserted a piece of tape beneath his lips and stuck his gums together so that to the casual gaze he looked OK while lacking the power of articulate speech.

I quite enjoyed the ride after that. If you have to drive a couple of hundred kilometres on a red hot Italian day, then an air-conditioned Merc ambulance is the vehicle to do it in. The driver had thoughtfully provided a hunk of *crespone*, a couple of peaches and a flask of iced coffee, all of which I found in the glove compartment and enjoyed as we bowled along. Eventually the driver woke. I assured him casually that if he made the slightest effort to draw attention to himself as we went through the tolls, I would put two toy bullets from his toy gun up each of his nostrils.

I was going to need somewhere quiet to talk with this fellow eventually and a parked ambulance tends to attract attention. I'd been lucky once, but I didn't want to push it unless I had to. I thought of turning off the autostrada somewhere in the Castelli and finding a nice quiet little sideroad, but my recent experience with the peasantry had reminded me what a suspicious, inquisitive race they are.

Eventually it occurred to me that the one place in which no one would take any notice of an ambulance was outside a hospital. So I did what the driver's papers had said he was going to do and headed for Rome Policlinico.

Here I parked in an area marked 'Private' alongside another ambulance and spoke quickly but firmly to my passenger.

I told him I was going to take the tape out of his mouth and that when I did, he had thirty seconds to tell me what his orders were. If he obeyed, I would leave him to be found eventually. If he didn't, I would still leave him to be found eventually. The only difference was the state in which he would be found.

I took the gun from its holster, ripped loose the tape and glanced at the dashboard clock.

'Talk,' I said.

He talked extremely rapidly. I listened. When he stopped I said, 'Liar,' and pressed the gun to his ear.

He talked again. I thought he'd set an all-time record before, but this beat it with seconds to spare. In essence it was the same as he'd said the first time, with assurances on his mother's grave that no one had spoken truer since the Archangel Gabriel had forecast the Virgin Birth.

What he told me sounded a little more likely than that.

He was merely a hired hand and he'd taken his instructions from Reilly (he didn't know her name, but there was no mistaking the description). He had been given a telephone number to ring from the Frascati self-service about ten kilometres outside the city, where he was to have received final instructions about his destination.

I noted the telephone number. There was a room number with it so it probably belonged to a hotel. Then I cut another piece of tape and sealed my driver's mouth.

I said, 'I'm going to make a phone call. I won't be more than ten minutes. You'd better have been telling the truth.'

Making sure I'd locked all the ambulance doors, I moved swiftly away from the car park like a man who knew where he was going. Once out of the hospital precincts I slowed down. I was a lot stronger than I'd pretended when I was picked up that morning, but a lot weaker than I'd realized. Other pedestrians glanced at me strangely as they passed. It was hardly surprising. The ambulance driver had been a shorter, fatter man, and the difference showed in my borrowed clothes. Fortunately investigation revealed he'd also been a richer man. His wallet was bulging with notes. Reilly must have paid him in advance. No – knowing Reilly, *half* in advance!

I was drifting along the Viale de Policlinico which intersects the Viale dell' Università. There was a great deal of pedestrian movement down this latter road, with banner-waving and a lot of noise. As I got nearer I realized it was the tail-end of some student protest march which must have started in the nearby university complex. There were several police cars cruising slowly around and my first instinct was to retreat before my odd apparel drew their attention, but it struck me that the best place for an eccentric dresser to hide is among a crowd of the eccentrically dressed and I joined the march. It turned right when it reached Stazione Termini, Rome's mainline station. Here I dropped out, noticing a small, rather scruffy men's outfitter's in a side-street. Clearly it catered mainly for small, rather scruffy men but I eventually found an awful battle-ship grey suit which almost fitted me. I also bought a straw hat and at a neighbouring chemist's the biggest pair of sunglassss I could see.

By now I needed a pick-me-up. I went into the station, dumping my borrowed clothes in a wastebin en route, and made for the refreshment room. I ordered a *grappa*. I'd have preferred whisky but feared that my preference might tempt me to excess. After one *grappa* I was able to turn to coffee and food. And finally I felt fit enough to go in search of a telephone.

It rang for five minutes and I was beginning to think I'd been wrong about the hotel. But it must only have been a receptionist taking a long siesta, for suddenly the phone was lifted and a voice said with all the resentful contempt of the breed, 'Hotel Cristallo.'

I asked if they had a room. I was told that it was the height of the tourist season, and that vacancies were rarer than Papal errors, before this devout shit admitted they had. I was suitably, that is grovellingly, grateful, booked it in the name of Albino Ratti which I'd found on the papers in the ambulance driver's wallet, and asked for directions from the station, saying I'd just arrived from Brindisi.

The Cristallo proved to be in easy walking distance, only a loud prayer's length away from the church of Santa Maria Maggiore. I invested some more of my borrowed money in a cheap suitcase, which I roughened up against the corner of a wall in a narrow side-street behind a *trattoria*. Kitchen rubbish had been dumped, on the pavement for collection later in the day and I shoved a couple of cardboard boxes containing what looked like non-noxious matter into the case as ballast.

The Cristallo proved to be a pretty modest establishment of the third or fourth class. The young man on reception was obviously rehearsing for better things. Like most Romans, he thought that anything from the deep south was three-quarters African and my scruffy luggage, cheap suit and strange gruff accent (I affected a heavy cold) merely confirmed his prejudice. I signed in as Albino Ratti, inventing an address in Brindisi, and accepted my key with bobbing servility. The key to 211, Reilly's room, was missing I noted.

The receptionist started sniffing as I turned away and for a moment I wondered if by the power of suggestion alone I'd given him my imaginary cold. Then my own authenticating sniff caught a wisp of some foul odour like the stench arising from a midsummer midden. It took only a second to trace it to my suitcase. My ballast can't have been as hygienically based as I thought, and heat and confinement must have triggered off a reaction. Fortunately it wasn't the kind of place where porters leap out to assist guests, as by the time I reached the Fourth Floor, I was trailing a visible miasma.

In my room, I opened the window wide and set the case on the sill. I hoped to God Reilly and the Brigadier were both here so I could get finished and away quickly.

Then the ghoulish humour of the situation struck me. I was planning to commit a double murder and my mind was mainly occupied with a suitcase full of garbage!

I checked the Makarov. Like I say, it's not much of a gun, but it fitted snugly into my pocket so I wouldn't have the awkwardness of drawing it from the shoulder, and at close quarters it would be as effective as a Magnum.

I left my gently rotting room and descended the stairs to the second floor. My plan was vague. People like Reilly and the Brigadier didn't open hotel doors casually. I had a thought of setting off the fire alarm and blasting them both as they came running out, but that was quite literally a hit-or-miss scheme and besides I couldn't see anything in the corridors of the Hotel Cristallo vaguely resembling an alarm system.

But as I reached the second-floor landing, my problem was solved.

Down the corridor, a door opened and I heard Reilly's voice. I couldn't catch what she was saying, but I'd recognize that double-bass brogue anywhere. I went into retreat faster than a nervous novice. Then the door closed and her footsteps came towards the stairs. By the time she reached them I was out of sight on the next landing. I heard her going down, gave her a few seconds start and followed.

She was at the desk talking to the receptionist. I guessed she was making sure there'd been no phone calls or messages for her. The receptionist was reassuring her in a manner far from supercilious. I smiled almost affectionately. Reilly wouldn't take any hireling crap.

I was ready to retreat again, imagining that Reilly and the Brigadier must be getting worried at the ambulanceman's silence. But she took me by surprise, picking up a small canvas grip which was resting at her feet and heading out into the street.

I rushed to follow her, tossing my keys on to the desk in passing. She turned left out of the hotel and set off towards Santa Maria Maggiore, skirting the church with a fine disregard for the speeding traffic and making down the long descent of Via Agostino Depretis. She was carrying the grip Roman-style, under her arm with the strap over her shoulder. Her hands were thrust deep into the pockets of a denim bomber jacket, and her head was bowed as though in solemn thought. But I kept my distance all the same. It would be second nature for Reilly to check for tails, and once she spotted I was following her, it wouldn't take long to penetrate the flimsy disguise of my hat and dark glasses.

Arrow-straight the street soared upwards now, till it became Via delle Quattro Fontane and plunged down into Piazza Barberini where I'd been staying what felt like a lifetime ago. I thought perhaps Reilly might be making for the same hotel, but she kept going at an unchecked pace up Via Sistina which ends at the piazza in front of the church of *Trinità dei Monti* overlooking the Spanish Steps. I was beginning to labour heavily up this last hill and I didn't take much notice at first of a new noise which was being added to the usual Roman cacophony. It sounded like a rhythmic chanting with its beat marked by a clashing of cymbals. It wasn't till after I'd seen that there was a marked thickening of the crowd ahead and forced myself to speed up in order not to lose Reilly in the crush that I put the two things together. This must be the focus of that student protest I'd briefly joined after I left the Policlinico.

I got within a couple of yards of Reilly by the time we reached the piazza. She shouldered her way to the balustrade and paused. I squeezed in two or three people away. From here the view over Rome is magnificent. But no one was admiring the distant prospect today. It was the foreground that held our attention.

The Steps were jammed with students. It was like the Kop on a cup-tie day, except that most of these faces were turned upwards towards the leader of their revels, who was on the terrace immediately below us leading the chanting through/a loud-hailer. The accompaniment came from the beating of fists against dustbin lids, tin boxes, anything that gave out a resonant noise. The crowd was far too large to be contained on the steps and had spilled over into the Piazza di Spagna below. The 'old barge' fountain and the flower-sellers' stalls were small oases of freshness and fragrance in this wilderness of human sweat and frenzy. The traffic in the piazza was at a halt and there were signs of the beginnings of a large police build-up at the head of Via Condotti, the fashionable shopping street running off the square. The precise object of the protest wasn't clear to me but I sensed a general disapproval of those who were middle-class, middle-aged and rich enough to shop at Gucci's, whose humble stall in the Via Condotti was within stone's throwing distance.

The phrase filled me with alarm. Whatever its initial intent, this did not look to me like a gathering about to disperse peaceably. I'd once had the chance of studying the Roman police crowd-dispersal tactics from the safety of a high office window. It had been like sitting in the Imperial Box at the Colosseum.

I looked towards Reilly in a fury of resentment. Perhaps she'd simply come down here to buy herself a new golden knuckleduster at Gucci's. Perhaps the Brigadier had been sitting in Room 211 at the Cristallo and I could have taken them both at once.

I certainly didn't want my great revenge trail to end with an eyeful of tear-gas and a headful of baton. I willed her to move and, for once obedient, she turned and began to push her way back through the crowd. One thing about following Reilly through a press like this was that you could keep in touch with her progess just by watching the violent parting of the tightly crushed people ahead. She'd have made a fortune in Rugby League.

She was making straight back past the Obelisk in the centre of the square towards the church. In fact, it began to look as if this must be her destination. A sudden conversion, perhaps? I wondered light-headedly. If so, it looked as if she was going to be disappointed in her search for spiritual solace. The main doors of the building looked firmly and solidly shut. The old days of sanctuary are long past. Nowadays when the Church sees a riot developing on one of its doorsteps, it knows what to do, i.e. ram home the bolts and lock up the silver.

Reilly ignored the main door, however, and went unhesitatingly to a small side doorway and rang a bell. Almost instantly this door opened and she slipped inside. I followed, feeling close to the end of my strength and my patience. I was ready to ring the bell too and go charging in, even if the Pope himself answered it. But when I reached the door, I saw it was slightly ajar.

That should have alerted me. Not that I've been trained in the arts of security, but you don't have to be James Bond to spot a trap when it's advertised in neon. But all I did was take a firm grip on the Makarov and step inside.

It was a farce. I'd forgotten to take off my sun-glasses and it was like putting my head into a sack, an impression reinforced when almost immediately my straw hat was forced down over my forehead, the canvas grip was rammed with disabling force into my plexus and the pistol was plucked from my pocket with a Faginesque ease. Whether it was the Makarov's muzzle or Reilly's own that was thrust under my jaw I don't know, but it made it difficult to obey her instructions when she said, 'All right, creep, who are you? Why've you been following me? Now *talk!*'

I managed a groan. This seemed to offend her, for she back-handed me across the face, dislodging my hat which I was beginning to fear was permanently jammed and also knocking off my glasses so that I could see again. I looked up at her. I was on my knees like a postulant before the Mother Superior. In that dim religious light I could see astonishment struggling through the mask of her make-up. It struck me that this was possibly the last satisfaction I was every likely to have. I ought to try to produce a good exit line.

I gasped, 'Yes, Reilly. It's a true miracle. It's really me, you lousy bitch!'

Well, I suppose the staircase to Paradise is thronged with souls all morosely rehearsing the elegant witty things they ought to have said on their deathbeds. In the circumstances I felt I did well enough. I closed my eyes and waited for the curtain and the distant ripple of polite divine, or diabolical, applause.

. . . wounds on the front . . .

If my exit line was feeble, Reilly's response was positively banal.

'It's you!' she exclaimed.

Then another familiar voice added its contribution to the bathos.

'Miss Reilly! For heaven's sake, remember where you are! Put that thing away before someone sees it.'

I opened my eyes again. I had adjusted completely now to this new dim light. The Brigadier was standing close, very English and military in a dark blue blazer and grey flannels. Reilly, with what I felt was unbecoming and unladylike reluctance, withdrew the gun from deep inside my thyroid gland and I slowly stood up.

'Thank God you're here,' said the Brigadier piously.

Reilly began to say something but he cut her off imperiously.

'Not here,' he said, picking up the grip. 'This way. This way.'

We set off at a swift march, myself sandwiched between the pair of them like a prisoner under escort. *Like*, I say! That's just what I was. I don't know if prisoners on trial at the Old Bailey ever take in much of the architectural features of that historic building, but I personally have very little recollection of the beauties or lack of them of the Church of Trinità dei Monti. My æsthetic sensors had not time to re-adjust before we diverted through a narrow door between two side-chapels into what looked and smelt like a small vestry.

The Brigadier glanced at his watch and shook his head.

'We're very short of time,' he said. 'Let's have a look at you, Mr Swift.'

He opened my jacket and looked with some distaste at the label, then removed my stolen wallet and studied the papers.

'This will never do,' he said. 'Would you mind changing into these, please, Mr Swift?'

These were a lightweight English-made suit, shirt, and shoes. I saw no point in provoking any greater antagonism at that particular moment and began to remove my clothes.

'We don't seem to be able to get through a meeting without me undressing,' I remarked.

'What happened?' said the Brigadier to Reilly. 'You're an hour late. Our friends have become extremely impatient. I don't blame them. They suspect a cross.'

'Where are they?' asked Reilly, who was more subdued than I'd ever seen her. This upset of plans seemed to have knocked her back a disproportionate amount. Perhaps she was worried about her promotion hopes.

'They've popped out to check on things out there. What *has* been happening, Miss Reilly?'

'I don't know,' confessed Reilly helplessly. 'There was no contact so in the end I thought I'd better come here myself in case the plan had been changed. I spotted I was being followed but I'd no idea it was the man himself.'

'I see. I presume these papers belonged to the man who picked you up in the ambulance, Mr Swift?'

I nodded, fastening my flies.

'You really must be more careful about the help you hire, Miss Reilly,' he reproved gently. 'Your argument that we couldn't trust a Red Brigade man was valid only if his substitute was perfectly to be trusted.'

'Red Brigade?' I said, suddenly alert.

'That's right, Mr Swift. Look, no use beating about the bush. You've been very useful to us, thanks for that. We've stuck to our end of the bargain, you saw your daughter, I'm sorry it all ended so unhappily, but you did see her. Now it's over. Put these into your pocket, please.'

He handed me my Alexander Evans passport and a wallet. I opened it. It contained money, a lot of papers and a small diary. I began to examine the contents more closely but he shook his head saying, 'Don't bother. No time. Ah, signori. Is it all set?'

The door had opened and two young men came in, dressed in their young men's uniform of T-shirts, jeans and open sandals.

'You have him?' said one of them in a voice full of pleasure.

He came across to me, studied my face as though to reassure himself, and then spat right into my eye. Instinctively I swung at him. He blocked, and punched me in the belly. It was clearly target for today.

I doubled up once more, retching. The young fellow looked ready to continue the dialectic but his companion intervened.

The Brigadier said, 'This is Pietro. I think you knew his sister, Monica. Signori, if you please.'

Pietro's friend was carrying a zipped-up leather wallet which he now handed over to the Brigadier, who opened it and examined the papers it contained.

'Excellent,' he said.

'Why are you dealing with these animals?' I croaked.

'Why not?' said the Brigadier. 'You had to go, you see that, Mr Swift? In any case, you didn't have very long to live, so it's not a very great loss to you, is it?'

I suppose it was a kind of humanitarianism, keeping up that pretence. I opened my mouth to protest but he didn't give me the chance.

'We like our operations to be as cost-effective as possible. Ultimately, like all government departments, we have to justify expenditure and make savings, especially in times of economic stringency. The Red Brigade are very keen to see you put underground so, not to beat about the bush, we've sold you to them. Not for money, just information about the odd politician and also one or two of their former friends. And between us we've concocted a little package of papers and diary notes which will stir up all kinds of hornets' nests when the police go through your wallet.'

'And when are they going to do that?' I asked.

'Not long,' said the Brigadier. 'Shortly there's going to be a riot out there, viciously put down by a brutal police counter-attack. When the flak dies away, you'll be found among the other wounded and dying.'

'With a bullet in me? That should certainly rouse curiosity,' I said.

'With your skull fractured,' said the Brigadier gently. 'Signori.'

Pietro's friend had come round behind me and suddenly he dropped a noose of rope over my shoulders and drew it tight, pinioning my arms to my sides. Pietro opened a cupboard and from it produce a long and viciously weighted truncheon.

'I'm sorry,' said the Brigadier. 'It had been our intention that you should be drugged at this point, but as we seem to have lost our medical man ...'

Pietro came at me, swinging. I ducked away desperately.

'Miss Reilly!' said the Brigadier.

Reilly produced her gun. Or rather my gun. Or rather the ambulance-driver's Makarov. I might have laughed if I'd been given a last wish. Did they think the threat of being shot was going to make me stand still so they could beat me to death?

I twisted away again. The youth hanging on to the rope drove his knee into my kidneys. Pietro swung the baton high into the air. I think he cried, 'Monica!'

I'd had trouble with last words, but I saw now I should have gone for simplicity. What more moving way for a lad to die than in church with his sister's name on his lips? It gets you right here, in the heart. That's where it got Pietro certainly. He wasn't exactly bowled over. The 9mm Makarov doesn't pack that kind of punch. But when a lump of lead of no matter what weight or velocity ventilates your ventricles you stop what you're doing and sort of fold up.

Pietro's friend stopped what he was doing too and looked round at Reilly in bewilderment. Any suspicion I'd had that getting Pietro plumb in the metronome was fortuitous disappeared with his friend's left eye. Or perhaps she was aiming at the right.

I staggered round like a roped steer trying to get rid of the lasso.

The Brigadier said, 'Miss Reilly, what the hell are you doing?'

He looked extremely cool, I must say, with that unique

British Officer-class coolness which allows its possessors to stroll towards the enemy with walking stick in hand and bull-terrier at heel.

Reilly said, 'Hold very still, Brigadier.'

'Indeed I shall,' he replied. He was no fool.

There was a hiatus in the conversation which gave me time to get myself unroped. I checked the two youths for signs of life but it was like checking a couple of lamb chops. They were clearly dead meat. I picked up Pietro's baton and looked speculatively at the Brigadier. Reilly I'd become ambiguous about, but the Brig was still in the ring.

Reilly said. 'You too, bucko. Hold still.'

It wasn't really a declaration of enmity, I decided, but just a time-filler. The poor girl was not completely certain that she was making the right move. I had no doubts.

'Blow the bastard away and let's get out of here!' I urged.

Unoriginal, perhaps, but it came from the heart.

'What seems to be the problem, Miss Reilly?' asked the Brigadier.

'I don't like the company we've been keeping,' said Reilly.

The Brigadier and I glanced at Pietro and his mate. I think we shared a thought. When Reilly didn't like the company, she was certainly adept at speeding the guests' departure.

'In our work, we can't be choosey,' said the Brigadier reasonably.

'I don't just mean this scum,' said Reilly. 'Though they're insects. We should stamp on them, not deal with them. I mean the Russians.'

'In the face of a common foe,' murmured the Brigadier. 'My enemy's enemy is my friend … remember?'

'I remember,' said Reilly. 'And the Russians were Billy Bessacarr's enemy? There's no disputing that, the way things turned out. But Billy Bessacarr had to be *our* enemy too, that was the nub of the thing. Well, to be sure, at first I had no difficulty in believing it. The whole Profumo business was ancient history to me. I was just getting into my teens at the time, too young even to get myself a Christine Keeler hair-do, though I recall I was mad for one. But I could well believe there were a great number of very respectable and influential people, now leading worthy, God-fearing lives, who would look very sick if the whole affair was dredged up again. And of course there were security considerations, didn't you tell me that? People we'd turned around or let the Russians think they'd turned around? Oh, it was all very believable.'

She spoke reflectively, as if really addressing herself, but her gaze and the Makarov remained firmly on her leader.

'And where is the difficulty now, Miss Reilly?' asked the Brigadier.

'I suppose it started after I got to know the noble lord here. I was surprised. For an egotistical, unbalanced aristo, he didn't seem such a bad fellow.'

'Gee, thanks,' I murmured. She ignored me.

'I thought that if I really was going to put him in the way of killing his own father, I ought to know just a bit more about the old monster. So I started a bit of quiet research into what was really going on back in 1963. In particular, I dug around and found out what the late Lord Bessacarr had to say when he got to Moscow. No one took much notice of it at the time. He was saying he was innocent, but then, to quote most aptly, considering the background of the affair, "he would, wouldn't he?" I heard him saying it again on the tape from the Villa Colonna.'

So Pa had been right. We *had* been bugged while we talked in the bedroom. Not that his care had done the children any good. I felt the surge of grief sweep over me again.

'So you heard that tape?' said the Brigadier. 'I thought Major Krylov, the late Major Krylov, kept it.'

Reilly suddenly grinned.

'I borrowed it before I left the villa. Not that there was much on it.'

Just a record of a fool finding his father and his daughter when it seemed he had lost them for ever. And then losing them for ever.

'But you know what I was thinking now? Suppose the old man didn't do it. Then who did? Either them or us. If *us*, no wonder we didn't want it advertised. If *them*, why were we so worried? Mind you, if *us*, why were *they* so worried? Unless, of course, in some way, *them* and *us* were one and the same thing.'

'Oh dear,' said the Brigadier. 'I think I see where this interesting speculation is taking us.'

'I don't,' I burst out. 'Reilly, if you're on my side, shoot this sod and let's get out of here.'

'Shut up, Lem,' she said. 'And it's not speculation, sir. You see, I've read the woman Kim's confession. Or, at least, old Bessacarr's account of it.'

That set the Brigadier back, though he only showed it for the briefest flash.

'How the hell have you managed that?' I burst out.

'I looked in the obvious place. Teresa's flat. Who else did your father trust?'

'But it was meant for me!' I protested childishly. 'How could Teresa …'

'I didn't ask Teresa,' said Reilly. 'She's in hospital, remember? So, the question I want to ask you, sir, is, how come our boss, our recently retired boss I should say, was able to give an admitted KGB agent instructions over the phone that night? For that matter, how come our recently retired boss seems to be in sole charge of this operation?'

'Miss Reilly!' cried the Brigadier as if the light of understanding had suddenly been switched on in his mind. 'Now I see your problem. But it's all quite simple. Unfortunately you didn't have the clearance to be told, but as you will readily appreciate, the fewer the better. It's Anthony Blunt all over again, you see. He was spotted years ago. At first the idea was merely the usual one of offering immunity from prosecution in exchange for a full confession. But then, by a master stroke, he was allowed to remain in the department and apparently flourish! He became the greatest double of all time. You can see why the Russians should be as concerned as we are that he shouldn't be exposed. They're still completely fooled. But we're the only winners, please believe that, Miss Reilly.'

He was getting to her, I could see that. The gun wavered slightly and she began to look uncertain. Whatever the Brigadier was telling her made some sense, but the only kind of sense it made to me was no sense at all.

'What the hell are you talking about, Brig?' I demanded.

Reilly said, 'Later, Lem. Leave it alone for now.'

Perhaps the Brigadier read this implied promise that for me there was going to be a 'later' as a sign that he'd failed to persuade Reilly. In any case, he suddenly switched tactics.

'No, he has a right to know,' he said sneeringly. 'Every fool has the right to study his own folly. And I think he's guessed anyway, haven't you, Mr Swift?'

'Guessed what?' I cried.

'That we're talking about Sir Percival Nostrand, your beloved godfather, Uncle Percy.'

'Uncle Percy?' I echoed. 'But he's … he's…'

'He's what? A fat old civil servant, with a taste for mature brandy and immature boys? The loyal defender of the Bessacarr clan? Oh, Mr Swift, how you have let yourself be deceived!'

Reilly said, 'For God's sake, let it alone, Brigadier!' as I stood paralysed. But the Brigadier did not want me paralysed.

He continued harshly. 'He deceived you even in his alleged taste for young men, Mr Swift. His tastes were much more catholic than that. Hot, lush, and Latin Catholic, you might say. Oh, he was a good friend to at least one of the Bessacarrs, a very good friend, as close as you can get. Who introduced your mother to your father, Lem? And who was your mother with on that last night?'

The provocation was deliberate and irresistible.

Reilly grasped what was happening but that itself was part of the Brigadier's tactics. With a scream of rage, I bent to grasp Pietro's discarded baton. Reilly cried, 'Lem!' and put out her hand to restrain me. I grabbed at it and tried to fling her aside, but she was too well balanced for that. But she did stagger a couple of paces, the gun moved off line, and the Brigadier saw his chance.

He came at a low run, incredibly fast for a man of his age. His right shoulder held low like an American footballer carrying out a block crashed into Reilly and set her cannoning against me. I fell backwards over Pietro's body. Reilly came down hard on top of me. And the Makarov went skittering across the stone floor.

The Brigadier was too bright to be interested in a catch-as-catch-can contest with two of us. He backed off towards the door, his right hand scrabbling for the butt of a pistol holstered in the small of his back. But old muscles decay, and he must have damaged his shoulder against Reilly's solid hip and he was winning no prizes in a fast-draw competition.

Reilly went diving in pursuit of the Makarov. I seized the late Pietro's baton and started to rise, eager to conduct a little elegiac music on the Brigadier's head. He'd got his pistol out at last but before he could raise it, the athletic Reilly had reached the Makarov and rolled round, firing.

The Brigadier was hit. I saw a line of blood drawn across his left temple as though by a felt-tip pen. He raised his hand to the wound in a weary saluting gesture. It could only have broken the skin, but it seemed also to break his spirit. Or perhaps there was another of Reilly's slugs elsewhere in his body.

Whatever, he made no attempt to return the fire but turned and fled.

'You OK, bucko?' panted Reilly.

'Yeah. That was lousy shooting,' I said.

'Ha ha. Come on.'

We went running through the echoing church. There's a thing called the multiplication of sins which give you two or more for the price of one, as for instance if you rape a nun. I wondered how high Reilly had already sent the divine till clicking by blowing away those two Red Brigade yo-yo's in the vestry. She was clearly bent on pushing her credit to the limit, but either the Makarov had jammed or the clip was empty, and ahead of us the Brigadier had reached the exit without further perforation. But we were closing fast.

Reilly reached the open door just ahead of me and stopped so quick that I ran into her.

'Hold it!' she ordered, pulling the door to so that just a crack remained.

I peered through and saw that she'd been wise.

The promised riot had just exploded out there. What precisely had triggered it off, God knows. Eventually everyone would blame everybody else, but the one explanation no one would come up with was that the Red Brigade had orchestrated it so that the body of an English crook could be found among the other debris with his head beaten in.

I shuddered and watched.

The police were coming in from both sides of the small piazza in front of the church. The tactic was obvious. Drive those in the square and the terrace down on to the Spanish Steps, forcing the crowd there to descend into the waiting arms of the police below. The riot shields flashed in the sunlight and the flailing batons were already bloody. The air was filled with missiles and shrieks of terror and of rage.

Right into this maelstrom of panicking bodies plunged the Brigadier. Normally the Italians have a great respect for the silver hairs of age, but not here, not today. No one was guaranteed safe conduct and a fast running man with a bloody head and a pistol in his hand didn't even begin to qualify.

A baton-blow which must have shattered his arm sent the pistol to the ground beneath the obelisk. I saw him take another blow along the jaw, then he was swept up in the fleeing crowd and borne out of sight towards the Steps.

The line of police advanced in inexorable pursuit, much as a Roman Legion must have advanced two thousand years before.

'OK,' said Reilly. 'Let's go.'

'Out there?'

It was the last place on earth for a sensible man to be, it seemed to me. But she too was as inexorable as any legionnaire and dragged me out.

She'd at least put the pistol out of sight and once in the piazza she grasped my arm and together we tried to give the impression of a pair of terrified tourists inadvertently caught up in this dreadful riot. It wasn't difficult in my case. I really was terrified. But I soon realized that, in fact, up here in the piazza, the main danger had passed. There were still police around but they were mainly attending to the needs of the numerous wounded who littered the square.

We teetered through them to the balustrade overlooking the terrace. The scene below was like the famous Odessa massacre sequence in *The Battleship Potemkin* and I'd no doubt the left-wing press would work the parallel to death. A double line of riot police was descending the Steps in strict formation, driving the crowd before it. They didn't need to use their batons. The barrier of their shields was like the shovel of a snow-plough and its irresistible pressure was avalanching the protesters into the square below. There they were being allowed to disperse with no more than a few valedictory swings from the police contingents stationed at each of the exits. The main physical danger to the demonstrators came from their fellows. Anyone slipping or being knocked over on the Steps was in real peril.

'There!' said Reilly. 'There he is!'

She pointed. Her eyes were better than mine. At first I found it quite impossible to make distinctions in that torrent of heads, seething and bubbling like a cobbled street in an earthquake, then I had him. But just for a moment.

'He's down,' said Reilly.

'How can you be sure?'

'Oh, I'm sure,' she said.

The uniformed line continued its descent, passing over the bodies of the fallen with scarcely a hiccough. Some of these moved and sat up and began to explore their wounds. Others stirred or simply twitched. And a few lay quite still.

'I see him,' said Reilly.

'So did I. His body lay athwart the Steps, his head lower than his feet, but he was unmistakable.

'He's dead,' I said.

'Let's take a look,' she said. She was a real doubting Thomas, that Reilly.

'As we descended the Steps, a policeman tried to stop us. Reilly spat a couple of obscenities at him and waved a card in his face and he sullenly retreated.

'Still *persona grata*?" I said.

'For a little while,' she said.

We reached the body. There was no doubt it was a body. That immaculate blazer was covered with footprints and stained with a dull red and those piercing eyes were wide open and trying to intimidate the sun.

'He died with his wounds on the front,' I said asininely.

'You want to look at his back?' asked Reilly.

I shook my head.

She dropped own on one knee and began going through his pockets. I studied the scene in the square below. The police had swept the Steps clear and the remnants of the demonstration were running out of the piazza. There was still a lot of trouble in store, I guessed. I could hear the noise of distant shouting and the breaking of glass. I suddenly felt very tired.

'Reilly,' I said. 'I came back to kill you. Both of you.'

'And why not, bucko? But not here, not now, OK?'

Why not? I wondered. Another death would hardly be noticed.

Reilly said, 'Oh shit!'

She too was looking down into the Piazza di Spagna. The *carabinieri* she'd waved her card at was returning with an irritated-looking officer.

'Let's not complicate things by getting you arrested,' she said. 'I'd better stay here to clear up. You take off, bucko. Go on, scat!'

'Where?' I said helplessly. 'Where shall I go.'

She looked at me with an expression of almost Pa-like exasperation.

'Back to the Cristallo,' she said. 'Go to 211, knock at the door, say who you are. Hurry!'

I hurried, half trotting till I reached the Piazza Barberini where I picked up a cab. My return to the Hotel Cristallo was greeted with far less indifference than my first arrival. The receptionist's face showed real emotion as he rushed from behind to greet me.

The reason wasn't far to see. Or rather to smell. Whatever it was I'd put into my case had now achieved a ripeness second only to very, very old gorgonzola, and its emanations must have been heavier than air for they had descended all the way from the fourth floor to the vestibule.

I shook my head and pushed him aside, making for the staircase. He probably thought I was going to do something about it, but he was crazy if he imagined I was going to go into a room smelling like that! I reached the second floor and knocked at 211.

There was no reply. I knocked again.

Then I said in Italian, 'Excuse me, this is ...'

This is who? What had Reilly meant when she told me to say who I was?

I tried my borrowed Italian name.

No response.

Then I tried Alexander Evans.

Still nothing.

Finally, feeling by now extremely light-headed, I banged hard on the woodwork and almost shouted, 'This is Antonio Lemuel Ernest Sebastian Stanhope-Swift, 6th Viscount Bessacarr. Open up!'

Now there was movement inside. The sound of a key turning.

And slowly the door opened, just a fraction.

I looked incredulously at the face which peered through the crack.

'You?' I said. '*You?*'

I thrust the door open, a wild hope welling up inside me. So wild it was that even when it was realized, I still hesitated, suspecting illusion or deception.

Then I was pushing past my nephew, Vasco, and running towards my daughter who rose from the edge of the bed to greet me.

26

. . . grave lack of trust . . .

Reilly and I sat together high above the sunlit Alps. The pilot
was waxing enthusiastic about them but to me they were just
pink and white rock.

I'd left Angie in Rome, safely lodged with the family of one
of Vasco's brothers. I'd have liked to stay longer with her and
to see Teresa who was doing well and would soon be out of
hospital, but Reilly had advised that the quicker I made my
exit, the better. So in twenty-four hours, Alexander Evans
was on his travels again.

I said, 'She will be OK, won't she?'

Reilly nodded as if she hadn't heard it ten times already.

'In the first place, it's too late to shut them up.' She said.
'And in the second place all those who ever thought it worth
while shutting them up are shut up themselves.'

I nodded. Certainly the men who'd been given the job of
contriving the accident on the Amalfitana were shut up.
Reilly had shut them up in their car before sending it over the
edge.

When I'd thanked her with an emotional fervour she
clearly found embarrassing, she'd said dismissively, 'The
whole thing was beginning to smell like O'Leary's pigs. So I
came back alone to have a poke around and when I saw the
kids being taken off like that, I thought I'd like a word with
them myself. And I couldn't talk with them if I let them be
pushed over a cliff, could I?'

I still found it hard to believe what I'd heard about Uncle
Percy, even though Reilly gave me chapter and verse. It
wasn't till she gave me Kim's confession that I was totally
converted.

'Why didn't Pa mention him when we were together?' I
wondered.

'In the bedroom while the kids were there, he knew that any reference to Percy would make it absolutely certain they had to be dumped. And afterwards, you were a bit busy from the sound of it. Though at the very end when he told you to swim to the Emerald Grotto and "still persevere", it wasn't just your lily-white body he was worrying about. After all, at that juncture he thought you were a dying man too. No, I suspect what he really said was something like *kill Percy*. That's what I guess his plan was. All this business about trials and press conferences was a misreading. He just wanted to sort out the man who'd betrayed him before he died.'

'Betrayed,' I echoed. 'All that stuff about Percy and Mama that the Brigadier implied, what about that, Reilly?'

'Can't help you there,' she said firmly. 'Yes, he did have lady friends as well as young men, I've picked up that on the departmental grapevine. But as for your ma, Lem, that's up to you to decide.'

'The bastard,' I said. 'No wonder Pa found the strength he did to try and get back at him. Some things need to be done personally.'

Reilly looked at me warningly.

'Leave it to the experts, Lem. There's two or three I know I can trust. I'll be talking to them when I get back. They'll sort the old sod out.'

I settled back in my seat, saying, 'You're the boss.'

At Heathrow we got a taxi. Reilly told the driver to make for the West End, adding, 'And let's not be having any of your scenic tours.'

The driver rolled his eyes in mute indignation.

'Nice to see you saving public money, Reilly,' I observed. 'Where *are* we going, as a matter of fact?'

'I'm going to put you somewhere safe. They'll likely want to talk to you when I tell them what's happened.'

'Likely,' I agreed. 'And after they've talked, what then?'

'Drop you in the sea half a mile off Margarita so you can swim ashore and tell the authorities you've been kept bound and blindfolded by the FALN till just now you made a miraculous and heroic escape,' she said.

She didn't sound convincing or convinced. I felt she'd got it almost right, only it wasn't half a mile *off* but half a mile *above* Margarita they'd be dropping me. I found myself thinking a lot about the island which I thought I'd said goodbye to forever. Dr Quintero must have thought he'd said goodbye to me forever also. Well, he was in for a shock, not to mention Numero Siete who, according to Reilly, had helped doctor my food to produce the early symptoms.

'You can't expect loyalty from a number,' commented Reilly.

'I've not done so well with names either,' I said and went on, 'Reilly, what was the plan for me if I'd actually played along and killed Pa?'

'What? But you didn't, bucko! I knew you never would. You're not the pa-killing type. You have to be either crazy or fitted up by the gods to do a thing like that.'

'I acted as gun-dog,' I said. 'And there must have been some contingency plan. So, what *would* you have done with a patricide who thought he was dying of cancer? Would you have told me it was all an April Fool after all?'

She shook her head.

'Not me. I'd have set about curing you, put you on a course of Interferon perhaps.'

'How kind. On the National Health? It's rather expensive stuff, I believe.'

She shook her luminescent locks.

'No way. I'd have sold you the stuff, bucko. Top rate.'

I laughed, but I wasn't sure she was joking.

Our destination proved to be a stale-smelling bed-sit in Earl's Court. The stairway and landing weren't exactly fresh, but I'd grown used to that by the time Reilly got the door open and by contrast the smell from the room was like opening an old coffin.

Reilly went in and did what I took to be a series of checks.

'It's OK. No one's been here,' she said.

'I don't doubt it. We'd have found them unconscious on the stairs, else,' I rejoined. 'What is this place? What you call a *safe house*?'

'My own personal safe house,' she said. 'Not the department's. I'm sorry about the pong, bucko, but I seal it up really tight, that's part of my security system, and I think when they stuffed the sofa with horse hair, they left some bits of horse attached. Well, make yourself at home.'

It wouldn't be easy, I thought, looking around. Besides the offending sofa there was a narrow truckle bed, a balding card table, a single cane chair and an old fashioned hat-stand, seven foot tall, which held what looked like an Arab's head-dress and a brand new bowler.

'Entertaining the bosses?' I said, nodding towards this last.

Reilly opened a cupboard.

'You'll have to starve for a while,' she said. 'But there's some scotch here. I've only got half-pint tumblers, but I dare say you'll not be complaining at that?'

She tossed me a full bottle of Tomatin and a glass. I caught them, but only just.

'Now I need a drink,' I said pouring myself a good quarter-pint. 'One thing, though, Reilly. I'm not going to start showing all the symptoms of bubonic plague as soon as I taste this, am I?'

To my surprise she didn't reply with her usual cynicism but said, 'I'm sorry about that. It was a disgusting thing to be doing to anyone.'

I raised my glass to my lips and said, 'Here's health.'

She dug further into her cupboard and came up with a small automatic which she slipped under her blouse. Our other weaponry had been dumped in the Tiber prior to departing from Rome.

'Prettying yourself up,' I said. 'You must be going out.'

'That's right. I've got people to contact,' she said. 'Listen, Lem, this is serious. In here you're safe, so stay in here. We'll both be safe once I get word about Uncle Percy to someone I can trust. But he's a very big gun and I'll have to get some very big guns on our side before we can relax. So stay put, will you?'

'Brownie's honour,' I said. 'As long as you promise to bring me something to eat.'

She came across the room and gave me a quick peck on the cheek, like a husband on his morning way to the office.

'I won't be long,' she said.

I set my whisky on the table, looked at my watch and gave her ten minutes.

Very carefully I opened the door about eighteen inches and slipped out on to the landing. Or rather I slipped my left leg out, but before my right could join it, there was a movement in the shadows of the stairs running up to the next floor and a sound like a deep exasperated sigh.

I froze. Reilly descended, gun in hand.

'Lem Swift, you're a trouble to me,' she said. 'I hoped I could trust you this once. Or at least trust you to drink your whisky.'

'So there is something in it?' I said.

'Just a little sleeping potion,' she said. 'I should have known you wouldn't take it.'

'I should have known you wouldn't trust me,' I said.

She motioned with her gun and I slid back into the room. Reilly followed, pushing the door fully open to keep me under the restraint of her gun. The old hat-stand which I had balanced at an angle of seventy degress so that it rested against the edge of the door toppled slowly towards her and I gave her the glassful of tainted Tomatin in the face. Anyone who so mistreats that precious fluid deserves no less. Besides, I was hurt by her grave lack of trust.

As she grappled with the hat-stand and blinked at the whisky, I took the gun with my left hand and chopped at her neck with the edge of my right. I remembered my assault on her in Rome – this was getting to be a habit! – and didn't want to repeat my fears of having fractured her skull.

Happily she went out like the cat on a summer's night. I carried her to the bed, ripped all the bedding off and laid her on the thin hard mattress. Tying her up didn't appeal. It could be dangerous and besides, I'd no certainty that I'd ever be returning and if this place were as safe as Reilly claimed she could lie here for days. But I didn't want her coming after me as soon as she recovered. So I stripped all her clothes off, bundled them up with the bedding, and left the room.

Again, as in Rome, I glanced back, wishing I didn't have to go. This time I had the sight of that splendidly rugged body naked on the bed to persuade me to stay. Sometimes, I thought, a man doesn't have to do what a man has to do.

But I left.

I dumped all the bedding and Reilly's clothes in a dustbin

below the steps which ran up to the terrace house. And then I strode off toward the underground with no more urgency (I hoped) than what was proper to a man who was a little late (about twenty years) for an appointment with his godfather.

. . . with forked tongue . . .

Uncle Percy greeted me as if I'd just dropped in to see him during the school holidays as I used to do all those years ago.

'Lem,' he said, his round, benevolent face alight with pleasure, 'I was hoping you'd call again. Come in. Come in. Sit you down.'

I came in and sat me down. The temperature was as high as ever and the room just as musty, though not with the depressing mustiness of squalor which I had just left in Earl's Court, but with an odour compounded of old books, old leather, old mahogany, and extremely old cognac which glowed like evening sunlight in a crystal decanter in Percy's hand.

'You'll join me in a snifter?' he asked, setting out another glass alongside the one he had just been filling.

I didn't reply but let the silence grow between us. At least I would have done but Percy poured the cognac and nodded and smiled as though I were making lively conversation. So finally I spoke.

'Uncle Percy,' I said seriously, 'let me tell you what I know and about which I will brook no discussion or argument. You are or were something very important in British Security. You were and doubtless still are something even more important in Russian Security. It was by your contrivance that I was inveigled into leaving Margarita and sent to Italy to join in the hunt for my father. These things I know beyond denial.'

He put a balloon of brandy on the arm of my chair and said mildly, 'Knowing all that, Lem, what on earth does it leave you to be inquisitive about?'

'About why my mother died and why my father and I between us had to waste four decades of our lifetimes. That's enough to stimulate a growing boy's curiosity, wouldn't you say?'

'Point taken,' he said, sinking into a huge leather armchair opposite me. 'Lem, I was sorry to hear Billy was dead, believe me. That may not sound all that convincing in the circumstances, but it's true. We went back a long, long way. I was genuinely fond of him. We were true friends.'

His curtains were drawn despite the fact that beneath his window Gloucester Place was still brimful of a summer evening as golden and warm as his excellent cognac. A reading lamp trained on the table beside his chair painted half his face with shadows. The old gas fire hissed and popped. Across its broad top lay a long, elaborately wrought brass toasting-fork with a handle shaped like a writhing snake from whose gaping mouth protruded two needle sharp prongs on which was impaled a muffin.

I drank in the scene with all its strange savour of English tradition and privilege and eccentricity and said, 'Bullshit, Uncle Percy. I think you hated Pa. I think from your earliest acquaintance you probably envied and resented him and resolved to do everything in your power to destroy him.'

He looked at me in round-eyed, round-mouthed shock.

'You're so wrong, Lem,' he protested. 'Exile's made a cynic out of you. I respected, admired, even hero-worshipped Billy. His qualities of mind and spirit shone like a beacon. Naturally they attracted attention from the same people who recruited me at Cambridge. They'd have swopped a dozen Anthony Blunts for Billy Bessacarr but after a few tentative approaches, they soon gave up. It was not that he was unsympathetic to radical ideas, it was just that it quickly became apparent he was incapable of subterfuge! He'd have had the lot of us declaring our new allegiance from the rooftops, with his own declaration topping the bill, of course. There was another thing. There was no way he would take orders. He had to feel independent. It's a quality of the Bessacarr family which you will not find it difficult to recognize, Lem. You need to be gently nudged. Anything stronger provokes immediate resistance. Well, Billy Bessacarr had far too much to offer to be abandoned completely. I was close to him and I was given the job of nudging. But my motives were pure, Lem. Admiration, affection, and a simple desire to have this man's fine qualities working for the right side, the side to which he spiritually belonged.'

He spoke so earnestly I could almost believe him. But it still made me feel sick.

'Tell me about these nudges,' I said. 'Start by telling me about my mother. You introduced her to Pa, didn't you?'

'Yes, that's true. A fine woman. Fine woman. Fine.'

A feeling of revulsion so strong arose in me that it took a great effort of will not to pull Reilly's gun from my pocket and add another red O to this rotund rubicund face.

'Were you and she lovers?' I asked as unemotionally as I could manage.

'Lovers?' he said in alarm. 'Surely you've heard some small rumour of my tastes in that area, Lem?'

'For God's sake, don't treat me as a naïf!' I shouted. 'Everything about you is fraudulent. I know it. Understand me, Uncle Percy. I *know* it!'

'My dear boy,' he said, shaking his head. 'My dear boy.'

He took the serpentine toasting-fork and held the muffin out to the fire. He looked hurt and bewildered. Muffin and snake, how well that odd conjunction summed him up, I thought.

'You were with her the day she died,' I said, regaining control. 'You spent the weekend at Bessacarr House, then you drove back to town with her. I rang you here and you said Mama had just gone.'

'That's true, I remember,' he said. He turned his mild gaze on me and added, 'We were just talking, Lem. Just talking.'

'But were you her lover?' I repeated fiercely. 'Come on! I have to know!'

'Not then, believe me, dear boy. Not at all after they were married,' he replied. 'But I had been. Yes, I admit it. Once. A long, long time ago. A long, long time ago.'

His voice died away. There was smoke arising from the end of the toasting-fork.

I said, 'Your muffin's burning.'

'Is it? Oh dear.'

He raised the fork to the vertical, smoke drifting up from

the charred remains. He looked like the torch-bearer at some Geriatric Olympic Games. With a sigh he removed the burnt muffin, extracted another from a large paper bag on the floor by his chair, impaled it and resumed toasting and talking together.

'Of course, the thing about the Bessacarr mind is that, while it is so proud of its independence that it rejects any obvious attempt to influence it, at the same time it is so egotistically certain of its superiority that it never doubts the wisdom of its decisions once made. The trick is to let it imagine it's in control. A quiet, unassuming friend can do a lot, of course, but when it comes to real professional nudging, you can't beat a wife. So I gave him a wife. Yes, I feel I can safely take credit there. I gave him a wife.'

He finished toasting his second muffin and started a third. He gave me a smile full of avuncular benevolence but I caught the malicious glint in his eyes.

'You *gave* him my mother?' I said. 'I hope you're not trying to tell me Mama was a KGB agent?'

'Oh no, positively not,' he said, alarmed once more as I leaned forward aggressively. 'But she was ferociously left-wing. So were we all in those days. That's how I first met her, through my CP contacts. Not that she was ever a Party member. She was like your father, essentially an individualist, one who needed to be nudged rather than directed. But she was much more politically aware than your father was at that time. Obvioulsy there was a deal of mutual attraction between them, but I think I helped make her aware of what a powerful force on the side of radical philosophy a man like Billy Bessacarr could be, and in *that* sense I gave her to him.'

I tried to digest this. He observed me with that same maliciously-edged amusement and continued toasting his muffins, expert now after that first conflagration.

'You want me to believe that Pa was somehow *controlled* by Mama?' I burst out incredulously.

'Only in the loosest sense, just as she was controlled by me only in the loosest sense. One hint of the leading rein in either case and they'd have been off. As both Bessacarr and a Madariaga, Lem, surely you recognize the condition? I mean, the parallels are not far to seek.'

I thought at first he was referring simply to recent events and then it came to me.

'Kate? You can't mean Kate?'

"She was one of my protégés, you'll recall,' he said with every appearance of self-satisfaction. 'Don't judge her harshly. When she found out she was pregnant by you, her first reaction was to say nothing and simply have a termination. But I said, 'Why not marry him?' She thought about it. She was never averse to the comforts of life, dear Kate. So she got a title and a steady income. And you got a wife and helpmeet.'

'Helpmeet!' I echoed bitterly. 'Some help!'

'More than you think,' he said. 'It was very useful having Kate keep us posted on your activities. Really, Lem, you've had ten years to think about it. You can't still imagine that your tremendous success and charmed life as an illicit arms-dealer was all the result of your own cleverness, can you? Nearly every one of your deals won the approval of one or the other of my masters. You path was smoothed with the silkiest of brooms!'

I should have been dumbfounded, I suppose, but my past awareness of incredible luck in my dealings had prepared me in some part for this revelation. Kate's role was harder to accept, but even here there had been preparation.

'And Kate?' I prompted, wanting to be sure I'd swallowed the whole draught. 'Was *she* an agent?'

'Oh no, not in the strict sense. More of an instrument. She worked in my department – my *real* department, I mean – as a collator and was flattered to be told off to keep an eye on you. I didn't want someone too expert, you see. She never had any idea about my Russian connection, of course, but, alas for her, she did meet Major Krylov coming out of my apartment when she called round unexpectedly just before she left for Rome. She had been familiar with his file at one stage while he was one of the innumerable KGB small fry at their Embassy here. I was able to explain his presence easily enough, of course, but when she ran into him again in your sister's apartment-block, well, he couldn't risk letting her meet you and identify him, could he? Even your blinkered brain might have started glimpsing something odd.'

'So she wasn't in on all this?' I said, watching the muffin pile grow. Was he expecting guests? Or did fear just make him hungry?

'Oh no,' he said. 'It was just unfortunate that her anxieties about your daughter should have taken her to that place at that time.'

'But she co-operated with you in hiding Angie in the first place,' I said bitterly.

'Why not?' he said in surprise. 'She became quite fond of you in those years of marriage, Lem, and your desertion of the pair of them genuinely shocked her. Also I fear that reports of your state of mind in exile were not reassuring, not reassuring at all.'

Dispassionately I said, 'You bastard. I thought you were my one point of human contact with them. Why did you do it, Percy? What was in it for you, keeping us apart?'

He shrugged and said, 'Letting you converse, even at a distance, would have involved some risk. I haven't survived all these years without learning that you take no risk that can be avoided. The Bessacarr mind is flawed by the Bessacarr egotism and is therefore easily deceived. But it is none the less a sharp mind and needs to be starved of nourishing ideas if it is not to become dangerously active. You see how relatively easily you have accepted all you have learned in the past few days.'

'The instruction's been given in a hard school,' I said. 'We seem to have drifted from my mother.'

'Yes. This proves the point. Already, having looked at your own marriage relationship, you are now much better equipped to accept that that process of radicalization which had your father voting socialist in 1945 and promulgating dangerous ideas about the universal sharing of not only the wealth but the scientific knowledge of nations thereafter, was triggered by your mother. Of course, she had to play second fiddle. Billy would bear no rival near the throne. And in any case your mother was an instinctive rather than an intellectual political animal and thought like many that with the end of the war, Fascism was dead and nothing remained but to sit back and enjoy the fruits of victory.

'Her job as far as your father was concerned was over. He

was now a dissident. Oh yes, they love Western dissidents in Moscow just as much as they love Soviet dissidents in Fleet Street. Of course they'd have preferred him as an agent, working on some secret Government research project. But failing that, he had great propaganda value and when he finally defected, as well as the propaganda kudos, they would get his brain.'

'His defection was planned?' I said.

'Projected,' he corrected. 'But it was a long-term project. Events, alas, overtook us and we had to improvise.'

'And what were these events, Uncle Percy?' I said gently.

He deposited another muffin on the pile which was assuming a Tower of Pisa-like elevation and inclination.

'Your mother precipitated the crisis, I'm afraid,' he said slowly. 'In some ways I blame myself. She was living a pretty separate life from your father by now, of course. The newspapers loved it. The dissident scientist and the society queen! Well, it had been a fairly open marriage for some years. It was you who provided the main point of contact, Lem, the main bond of union. Odd, that. But Angelica still had a great deal of respect and admiration for your father. Affection too. She often talked to me about him and the direction he was moving in. She had become rather more moderate in her own views by now. I was able to hint at my real work in the Home Office – she never suspected my former radicalism had ever been anything more than the youthful fervour we had once shared – and to assure her I'd keep an eye on Billy's well-being. And to keep her occupied I let her know there were all kinds of ways she could be useful to the cause of democracy in her own social circle. She ran with a very fast, very influential set, as you doubtless know.'

'The Profumo gang?' I said.

'The ones you read about were merely the slow runners,' he said contemptuously. 'Well, she was pretty disillusioned with them at this time and felt qualms about passing on information, starting rumours, effecting introductions, that kind of thing. The trouble was, she knew a great deal about what was going on, probably as much as any single person other than myself. She was greatly disturbed by the whole Profumo affair, but it was the Ward trial and his suicide that

243

really knocked her back. You may have noticed she was in a strange inward-looking mood at the end of that summer and into autumn. It came to a head that last weekend down at Bessacarr House.

'I stayed till the Monday, then drove her into town. She was really most distressed and when we arrived, I brought her here, and gave her a cup of tea. There were muffins too, I remember, but she didn't eat any.'

He looked sadly at his unsteady column.

'Finally she left, saying she was going to go round to your town house in the hope of finding Billy there and talking things over with him. Naturally I didn't think that was a very good idea. There was no way of knowing how Billy's volatile mind would react to this proposed confession. I was worried about Angelica too. The dear girl hadn't eaten anything, but she had drunk a great deal of brandy. Just like you. I don't suppose you would fancy a muffin?'

I shook my head.

'Just say if you change your mind,' he said. 'Well, I was in a bit of a panic, I must admit. As soon as she left, I rang your house. It seemed to me that if Billy was there, I had to make an effort to get him out of the way and gain time. To my relief Kim answered the phone. I'd better explain about Kim. I knew about her though she didn't know about me. She'd been one of hundreds of 'plants' the North Koreans fed into the refugee camps in '52 and '53. Most got detected, but Kim, even though she was sixteen or so at the time, could pass for ten or eleven and they didn't vet children so thoroughly. It was just sheer chance that Billy picked her up as part of his conspicuous charity drive. She really belonged to the Chinese, of course, but they had no proper control set-up in England and the KGB took her over. Soviet-Sino relations were much happier in those days, you'll recall.'

'Spare me the political history,' I grated. 'What happened?'

He shook his head.

'All I can tell you is what I did. I identified myself to Kim. There's a code. I used it. She knew me as a friend of the family, of course. She called me Uncle Percy, just like you. So it must have come as a shock to her but she took it in her stride. I told her quickly it was essential that Angelica didn't have any contact with Billy that night. I was really just hoping that in the morning after a good night's sleep with the brandy out of her system your mother might be more amenable.

'Kim told me they were going to Paris. That gave me an idea. When Billy came on the line I told him I'd got a whisper that Special Branch were coming round to see him that evening. It was true that he was under investigation. I'd organized it myself. And the leaks to the Tory press to keep up the cries of outrage. And the leaks to the radical protest to keep up the cries of witch-hunt! It was all going rather well.'

There was a self-congratulatory tone in his voice which filled me with fury, but I held it in. Action must wait till words were finished.

'He thanked me, said he was on his way to Paris and didn't fancy being held up, so he'd shoot off tooth-sweet. I rang off. Just to be on the safe side with my story, I then contacted the Department and arranged for an interview team to go round to the house an hour later.

'And that was all I did, Lem. I swear it. I don't know what happened there or who was responsible. All I can guess is that Kim contacted her own control and got instructions. Or perhaps she acted off her own bat. Or perhaps there was simply an accident. I just don't know!

'But when I found out what had happened, though I was personally devastated, I had to take advantage of it, you see. I arranged for Billy to be given the news in Paris and put under cover. Moscow were quite happy with they way things had fallen out. A straightforward defection would have been preferable, but this did almost as well. So they got him and they fed him with some story to keep him happy. He always had the capacity to arrange things around him for his greatest happiness, you must recall that.

'It's a capacity I lack, Lem. I don't think I've been truly happy from that day to this. Angelica was a true, a dear friend. Perhaps no one else has ever been so close to me. And now, certainly, no one else ever will.'

He sat there with the last muffin on his fork and tears in his eyes. At least I assumed it was the last muffin. It would take the pile up to twelve and surely no one bought more than a dozen muffins at a time? Or did bakers still give their own larger dozen in the interest of consumer satisfaction?

With such banalities does the human heart avoid being overloaded.

Percy turned his damp eyes towards me and said, 'Lem, can you find it in yourself to forgive an old man? I've had to make harsh decisions. I've had to tread a narrow path between my ideals and my affections. It hasn't been easy. Sometimes I may have been wrong. But at least believe this: never have I deliberately chosen to hurt someone I love. Never!'

It was a fine performance.

I said, 'Never? Not even when you arranged for Quintero to con me into thinking I had cancer?'

'The hurt wasn't permanent,' he argued. 'Besides, it wasn't my idea or my doing.'

'You mean you didn't make the arrangement yourself when you were so fortuitously 'passing through' Margarita in the summer?'

'Why should I have done?' he cried indignantly. 'If you won't believe my fondness for you, believe facts. Billy didn't do his disappearing trick till nearly two months later. What reason could I have had when I visited you for initiating that grisly charade?'

'The best reason in the world,' I said quietly. 'You wanted me dead.'

He suddenly looked alarmed, but his voice was steady as he answered. 'Dead? Why should I want you dead?'

'Why should the symptoms have started so long before Pa disappeared?' I countered. 'That's been puzzling me ever since I got the dates sorted out in my mind. But eventually I got the answer. You'd heard from Krylov that Pa claimed he'd smuggled a transcript of Kim's confession to the West to be delivered on his death. But delivered to whom? You knew Pa well enough to work that one out, didn't you? It had to be me. Who else would he trust to react properly to what it was he had to tell? So I bet you had your bloodhounds sniffing at every law firm and bank that Pa or I had ever had any dealings with. When that failed, you suddenly found yourself impelled by love and affection to drop in on your errant godson and take an avuncular interest in his well-being. I bet you went through every scrap of paper you could find in the house! Nothing – so it had to be the final solution.'

'But why should I want you *dead*, Lem?' he asked plaintively. 'It was all a charade, the cancer. You were in no real danger!'

'You didn't want to risk an embarrassing investigation by poisoning me straight off,' I said. 'In any case, even a crook like Quintero would probably have balked at murder. No, the idea was simply to flush me out of cover so that your Communist friends in the FALN could finish me off, no questions asked. How long had they known about poor old Dario? It must have amused you, thinking of my surprise when they told me. First the good news, Mr Swift, you haven't got cancer. Now the bad, we really are going to kill you!'

'But why, Lem? Why should I want this?' he protested once more.

'Because if I died immediately after Pa's death, which seemed imminent, any mysterious package would pass into my estate, and you are my executor. A not unfitting term, Uncle Percy. More than that, Angelica is my sole heir and during her minority, you would have been her appointed guardian and trustee. You'd have had every chance in the world of getting your hands on that package, wouldn't you?

'But before I did my disappearing act, Pa performed his and the case was altered. With him loose, it was pointless killing me. In fact your clever little mind saw there might be an advantage in letting me loose in Rome where you believed Pa was hiding. If I flushed him out, you'd get two birds with one stone. If Krylov and the Brigadier got him first, then I was readily disposable and you were back to plan one. And even if by some miscalculation, the package was delivered directly to Angelica, well, a sixteen-year-old girl wouldn't put up much resistance, would she?'

'Lem, this is utterly outrageous!' he protested, all red and hurt. 'How can you imagine I would ever let the slightest harm come to Angie?'

'Why not?' I enquired. 'After all, you murdered her grandmother, didn't you?'

I said it quietly. If I'd had any doubts about the truth of the accusation, they disappeared in that briefest of moments when guilt started up on his face before vanishing beneath the cosmetic of shock and indignation.

'*What*? This is too much. Lem, you cannot believe such a thing! I had no idea ... I was prostrate with grief when I heard the news. Prostrate. If this mysterious package should ever turn up, I'm certain not even the fevered imagination of that Korean whore could devise such a foul slander!'

'Bravo,' I applauded mildly. 'And you're quite right. She doesn't. Oh yes, Uncle Percy, the package has turned up. It was with my sister, Teresa, all the time. It must have been within a few yards of Krylov when he was working on her fingernails, but he never asked. All that Kim told my father on her deathbed was that she never saw Mama that night. But she let two men in at the back door and they were carrying what looked like a roll of carpeting. They told her what to say and she left for the airport. But my father knew what it meant, Percy, just as I know. He might still have believed you just gave the orders, but not me. I know now what you're capable of. I've no doubt at all that you killed Mama yourself, right here in this snug, warm, little apartment. Perhaps she was lying here awaiting collection when I phoned that night. Right here in front of the fire, to delay rigor mortis!'

Percy gave a little birdlike twitter of fear, or perhaps simply distaste. With trembling fingers he removed the twelfth muffin from the toasting-fork and placed it on the perilous pile. His shaking hand went into the paper bag. A baker's dozen after all.

'Nothing to say, Uncle Percy?' I mocked. 'Oh, you knew why Pa did his escape act, didn't you? You knew his mind wasn't concerned with trials and press conferences. He wanted one thing only, that tireless servant of reason and worshipper of truth. He wanted to perform the most rational and truth-advancing act of his life, which was to get his fingers round your throat and squeeze the last gasp of treacherous, pusillanimous, prevaricating breath out of you. Well, he couldn't make it. He got diverted en route. But at the end, for the first time in his life, he delegated me to do a job that was beyond him. He was drowning and his hands had been chopped off by a propeller, but he raised those bloody stumps towards me and told me his dying wish. "*Kill Percy*," he said. "*Kill Percy!*" '

'Lem,' the old man cried brokenly. 'Dear boy ... how can you ... I loved ...'

He choked on his words. His left hand flapped ineffectively at his tear-stained cheeks. And his right hand came out of the paper bag.

But I was already launched out of my deep leather armchair and my fingers closed like a manacle round his skinny twiglike wrist. I hadn't really believed that in this materialistic society bakers gave their inflated dozens any more.

'Mustn't be greedy, Uncle,' I said. 'Too many muffins will give you indigestion.'

Roughly I prised his fingers loose from the butt of the Smith and Wesson 61 Escort which at about twelve centimetres is just the right size for hiding in a bag of muffins. He looked up at me with his round philanthropist's face still reluctant to contort its lineaments into the terrified acceptance of malicious intent.

Now at last he believed and with a squeal of fear he swung the toasting-fork at me, but he had only the cunning, not the speed, of the serpent whose form it took and I had no difficulty in intercepting the blow and wresting the fork from his weak grasp with my free hand.

I pressed the gun against his brow. He retreated in his chair till the leather upholstery had absorbed as much of his frame as it could. The only sounds were the gas fire and his shallow rapid breathing.

The doorbell rang.

He screamed as if the gun had made the sound and in truth I too was so startled by it that I almost pulled the trigger.

'The US Cavalry,' I said. 'Or the Indians. Either way, they've got here too late this time.'

'Lem, for God's sake, you don't know what you're doing!' he pleaded. 'You mustn't do it, for your own sake.'

'For *God's* sake? For my *own* sake?' I cried, feeling my

rage bubble up to boiling point. 'Why not include for my *mother's* sake? For my *father's* sake?'

'I do include them, Lem. Believe me, I do,' he gabbled. 'Lem, I knew your mother first. I knew her very well. Remember, I didn't deny that we'd once been lovers. How could I harm her, Lem? How could I? Lem, listen, she was pregnant when she married your father. She didn't realize it till too late, but she was, *she was!* Check their wedding date against your date of birth, you can see she was!'

I recoiled from him. I'd thought I was past shock but this was the worst yet.

'What are you saying old man?' I shouted.

Behind me, the door burst open. Startled, I looked round.

It was Reilly. She must have borrowed or stolen her clothes for she was wearing a man's dress shirt, tight running shorts and floppy basket ball boots. In other circumstances I'd have fallen about laughing. But Charlie Chaplin couldn't have made me laugh just now.

'Lem!' she screamed.

I felt a crashing blow on the side of my head and, as I fell, a gushing of liquid over my face. I cried out in pain as it hit my eyes, then had time to feel relief as it reached my lips.

It was cognac. Percy had hit me with the crystal decanter. Instinctively my hands went to my face, letting the gun and fork fall from my questing fingers.

I rolled over, rubbing at my eyes. I heard Percy's voice cry, 'Hold still,' which was, probably, literally, the last thing I was going to do. I kept rolling but as vision returned to my left eye, I saw that he wasn't talking to me but to Reilly. She was coming at him in a headlong rush but her overlarge boots and the clutter of furniture weren't helping.

Percy had retrieved the Smith and Wesson. He raised it and fired. Reilly cried out and went down. The revolver swung round towards me. Now I reversed my roll, trying to keep just ahead of the smoking muzzle's arc, but by the time I reached my starting point, it had caught up with me.

I felt something hard and metallic under my forearm. I grasped it in my left hand. And pushing myself off the floor with my right hand, hurled the serpentine toasting fork at Percy.

The twin prongs of snake's tongue took him in the throat. He crashed back against the fire, whose hisses and pops were minimized by the awful bubbling noises coming from his mouth. The gun dropped to the carpet as he tried to grip the fork with both hands.

Then he sank down to the floor, still twisting, still turning, but with progressively less force. I lay there and watched, paralysed by emotions I did not yet dare contemplate.

Finally he was still. And from the top of the fire tumbled the tower of muffins, scattering themselves across his belly and chest.

I stood up, crying, 'Reilly!'

To my momentary relief she pulled herself to her knees by the side of an armchair. There was blood all over the dress shirt. She looked down at Uncle Percy with the brass snake at his throat.

'Well, little Tonto,' she said, 'white man speak with forked tongue.'

And slid back out of sight.

28

... the Spanish for nine ...

It was early evening, my favourite time on Isla de Margarita.

I lay in my *chinchorro* on the verandah with a long whisky in my hand. Distantly I glimpsed my new foreman doing his dusk check of the inner perimeter fence. Inside the house I could hear Numero Ocho singing a tuneless Amerindian song as she prepared my meal. Soon the scarlet ibis would glide by towards the long lagoon. It was a blessed time, a time of peace, a time when the past had least power to pain.

I had got Reilly to hospital and stayed just long enough to have my own diagnosis confirmed, which was that the bullet had shattered her shoulder and the wound was serious but not dangerous. When interest began to be shown in me, I clasped my split head and swayed on my feet. They put me in one of those treatment cubicles where the first rule in a NHS hospital is that the patient must be completely ignored for at least fifteen minutes.

When they came back, I was gone.

I returned to the hospital next day, vaguely disguised in dark glasses and a hat – not an Italian straw hat this time but a trilby. I knew that telephoning or enquiring at reception was likely to get me nowhere but an SIS cellar. All I wanted was a glimpse of Reilly to check that she was all right. All I got was a glimpse of Commander Hunnicut deep in conversation with a small grey-suited man who looked too authoritatively ordinary to be anything but Security.

Honey glimpsed me too, over the Security yo-yo's shoulder. His eyes registered my identity. Then he yawned as if he'd had a long night and knuckled his eyeballs.

I got the message. In Honey's book, I deserved one flicker of sympathy for what I'd been put through.

But it would only be one.

Alexander Evans was on the next flight to Dublin and thence by various routes to a joyous homecoming in Venezuela.

Well, perhaps not exactly joyous, but I stage-managed things so that an anonymous telephone call led the police to a rat-infested Caracas cellar where they discovered and rescued their currently most famous terrorist kidnap victim. There was no doubt the authorities guessed or had been tipped off that something odd was going on, but when you've got a grateful guest assuring the world's press that Venezuelan police, government, and society generally are the greatest in the universe, you don't knock it.

In Porlamar, the Chief of Police led what was a sort of civic reception, assuring me that if there was any more shooting on his island he'd make damn sure I was on the receiving end of it, then he graciously allowed me to split a couple of bottles of champagne with him.

Dr Quintero, I gathered, had during the last twenty-four hours experienced an irresistible humanitarian urge to practise his craft among the poor deprived Indians of the Gran Sabana. I had just missed him. Numero Siete had likewise disappeared, taking with her as many of my household possessions as she could pack into the set of leather suitcases she stole.

Well, their departure saved me the bother of being angry. I'd had enough of anger. Besides, I felt so well I had no expectation of needing a doctor ever again, and as for Numero Siete, she'd been coming to the end of her service and in a few weeks I'd have been trading her in for Numero Ocho anyway. Not that I'd been in any hurry to choose a replacement. I wanted to be quite sure the next one wouldn't be grinding glass into my *chipi chipi* soup!

In fact as it turned out, Numero Ocho chose me. She came out of the house now with a tray holding two steaming platefuls of *sancocho*. I smiled up at her and remembered her first appearance at the *hacienda*. I'd been lying here in this same position except that I was about ten times more bottled. There'd seemed to be little else to do in the months since my return and I suppose I'd taken fairly large steps towards alcoholism.

I'd heard a step on the verandah and through my drink haze assumed it was one of the guards. Then suddenly I felt my *chinchorro* being twisted round and as I crashed out of it to the wooden floor, a familiar voice said, 'Don't you know to stand up when a lady comes visiting, bucko?'

'Reilly!' I groaned. 'How the hell did you get here?'

'Just walked through your defence system, Lem, if that's what you call it. I'd kick a few bums if I was paying anybody good money to defend me.'

I stood up and looked at her. She was changed but as extraordinary as ever. Her hair was now a dull ochre and had been cut very short and plastered against her skull. She wore no make up except some very dark eye-shadow. She was wearing Bermuda shorts and a sun-halter which only just succeeded in halting anything this side of decency.

Beside her on the verandah was an old battered suitcase.

'Why've you come, Reilly?' I asked.

'Have you forgotten, bucko? I told you a long time ago soon after we met, if you beat me three times, you got to keep me. You did it. Here I am. Broke and out of work, I may add.'

We locked gazes. Gradually it dawned on me that, Angelica apart, there was no one else on earth I'd rather see.

I grinned widely and said, 'Reilly, by a strange coincidence there's an opening here that might just interest you.'

And that's how I got Numero Ocho. Occasionally she asks me what the Spanish is for *nine* and I think for a while and then shake my head and say I don't know. She seems very happy. I know I am. I correspond regularly with Angie, who has settled more or less permanently with her Carducci relatives in Rome. I've sent them the money and she and Teresa and Vasco are coming on a long visit next month and I wake up counting the days, like a little boy longing for Christmas. But each day I count is a happy day too, and the past is slowly becoming bearable again.

Reilly and I respect each other's privacy. Neither of us probe. Gradually little by little I'm learning about her early life. As for her more recent past, when she came out of hospital she knew her shoulder, though mending, would never be as strong again. She also knew that in the Department she was an object of much resentment. There was little absolute proof against Percy, none at all against the Brigadier. And though it was generally agreed that she'd been right, it was generally preferred that she should have been wrong.

'I can't be looking over my shoulder all the time, especially when it's busted,' she'd explained. 'I wanted somewhere safe, with someone I liked, someone who's as good as me at the things that matter.'

Now we ate our meal together in companionable silence.

I broke it, saying casually, 'Reilly, did I ever tell you what old Percy told me just before he died. Before I killed him?'

She shook her head. It was unnecessary. Both of us knew I'd never mentioned that day since her arrival on Margarita.

'He told me that he and Mama were lovers before she met Pa. He told me that after she got married – it was one of those whirlwind affairs, only a couple of weeks' courtship – he told me Mama discovered she was pregnant.'

'By Percy?'

'That's what he told me,' I said.

'And so?' she said.

'I just wonder sometimes,' I said. 'I just wonder if after all they got me to do what they said – what you and the Brigadier said you wanted me to do in the first place. Kill my own father.'

'Now that'd be really something, wouldn't it?' said Reilly softly. 'But ask yourself this, Lem. What do you think your ma would have done in the circumstances? Being the kind of woman she seems to have been.'

I thought.

'Told Pa, I guess.'

'Right. And did your Pa ever treat you unlike his own son? Or rather do you think he'd have treated you different?'

I shook my head.

'No. Pa treated me like his son, all right. That's for certain.'

'Well, then. Add to this that dear old Uncle Percy was probably the biggest liar either of us will have the privilege of meeting. Add all that up, and see what you get.'

I lay back in the *chinchorro*, rocking gently. Overhead the sky was a deep rich blue. Soon the stars would come pricking through.

Reilly said, 'Hey, milord. Isn't that what they call a Viscount? Though there's still a strong school thinks you should lose the title, you know that?'

I said sleepily, 'Who cares? Anyway, don't forget that under Italian law I may be a *Conte* now.'

'I never doubted it.' She laughed. 'What were you thinking of, *conte?*'

'I'm trying to remember the Spanish for *nine*,' I said.

She rose and came over to me and said throatily, 'I'm going to stunt your education, bucko. Move over.'

I said, 'For God's sake, Reilly. Not in a *chinchorro*. You'll bring the house down!'

'That's always my aim,' she said. 'Move over.'

She climbed in on top of me. Over her shoulder I saw a flight of scarlet ibis winging their way across the darkling sky, their wing-beats as strong as a swimmer's arms driving his body through the flashing water, their movement as graceful as a sail-boat's surge before a rising wind.

Then I saw no more.